CM 2310

D1446737

You Can Sleep While I Drive

OTHER BOOKS BY LIZA WIELAND

The Names of the Lost
Discovering America

You Can Sleep While I Drive

Stories by
LIZA WIELAND

SOUTHERN METHODIST UNIVERSITY PRESS
Dallas

These stories are works of fiction. Names, characters, places, and incidents are either the product of the author's imagination or are used fictitiously.

Requests for permission to reproduce material from this work should be sent to:
  Rights and Permissions
  Southern Methodist University Press
  PO Box 750415
  Dallas, Texas 75275-0415

Grateful acknowledgment is made for permission to quote from "My Fifty-Plus Years Celebrate Spring" by Luis Omar Salinas. Used by permission of the author.

Some of the stories in this collection first appeared in the following publications: "Laramie" and "The Loop, the Snow, Their Daughters, the Rain" in *The Journal;* "Purgatory" in *The Los Angeles Times* Magazine; "Salt Lake" in *North American Review;* "Halloween" in *Sycamore Review;* "Gray's Anatomy" in *Southern Review;* and a portion of "You Can Sleep While I Drive," under the title "Methode Champenoise," in *Georgia Review.*

Jacket art: Edward Hopper (American, 1882–1967), *Western Motel,* oil on canvas, 1957, 30¼ x 50⅛. Yale University Art Gallery. Bequest of Stephen Carlton Clark, B.A. 1903.

Jacket and text design: Tom Dawson Graphic Design

LIBRARY OF CONGRESS CATALOGING-IN-PUBLICATION DATA

Wieland, Liza.
    You can sleep while I drive : stories / by Liza Wieland. — 1st ed.
      p.   cm.
    ISBN 0-87074-441-0 (acid-free paper)
    1. United States—Social life and customs—20th century—Fiction.
  I. Title.
  PS3573.I344Y6   1999
  813'.54—dc21   99-18493

Printed in the United States of America on acid-free paper

10   9   8   7   6   5   4   3   2   1

This book is for
Alexis Khoury
and
Dan Stanford

On the road, the mountains
in the distance are at rest
in a wild blue silence.

LUIS OMAR SALINAS
"My Fifty-Plus Years Celebrate Spring"

CONTENTS

Purgatory / 1

Salt Lake / 17

Halloween / 49

Cirque du Soleil / 69

Irradiation / 107

Laramie / 129

Gray's Anatomy / 149

The Loop, The Snow, Their Daughters, The Rain / 181

You Can Sleep While I Drive / 197

Purgatory

Main Street in Durango, Colorado, makes me sad to the very core, the kind of deep loneliness I used to feel as a kid on winter mornings in Flagstaff when I'd walk to the bottom of the driveway to get the newspaper. Up and down the block, there'd be all those houses lit up against the cold, the buttery light of the neighbors' kitchens making me feel orphaned. All the way back up the driveway, my heart seemed like it would break open, and the pain of it got sharper and stronger until I thought it would kill me, right there on the back stoop, with all the news that's fit to print clutched in my hand. I'd let myself in the back door, into my mother's kitchen, and she'd turn away from the stove to watch me come in like she'd missed me for all of the five minutes I'd been gone. Everyone else was still asleep. I'd hand her the paper and see that same yellow light shining in our house too.

Now the only place to go back to is the Pine Aire Motel, and Charlie and the tired argument he's been trying to have with me the whole way across the United States from New York, then on to Flagstaff to my father and my brother and his exemplary life. We were going so Charlie could meet my family before we get married. But somewhere in the great ugly void of Kansas we seem to have decided what we really need to get is an abortion. I say "we," but I have plans of my own. I always have had plans of my own, I guess. It's what my mother hated most about me, that I wasn't your basic family-type person, wouldn't run with the pack, turned and snarled at the pack most of the time. Wouldn't she be surprised now. Maybe she is surprised, looking down from her front-row seat in heaven. Maybe she's saying to her heavenly cronies, that one's mine. Maybe she's thinking, hang on, there's hope.

I've come to the end of Main Street where it bottlenecks into the turnstiles for the Narrow Gauge Railroad to Silverton, passing through, would you believe it, the town of Purgatory. I have this idea: I will go to Purgatory, and I will get work in a bar. Of course there are bars in Purgatory, there'd have to be, but the glasses would always be just out of reach, or else you'd drink and drink, but never forget your sorrows, never even get drunk. Or you'd wait. And wait and wait. For your date, for the fog to lift, for a ride home. I could go there and have this baby that its own father doesn't want, and no one would ever find me. This baby could grow up in Purgatory and when it gets ready to enter the world, it will be one of the few humans truly equipped to live here. Charlie could drive the rest of the way to see my brother and my dad and he'd be happy for a way out.

That's when I start to feel scared. There's a solid wall of people moving from the McDonald's across the street past me to the railroad station and the ticket window, and at first I resist their jostling, but then I let myself be pushed into their number, close behind a man with an infant slung over his shoulder. I get packed in so close I can smell the sweet stink of talcum powder and sour milk that babies give off. I follow the baby and buy a ticket to

Silverton. Then I stand along the west wall of the depot watching the baby as its eyes begin to close down for the slow ride into sleep.

At 6:20, when the all-aboard whistle blows directly above my head, I open my mouth and give one long grieving wail, but it can't be heard above the whistle and the loudspeaker instructing passengers to have their tickets ready. My stomach heaves, and it's while I'm getting sick in the ladies' room that the train leaves for Purgatory and Silverton and all points in between. I know I'm going to ask myself sometimes what would have happened if I'd gotten on that train. What would have happened if my baby hadn't picked that moment to show off its early willfulness? I know, too, that I'll never stop asking because I'll never come up with a good enough answer.

We leave Durango at first light, heading west, then south, on Route 160, the two-lane highway that will run us through Four Corners, the wild and desolate convergence of Utah, Colorado, Arizona and New Mexico. We'll stop there, expecting fanfare and earth shifting under the weight of its own importance, but find instead only a few Indians selling their wares, and something like two hundred portable toilets. Then the road drifts gradually southwest, skirting first the Navajo then the Hopi reservation, then the Navajo again, bisecting and squaring the land until it dead-ends into 89 South to Flagstaff.

I point out to Charlie how this landscape looks like the moon or other places you would never think to go. The roads are deserted and so the land takes care of itself, makes itself up as it goes along, seeming to have never gotten the news about the way order and repetition make for what people back east call scenery. I wonder if the point of scenery isn't getting a lot of other people to see exactly what you've seen, which accounts for postcard sales and that red barn near Gloucester, Massachusetts, that's the most-often-painted piece of landscape in the entire free world.

Out here, though, I'm more alone, even with Charlie close enough to touch, even more alone than I felt last night on Main Street in Durango. This desert couldn't care one iota about my traveling through it on the way to Flagstaff and from there to my sorry old age, my puny death. It doesn't even care about its own name, much less mine. Names mean boundaries, and the desert has nothing to do with boundaries—they're somebody else's problem. I've never felt so much myself as I do now, driving through this desert, with Charlie sleeping next to me, his head turned away. I'm never so much myself as when I'm nowhere. This is especially true in the early mornings. We both like to be driving before the sun's up, and then hard, hot daylight begins to come on, come towards us, and that whole desert world turns blue, blue like it's underwater. So you can see, in some small way, that the desert had once been an ocean, that it had dried out, gone belly up, but hung on to its original color the same way we all die, holding on to the shadows of what we've been.

North Flagstaff was a long time ago given over to light industry. Railroad tracks guard the innards of the city and heavy-duty trucks fill the motel parking lots. I call my brother from a pay phone. When he answers, I tell him we're here, making my voice singsong and haunting.

"Good," David says, "Dad can't wait to see you."

"How is he?"

"So-so. We drove him around today so could see some of the painted desert. Lately he's started talking about maybe moving out to California."

"That's a good sign."

"No, it isn't. He thinks Mom is in California waiting for him. He drinks too much. Fell down and had to have stitches in his forehead, and now he's on crutches. It's like living with a hundred children. You can take over for a few days. I've had it."

"We're happy to stay in a motel," I say.

"No, no, the more the merrier. Arlene's about gone stir-crazy since she quit work. She says just get here as soon as you can."

"Dad's out of it," I say to Charlie when I come back to the car. I tell him about the stitches and my mother's putative whereabouts.

"You get this voice when you talk about him," Charlie says. "It's like that computerized instruction at the airport: 'Our next stop is Concourse B. The doors are ready to close.'"

"Yeah?" I say. "So?"

"It's just that it's not very nice."

Nice, I think. No, it's not nice. I'm not nice. I know a lot of people who are, but I'm not one of them. Arlene is nice. When we get to their house, I'll watch her and see how she does it. If I can't manage, well, she's nice enough for two. I tell this to Charlie. I tell him I always thought Arlene should be the name of a woman much older than my brother's wife is. Whenever I heard the name, all I could think of was Arlene Francis from *What's My Line,* and the way she had to sit there in her chiffon gown next to the likes of Soupy Sales and Nipsy Russell. So when David drove Arlene Fisher to Flagstaff to meet the family three years ago this Christmas, I was surprised to see somebody young and pretty, with this mass of blonde curly hair, and wearing a red dress like she knew how it was supposed to be worn.

It was a bad Christmas for everybody, though now I find it hard to say exactly why. I remember that no one was there to meet me at the airport, and when I did finally wise up and call a cab to take me home, the house was dark and locked. On Christmas Day, my mother finally told me why, told me that all my life I'd been selfish, not at all nice, and she was giving up.

Arlene got to hear most of it. The day was never mentioned between us again until the night before Arlene and David's wedding. At the rehearsal dinner, in the ladies' room, a very drunk Arlene put her arms around an equally drunk me and promised I'd never, ever be locked out of their house.

Six months ago, Arlene and David moved Mother and Dad into their house, because they were too old to be alone. Twice Mother had been found walking into the Coconino National Forest, shedding her clothes piece by piece as a trail to follow back. She died a month ago, and at the very end, she didn't recognize anybody, got the generations and bloodlines all confused. "Mother," she said to Arlene, "I hope I have a daughter just like you. And if I do, will you pay to send her to college?"

Now Arlene is eight and a half months pregnant, carrying high and walking swaybacked with her feet turned out. I think, in the first instant of seeing her, that Arlene looks used up, like the baby is already starting to take its measure of her, even before its official entrance into the world. Her skin has the flush of somebody who's been drinking or crying or both, and her eyes move quickly from my face to Charlie's to David's, as if she can't quite keep up with all that's being said. She says she's hated the last few weeks.

"Women talk about this glow," she says when I ask why. "All expecting mothers are supposed to have it. Bull, I say. It's not a glow, it's the frenzy of looking for yet another place to pee."

"You get a sort of bovine feeling," David says. It's a term one of the pregnancy books used. Charlie tries not to look at me. It's part of the deal he wanted to make in the motel in Durango before I took my little walk: no talking about our situation, no meaningful looks. It wasn't my deal, so I'm looking at him as hard as I can.

When my father comes into the room, I'm not sure he recognizes me. We hold each other in a formal way, like people just learning to ballroom dance. He balances on one crutch to shake hands with Charlie, says he is pleased to meet him. Then he turns back to me.

"Your mother was just wondering where you were," he says.

"So what did you tell her?" I ask.

"I said you'd been met with unavoidable delays."

"That's how come I talk like an airport," I say to Charlie and point at my father. Nobody else understands what I mean exactly, but they get the drift. Arlene changes the subject, tells my father he did a good job putting on the new bandage.

"Aren't we a pair?" my father says to her. "We could be our own hospital waiting room."

Arlene smiles. We talk about her doctor, Lamaze classes. My father says he'll wait around for the birth, but then he's off.

"So, Dad," I say, "what's in California that's got you so worked up?"

"Ask your mother," he says, and stops for a second. "I like the Pacific Ocean. Seems like I should see it again before I die."

"What's the rush?" David asks.

"And I got to be scouting retirement places for your mother and me. She never did like this desert out here. I know I don't."

"Well," I say, "I heard she already took off."

My father gives me a dark look. David waves his hand to mean I should stop egging him on.

"You know that's the best way to do it," my father says. "I have to look around by myself, and you know, I think she should look around by herself too. It shouldn't be that I run her life."

"You should have told her that before," I say.

"Maybe so," my father tells me, "maybe so, but I hadn't thought of it yet."

After supper, Arlene takes me upstairs to see what is still the guest room but will soon be the baby's room. Its walls are hung with colored posters of exotic birds and animals, toucans, ibex, peacocks. There's a windsock in one corner, its streamers all the colors of the rainbow fluttering against the freshly painted white walls. I want to tell her about Charlie and me, but I don't know where to start.

"The word is," Arlene says, lowering herslf to her knees, "babies go for bright colors and contrasts. No pastels, none of that Santa Fe style here. Help me fold some of these, will you?"

We sit on the floor with our backs resting against the bed. Between us, there's a pile of baby clothes and shoes, gifts from various baby showers, and hand-me-downs from relatives and friends. In the pile, I recognize some of my old favorites, Carter's pajamas with feet, the kind that snap together at the waist. There's a pile of stretch shirts and matching pants. I remember being the first kid on the block to wear one hundred percent polyester.

"Amazing how these lasted," I say to Arlene.

"Your mother told me it's because you both grew so fast, you hardly ever wore anything longer than a couple of months."

"I remember," I say. "I remember Mother crying after we'd been to the shoe store and my foot had grown two sizes. At dinner she said to Dad she cried because she had been jamming my feet into those old shoes. She thought I was just being stubborn about putting them on all the way."

"Your poor mother."

"No kidding," I say.

"She asked for you right at the end."

"It's called being delirious."

"She said to tell you hello."

It's not that I don't know where to start, it's that if I started, I'd never stop.

"Are you okay?" I ask Arlene through the silence. "You look dead tired."

"I am. It's supposed to be two weeks now, but all the books

say that first babies are usually late. I've got a kind of cooped-up feeling too. And it's only going to get worse. I keep thinking what if my water breaks in some public place. So I only go to the grocery store and I always make sure to buy a jar of pickles so I can drop it in case of emergency. I read where a pregnant woman always carried a jar of pickles in case her water broke in public."

We look at each other and burst out laughing. David comes running up the stairs.

"Oh," he says when he sees us folding baby clothes, "I thought you were crying."

"These days, it's a toss-up," Arlene says.

We've folded the sunsuits, the pinafores, smocked dresses, plastic pants, footie pajamas and piled them in the drawers of what used to be Arlene's desk. All that's left are two pairs of shoes, polished white baptismal shoes and tiny blue Nikes.

"Do you believe these?" Arlene says, holding up the Nikes.

"Where did those come from?" I say, pointing to the white pair.

"David bought those down in Mexico. From a woman sitting outside a church. She said they belonged to Santo Niño, the child saint who travels through the countryside at night and wears out his shoes. She said David should give these shoes to his baby to wear and then when the baby outgrows them he should bring them back to Santo Niño."

"That's sweet," I say.

"It is," Arlene agrees, picking up the two pairs of shoes and opening the bottom drawer of her desk. I crawl over on my hands and knees and as Arlene tries to shut the drawer, I reach in and pull out the shoes.

"No, no, no," I say to Arlene, shaking my head, getting up and walking to the closet where I've already hung up some of my own clothes. I bend down and line up the tiny Nikes next to a larger pair. Arlene is standing right next to me, laughing, but then she covers her face with her hands and it doesn't sound like laughter.

"What? What?" I say, and go to wrap my arms around Arlene's shoulders. It kills me that I made her cry. Arlene shakes her head and stands still against me. When she can speak again, she says the sight of those shoes in the closet just now made everything real.

Later, I'm lying there in the dark limbo of the guest room, soon-to-be nursery, listening to David and Arlene whispering together on the other side of the wall. Charlie's downstairs watching late-night TV. He'll probably stay down there too. It's really the beginning of the end, I can see it now that I've got some perspective, now that we're able to sit farther away from each other than the length of the front seat of a moving vehicle. I drift a little further toward sleep and into an old dream, one I had about David and Arlene's wedding, but years before they were actually married. In the dream, David, Arlene and I are all standing on our old front lawn, and I reach out to touch David's wedding ring, because I doubt it's real. *Like Thomas,* Arlene says in garbled dream language, *like Thomas into the wounds,* her voice sounding like it's coming out of a long metal tube. Then David says to me, he says, *this will never happen to you,* and it's right then that I always come bolt awake, breathing hard and feeling as if there's been a fist driven into my heart.

I can remember their real wedding like it was yesterday, even though I was hung over from the rehearsal dinner. I remember how David looked at Arlene in a way I'd never seen before, and then after the priest pronounced them man and wife and after he kissed Arlene, David looked up at me and made his eyes go huge, like he couldn't believe it any more than I could.

After that, I read from the book of Ruth, *Entreat me not to leave you or to return from following you; for where you go, I will go, and where you lodge I will lodge; your people shall be my people, and your God my God; where you die I will die, and there will I be buried. May the Lord do so to me and more also if even death parts me from you. And when Naomi saw that she was determined to go with her, she said no more.*

"Say no more" was a joke between David and Arlene ever since she said it to him when he asked her to marry him. So when I got to that part, they both laughed and Arlene dropped the shredded Kleenex she'd been hanging on to for dear life, dropped it right at the priest's feet, and it lay there for the rest of the ceremony. Everybody was happy. Even my mother and I declared a truce. We got drunk at the reception and fed each other pieces of the wedding cake, neatly and carefully, no messing around.

The next night, after supper, David takes us all out to The Grand Canyon, a club where four of his lawyer friends are playing in a band called "Power of Attorney." Their big hit is "Heart Balm and Tender Offers," which David says is an inside joke. The lead singer is a woman from David's firm whose voice is half Emmy Lou Harris, half Janis Joplin, a nicer-sounding combination than you might think. Between songs she tells lawyer jokes that run toward the indiscreet. She winks at David and Arlene, and says, "Did you hear about the lawyer who was so lazy he married a pregnant woman?"

"It's a good thing she's the best tax attorney in Flagstaff," David says, smiling, "or she'd be out tomorrow."

Dad sits at the table and listens to the first three songs, then stumps up to the bar for a refill. I watch him shift his good hip onto a stool and rest with his bum leg hanging down to the boot rail, three inches up from the floor. Arlene elbows me in the ribs and whispers how it's the most comfortable she's seen him look since Mother died.

"Maybe he's been wanting some other men to talk to," I say back. And not David either, I think. If David and Dad could be old men together, they'd be quite the pair. But right now, they're too much alike with too many years in between them, years that David would discover one by one and slowly, just as Dad was forgetting, leaving them behind.

"We haven't been much company for him, I guess," Arlene says.

We watch as Dad introduces himself to the man on his left, who then turns to look back at us when Dad jerks his thumb over his shoulder to show who he's with. Both men turn slightly to the left to watch the television over the bar. It's preseason football, the Broncos and the Chiefs going head to head in Denver, the sky-cam drifting high above the stadium to bring its view of the Rockies into a million homes and establishments just like this one.

I watch Dad and his new friend carrying on a kind of conversation, nodding sometimes, pointing at the TV without ever lifting their elbows up off the bar. There's a jangling part of me that admires men's conversation, always recognizes it above whatever else is going on in a room. The way it takes place with so little effort, that's what I admire most about the way men talk to each other, the way it always has to do with things of this world. Charlie's like that too: all during this trip he's loved talking to other guys on the road, store clerks and pump jockeys, about mileages and the names of towns and the exact distance we'd covered in a day.

Dad orders another beer and a shot of whiskey to go with it, then raises the shot glass to the television. I imagine he's making his old toast to Joe Montana, a guy he admires for having the name of the biggest wide-open state in the Union with the lowest population per square mile.

David gets up from the table and goes to stand at the bar next to Dad. He puts his hand on Dad's shoulder, but it's shaken off. I know what David's saying. He's telling Dad to ease up, checking to see if he wants to head back to the house. Dad turns back to the game, and David stands still for a minute with his hands hanging at his sides. Even without seeing his face, I know how David's slowly thinking through the situation like he always does. Then he moves around to Dad's right and sits beside him, nudging him with his elbow and signaling to the bartender at the same time.

I see Dad lean away to his left and say something to David, then swing himself off the barstool, kicking his crutches up under the boot rail. Without them, he stumbles, pushing off against people's backs and empty bar stools, heading toward the pool room at the back of the bar. David is right after him, and I get up to follow along the opposite wall of the room. Dad sees me and waves me back, but I keep coming.

Entering the poolroom from the bar is like walking out of a cave into full sunlight. Three naked light bulbs hang in a row over a pool table lined with pink felt instead of the usual green. Dad and David shield their eyes in identical gestures of salute. There are four women and one man standing around the table, alternating in and out of the game. They look up at their new spectators.

"Need a sixth?" Dad says.

"No, it's okay. We're okay," one of the women, a blonde, says.

"I could help out," Dad says. "That way you could all play. I'm not great, but I have my moments."

"Dad," I say, "let them be."

"Watch this," Dad says, taking a cue from the rack on the wall. "I'll call it too. Usually I shoot with my crutches, but I left them back in there with the lawyers. Five in the left center there."

Delicately, Dad lowers himself over the table, looking like a bird coming in for a landing, his hip bones balanced against the rim of the table. He slips the cue back and forth under his left index finger and closes his eyes. The table groans and shifts under his weight.

"Now, what did I say?" he asks.

"Five in the left center," says another one of the women. Dad lifts his head and looks at her for a long time. She's small, dressed in a white T-shirt and a denim miniskirt. She wears a small tan purse crossed over one shoulder.

"Hey honey," Dad says, "what's with that purse anyway?"

David comes to stand next to me.

"Dad," he says, then looks up at the other players and tells them he's sorry for the interruption in their game.

"Sorry about what?" Dad says, pushing himself upright against the table, lifting it up off the floor at the end so that all the balls roll forward toward the woman with the purse. She holds up her arms as if expecting to take the table's full weight.

"Don't you ever apologize for me, you understand? Ever. I'm not some old fart who pisses in public and has to answer to his own damn children."

"Dad," David says again, "we should be getting home."

"The hell you say. Just who do you think you are, dragging me off? Your mother will treat me a whole lot better than this, better than any of you. When I get to her in California she'll let me play pool if you won't. She'll let me do anything I want. Right now. I'm going. Right this minute."

Dad drops the pool cue and stumbles around the far side of the table toward the door. When he tries to pass through into the bar, David reaches for his arm, but Dad shoves him away, so hard that David's head snaps back against the door jamb. Dad stops and considers.

"Didn't know I had it in me, did you, son?" he says. "Neither did I."

We follow as he makes his way along the bar toward the door. Power of Attorney is doing a song I recognize but don't know the name of, and they're into the second verse before I get outside, singing about a wild card up your sleeve, and then I see Dad turn around in the parking lot, sway for a few seconds, then fall into David's arms. I can hear him saying he misses my mother, wishes she'd come back from California, doesn't understand why she went.

"It's you damn kids," he says when he sees me. "You drove her away. You fought all the time, you hung on her, made her drive you everywhere, all day long. You never said thank you. We would come home from a night out, and she would sit in the parked car and say to me, 'Do I really have to go back in there?' It might as well be that you killed her."

David shifts and leans Dad against the door of a car, like he's a potted plant, or something you don't expect will make a move against you.

"And you," my father says to me, "you especially. You're the worst. Other people's children don't do what you did, they don't go running off like that, over nothing, over a cross word."

"I'm sorry," I say.

"You have to make it up to her," he says. "You have to apologize before it's too late."

We're absolutely still. All around us, around this parking lot, is vast, shapeless night, and beyond that is the desert, its dark buttes and canyons waiting to turn blue in the early morning light, waiting to remember the strange truth of the desert's origin, which is that it was once an ocean. If I started walking now, I could be out in the desert, smack in the middle of it by morning.

I could watch its blue light turn slowly, softly to yellow, the yellow of kitchens in Flagstaff in the winter when only the two of us were up. If I started now, I could be in Purgatory in a few days, and not alone, at least not for long. If I started now, I would never stop.

But then I see it clearly, like a ladder, a strange marriage of the moon, the altitude and the sodium vapor lights outside the bar, and we're all on it, all but Charlie who's walked off because this isn't his family, and he doesn't want it to be, not ever. I can hardly describe it, the way I'm seeing this lineup: Dad, then David, Arlene, me, our unborn children, all of us waiting, waiting, for Mom to invite us up. She wants us all, even me.

In the morning, Arlene is up early, cursing her decaf, and I tell her everything.

"Woowee!" she says, tears filling her eyes and spilling over. She glances toward the couch, where she knows Charlie's been spending the nights. "Can't you just stay? Send him on back to the Big Apple?"

"It's his car," I tell her. "His apartment. It's all his. I don't want any of it."

We sit down at the kitchen table. The sun is coming up. We arrange the folds of our nightdresses modestly and settle our mortal bodies into waiting.

Salt Lake

When her mother was dying, the air would not clear. In Utah, this is called an inversion. Even at noon, the sky would be dusky, *dusky with grief,* she thought, in language that seemed to float into her head out of nowhere. *Like a net of souls over the city, hanging, eyeless desire,* she thought all this too, that's what the soul was, as yet unmet ecstasy, a ghostly peace. She had these ideas sitting by her mother's bed, holding her mother's hand, sometimes when washing the old body, so old and wracked as to be foreign, not a body but a series of protrusions and declivities. The sky over Salt Lake City, between the Wasatch and the far-off Cedar Mountains, turned itself inside out, became the unbreathable essence of air, obscurely felt, like a kiss.

Her name was Em, not short for Emma or anything else. In high school she said, *I am an initial,* and her friends laughed, but she didn't, herself, know what she meant, how she meant it to be funny. Now she drove a truck for United Parcel Service, tended children at St. Mary's Church during Sunday Mass. She had decided there was no difference in the two kinds of tending she did, children belonging to someone else, a mother who had worked to remain mysterious to her daughter, worked at it like a missionary, stalking the neighborhood, raising Em's questions to a fever pitch: where did we come from, when did we get here, why did we stay, and who is my father?

They had lived in Salt Lake for twenty-four years, since Em was four, but about time before that, her mother would never tell her. They were alone in the world, Em believed, except for her mother's brother in California. He had come to her high school graduation, ten years before, and that was the last she saw of him. His name was Teddy and he was a radio personality down in Bakersfield, a rabble-rouser on one of the country-and-western stations, a man who could say anything he wanted between the hours of 5:00 and 10:00 every weekday morning. He's much beloved, Em's mother said, shrugging her shoulders. He was master of ceremonies at cattle auctions, county fairs and local political fund-raisers. He used to be a beautiful carpenter, her mother said once, her eyes closed, a smile twitching over her face, he made that chair you're sitting in. It was a rocker, plain but solid, with thick slats like, Em always imagined, the arm and leg bones of a big man. Em remembered when Uncle Ted appeared at her graduation, he looked like a beautiful baby, his face round and soft, pink, clean shaven, so that it was hard not to kiss him a second time, hard to let go of his hand. His thin yellow hair lifted perfectly in the breeze and set back down again while everyone else's was frayed and punished by all that wind trying to get out of the valley. At the reception afterwards, he struck up a conversation with a girl named Paula Chess, a quiet classmate of Em's. No one had ever thought much about Paula—she was pretty enough, but she did her work and then seemed to fade back to North Salt Lake. One afternoon's banter with Ted Ames from Bakersfield seemed to change her life forever. People said this: on a windy day in early June in her eighteenth year, Paula Chess became a hot ticket. It was extraordinary. Boys appeared to be drawn to her against their wills. She worked in a restaurant called The Pie, and all that summer, the place was filled with young men, each one alone in a booth, slowly eating pizza, much more of it than anybody could want, waiting for Paula to finish her shift. Within four years, she was married three times. She had two children and a blowzy, tempestuous look when Em saw her at Harlan's, sniffing at the produce, handling it with a slow famil-iarity that made other women look away. A chance meeting with Uncle Ted had, it seemed, done that.

And now Em was going to have to call him, tell him her mother, his sister needed—what? To say good-bye? Settle the family fortune? She laughed to herself, one short *ha,* and sat down by the telephone in the kitchen. She could hear a buzzing in the living room, the home-care worker saying something to her mother. Her hands shook. She felt hot all over, sweaty. She would have to change her uniform shirt.

"Hello Uncle Ted," she practiced in a whisper. "It's Em Stanley. Your niece? Long time no hear from. Hi Uncle Ted. It's Em. Mary Anne's daughter? Uncle Ted? Hello. It's your niece, Em."

He would know that. He had only one niece. She pressed the buttons and waited, cleared her throat, listened to a scratching, then the sped-up, computerized beep of the numbers she'd dialed, and finally nothing, until the blat of the busy signal.

Then she was crying into her crossed arms on the kitchen table. She wanted to make a lot of noise, sob for hours, maybe whole days. But she had fifty-five minutes for lunch, and then afternoon deliveries over near the University. Easter baskets for college students from their moms and dads in Ogden or Provo, two-pound chocolate eggs, strands of green Easter grass floating out of the truck for weeks afterward. Delighted, unwashed graduate students over in the Avenues, who came to the door clutching a pencil. Intelligent, Em thought, and hung-over. She'd hand them the DIAD board to sign, and it was always the graduate students who noticed. They'd smile with a mixture of relief and pain and say, "Whoa, magic," or "Cool, an Etch-A-Sketch," like they'd been locked inside too long with their dissertations and couldn't believe what the world was coming to.

It took a couple of days, but she did finally get Uncle Ted on the telephone. She noticed right away that he had a radio voice, low but not growling, and perfectly unaccented. No one would ever be able to guess where he'd come from. She thought she could hear something like her mother's voice, or her own. She hardly knew how to explain—tone, maybe? Geography? Physics, which is all about motion and force? Something like that: both their voices had the quality of rushing ahead over the words to keep a secret, hide laughter or tears.

"Em. Sweetheart," he said. "How nice to hear from you."

"I know it's kind of a surprise."

"A good one, though. How have you been? How's your mother?"

"I'm fine. Just fine. But I'm calling about Mom. She's not well. I mean she hasn't been for a long time, you know. Well, I guess you don't know. But I think, I mean—God!—she's just so much worse. I can't— You should come and see her is all."

There was a long pause, and then Ted Ames said, *Wow,* his voice like a tire squealing against a high curb. The sound of it made Em wince.

"It's a surprise, I know," she said again.

"No, no. Well, yes, of course it is. You think I should come soon, then?"

"Yes. Soon."

Uncle Ted said he could get to Salt Lake at the end of the week. He would drive. Eighteen hours. No problem. His voice was smooth again, coming at you from radio land, this is Ted Ames, catch ya later, over and out.

When Em told her mother he was coming, her hands briefly uncurled on top of the blanket. She called to him, my Teddy, as if he were in the next room. The strength of her voice shocked both of them, an invisible force hidden among the sticks and empty tunnels and refuse her body had become. She smiled at Em.

"I was just dreaming," she said, still in that full, healthy voice. "I was just dreaming that Gertrude Himmelfarb was trying to smother me with a pillow."

"Oh Mother," Em said, laughing. She felt a wave of relief, then quick at its heels, terrible sadness. This was her old familiar Mother, mother of the non sequitur, mother of unlikely dreaming, mother of mysterious connection to what she read in the newspaper. "Why did you dream that?" Em asked, when what she really wanted to say was, I miss you already.

"Manners," her mother said, her voice smaller, shrinking. "Everybody's lost them." She sighed and closed her eyes. The last thing she said before she fell asleep was "Saint Anthony." Em followed her logic completely. Saint Anthony was the patron of lost things. You prayed to him, promised a dollar or two to get whatever it was returned. If people had lost their manners, well, maybe Saint Anthony could find them. In this way watching her mother die was like learning a new language. It was like talking to children, listening to children and their long stories about who did what, where and when, stories that were part wish, part television, part overheard conversation. When she read Bible stories to the children in the nursery at St. Mary's, she often asked the older ones to tell the stories back to her. She did this so they would learn the stories—it was a kind of memorization—but also for her own amusement. The children fixed their attention on the smallest details, what was the name of the donkey who carried the Virgin

Mary to Bethlehem, did the Good Samaritan have a wife and children, what kind of fish fed the five thousand. They wanted to see a mustard seed. Em thought their versions of events were better than the originals. More logical, the connections less mysterious.

In the usual nursery group, there was a two-year-old named Ellen Woolf. Though Em tried to resist the feeling, Ellen Woolf was far and away her favorite child. That Ellen was cute and talkative and sweet was part of it, but the attraction also had to do with Ellen Woolf's father, a widower about Em's age. He was a pleasant, good-looking man, a wildlife biologist. The handwriting was on the wall, Em told herself in the language of one of the children's favorite Bible stories. They found this story believable because it was, as the graduate students said, magic. Em could see herself and Daniel Woolf being drawn together like slow magnets. It seemed inevitable and, at first, horrifying, or like a dream in which she could do nothing to stop impending destruction, Gertrude Himmelfarb advancing with the blindingly white pillow clutched in her hands. Em imagined herself trying to get out of the way. She thought, here is one more person, two more including Ellen, that she would have to do things for, take care of. She would keep having to *deliver.* All those boxes, parcels, in the back of her truck, all that rushing up to the front doors of strangers, the face behind the screen, hands reaching, smiles, delight, serious nods of the head: *yes, I have been waiting for that.* Behind these people, Em could see a life, the television on, the smells of food cooking, dailiness that had been interrupted for a gift. But then, every once in a while Daniel Woolf made her imagine being on the other side, greeting someone who said, here, I brought this for you.

Uncle Ted arrived with flowers for Em's mother and a bottle of Glenlivet for Em. He told her if she didn't like a good slug of single malt now and then, well, it was time to learn. He'd driven overnight from Bakersfield because it was cooler, and there was something next-worldly about driving through the desert in pitch darkness. Em noticed he said it that way, *next-worldly,* and she crumpled a little and shot a look at her mother, who did not seem to be bothered. The three of them sat in the living room, now a bedroom because the stairs were too much trouble.

"You look wonderful, Ted," her mother said. "I guess California still agrees with you."

"It does," Ted told her, "though I want to move up north. Oakland or Sacramento. Have my finger on the pulse." He turned to Em. "You should come out, you know. To visit, anyway. You'd love it."

Em closed her eyes to shake off the sense of the floor tilting out from under her. Her uncle was talking about *later,* about *after.* She felt loneliness come into the room like it was a person. Uncle Ted smiled at her mother then, winked.

"So you took Pedro," he said.

"I've always had him," her mother said. "You just forgot."

"What Pedro?" Em said.

Ted got up from his chair and walked over to the lamp on the other side of the room. The entire base of the lamp was the figure of a bullfighter, in full dress, looking haughty and scared at the same time.

"Voilà, Pedro," he said, surveying the room. "You got a lot of her stuff. That fake Rembrandt, those sconces. *Sconces.* I can't believe I remembered that word. You got the desk, that rickety desk, and all the teacups."

"Who's *her?*" Em said.

"Your grandmother," Ted told her. "And those chairs, and the front hall table. And the piano. Hey, where's the piano?"

"Sold."

"What piano?" Em said.

"Didn't you know your mother played the piano?"

"I had no idea."

"She was quite good in her day."

"Weren't those player pianos something?" Em's mother said, and she and Ted laughed.

Em was stunned. Her mother had barely been able to speak for the last five days and suddenly now she made a joke.

"Don't be fooled," Ted said to Em. "It wasn't any player piano. It was a baby grand, and she could sit there and play all day with this funny expression like she was about to drool."

"Sort of like now," Em's mother said.

"No," Ted told her. "You don't look all that bad. I believe you could pull through."

"She *won't,*" Em said suddenly, and her uncle and her mother turned their heads and stared.

"Well," her mother said, smoothing the blanket.

"What else don't I know?" Em said then. "What else? Tell me everything."

"Did you know your mother once drank so many martinis that she fell into the oven?"

"It wasn't on," her mother said.

"Where was this?"

Ted and Mary Anne looked at each other. Guilty, Em thought. Guilty, guilty, guilty.

"Colorado Springs, maybe?" Ted said.

"Maybe," Mary Anne said.

"Mother. When did you live in Colorado Springs?"

"Oh, before you were born. I was just a girl."

Uncle Ted told the story this way.

When Em's father was a much younger man he fell in love with a woman named Mary Anne Stanley and they had a daughter. Mary Anne was a waitress in a steak house out on Nevada Avenue in Colorado Springs, far north towards the highway. All the itinerants ate there when they came to town, all the guys building for the government up in Bijou, because the food was cheap, and they sat together in packs because they had no one but each other. They got to know what you did before, everybody did something before their present line of work, and they kidded you about it. When the subcontractors and their crews heard Em's father had been at the Air Force Academy, they asked him why he wanted to learn to drop out of the sky, and then what changed his mind.

"Hey, Sky Boy," they said. "How come you gave up on flying?"

"Gravity," Em's father said.

He first noticed Mary Anne Stanley's hair, which was a shade of light brown that always looked like it was about to dazzle itself into red, before his very eyes. And the more beer he drank, the more worried he got that this transformation would happen when he wasn't looking, that her hair would suddenly catch up all the light when he was turned away to answer somebody's fool question or light a cigarette, so that he'd be missing heavenly fire for the sake of a goddamn wooden match.

So he left his name tucked under his plate with the tip. He said he'd be in later that week for supper.

"Thanks for your note," she said when she saw him again.

"You're welcome," he said, and then waited for whatever would come after that.

"You know what I especially liked about it?" she said.

"What?" he said.

"You didn't leave too big of a tip. That would have made me nervous."

"I have a car," Em's father said, thinking that was probably not the beginning, but more like the middle, of the sentence he ought to have said.

"Fine," Mary Anne said. "I do too."

They went for drives in the general direction of Cripple Creek, along behind Pike's Peak. He liked seeing the Peak that way, a little foreshortened, then stretched out again as they drove on, made into something portentous, like the mouth of a tunnel, moving west and then dropping off as the tunnel itself fell into the earth, secretly, ominously. On these drives, Mary Anne Stanley told him all those things he needed to know: her age, which was twenty-six, that she lived with her mother, who was widowed young and used to drink too much, and was now about stone deaf. That she worked as a dressmaker during the daytime, alone with her mother and a mannequin in the deep silence of her mother's house. That she herself wasn't in love with anybody and hadn't been for years. Except maybe certain singers on the radio, who could make her feel like her heart had suddenly dropped a few inches, hooked itself onto one of the sharp parts of her ribcage and was swinging there like a star in the dark space of her chest.

She talked about her mother in slow detail, as if she hadn't spoken to anyone in a long time and had to feel her way back into words. She stared out the front windshield of the car while Em's father drove, and he noticed that her eyes stayed wide open, like they were stuck—she didn't ever blink when she talked, the way everyone else in the world did. He thought at first it made her look a little crazy. He waited for Mary Anne Stanley to blink the same way he waited for her hair to turn red, but with a new heaviness all along his right side, the side closest to her as they sat in the front seat of his car, as they faced the white peaks of Mount Princeton, Mount Harvard, Mount Yale. He thought about men, women and children heading west, and how they must have felt when they saw these mountains, the Collegiate Range, for the first time. He wondered if they thought about beauty or about being bone tired, but he thought he was too young to know the answer to such a question.

"In California, her relatives sometimes put her in the state hospital to do a treatment program," Mary Anne told him. "In the Napa Valley. Somebody's idea of a joke, right? Very funny. All those grapes turning into wine. And Mother sitting not a half-mile away, catching whiffs of the harvest, surrounded by women talking to trees and playing with dolls."

She told him that her mother used to point up at the weaving clouds of starlings in October and November, and say, *Drunk again.* When Mary Anne was ten, her mother taught her the exact word for what the starlings did to the vines after harvest, gleaning, she'd say, and her face made a kind of death's head as her mouth formed the word, exposing her clenched teeth in a horrifying grin.

"Then she would always point straight at me. I never did know why. But after a while I took it to mean she knew who I was. It was her way of making an inside joke. Far, far inside.

"When she got better, it was a different kind of joke, a play on words. When she was well, she was very funny, and very clever," Mary Anne said to Em's father. "I mean *is.* She's well now. But during the in-between times, she'd say, 'You've got to take my clothes to the gleaners,' and we'd about die laughing. She still says it sometimes now, and we still laugh, but we never talk about how the joke got started."

He took her hand and held it while she told him about living in Seattle, about coming home from school when she was fifteen and seeing her mother passed out in the park. It had happened two or three times, her mother setting out to meet her at school but unable to make the whole trip. Always Mary Anne sat down beside her and tried to look like a girl whose mother had fallen asleep. She'd wondered what in the world such a girl would look like. She'd try to arrange her features, make her face settle into a look of calm expectation. She'd lean back on her elbows, stretch out her legs and watch other children playing, their parents very much awake and watching *them.* She'd aim her body west, face into the sun and imagine the coast, not very far away, the fog banks drifting in from who knows where and boiling up to become the purplish clouds she could see in the distance. She said that was what she believed a regular fifteen-year-old girl would be thinking about, the coast, the weather. She worked to keep her face calm, to wait for her mother to wake up. She wished she carried a pocket mirror so she could check up on herself.

"Sometimes I thought about what I was going to make her for supper. I'd work my way through the meal forwards and backwards."

She'd reel off a night's menu, chicken, rice, green beans, chocolate cake for dessert, and Em's father wondered if she knew where she was right then, that she was with him.

They took these drives to Cripple Creek for a month, every Sunday afternoon. Sometimes they went fishing. On Friday and Saturday nights, Em's father would meet Mary Anne Stanley, and they would have something to eat and drink a beer in the back of King's, the restaurant where she worked, while the manager kept an eye on them and the busboys did the last sweep of the evening. She seemed so comfortable, and it made him wonder at times if she cared he was there. He asked her if this was how grown women were. There seemed to be whole lifetimes between twenty and twenty-six, those years filled with mysteries, shadowy presences.

January and February stayed cold and snowy in 1967. Em's father did finish work out at the Air Force Academy, north of Colorado Springs. After that, he'd build furniture or invent small repair jobs at Mary Anne's mother's house, or else they'd go skiing. He got to be a good skier. Sometimes they'd follow trails up behind Manitou, or around Pike's Peak, but if the roads weren't bad, they drove out to Green Falls or Woodland Park, places where they felt altitude and gravity more fiercely than anywhere they'd ever been. Mary Anne said it was like being hung on the side of the world.

They'd ski for an hour, then sit and drink a bottle of beer, not saying much, listening to the cold white world settle in close around them. Em's father liked the way snow and distance seemed to be able to freeze human time, while some other kind of time went on at its own speed. The sun moved over the trees, and no one aged a second or changed in any way.

"It's a little like being dead," Mary Anne said once, and then she asked Em's father if he ever wondered what that was going to be like, being dead.

"Never," Em's father said. And she asked him if he wasn't just a little bit curious, and he told her he guessed he'd have plenty of time to be curious about it when the time came.

"But what if it's not a stretch of time or a place you get to?"

"Then I'll be surprised."

"I hate surprises."

She said it with such force and outright anger that Em's father reached over and took hold of her hand. He promised never to surprise her. He knew he was telling the truth.

He asked her one last time: "When I go back to California, will you come?"

"No," Mary Anne said. "I can't move Mother and I can't leave her. And you can't stay, I know. There's nothing for you here."

"Ask me to stay. All you have to do is ask."

"I can't do that."

"Why not?"

"I can't."

"Why not?"

"Maybe I don't want it that bad."

The woods had darkened around them, imperceptibly, so that they were now half in shadow. They hated all this useless talk.

"Then I can't stay," he said as they gathered up their packs and put on their skis.

"I know," Mary Anne told him.

Mary Anne was working on bridesmaids' dresses in the early spring, the whole house full of lace, tulle and sateen and even bottles of nail polish to match, four or five nineteen-year-old girls being measured, pinned and hemmed. The conversation turned to whether Mary Anne was married, and then why not—not conversation, mostly long stories about husbands-to-be and fathers and brothers. At first, she would say that she didn't want to get married, but she could see it made other women uneasy, it wasn't usual, and she was afraid of losing business that way. So she began telling them that she just hadn't met the right man yet. The time she said it while Em's father was there, she looked back over her shoulder at him. She didn't make a face, roll her eyes or lift her shoulders in a gesture of *what else could I do?* She just stared. She knew something was breaking inside him, that he felt a coldness, a sudden frost at the very roots of his hair, like he'd put on a helmet of needles. It seemed to him that the light in the room changed, modulated somehow, and the colors of nail polish in the bottles on the table in front of Mary Anne seemed garish. He thought suddenly that nail painting must have originated out of some ancient admiration of bloodstains on the hands of the hunters, or the women who cleaned the animals and then cooked them. It seemed barbaric. He let himself out the back door, and stood in the cold.

"Sometimes I don't understand myself," he told her later. "I'm thinking about leaving a little sooner. Sorry to surprise you."

She said it didn't surprise her. She could tell once he'd made the decision to go, there wouldn't be much reason to wait.

They went fishing and built a fire low down on the trail near the Camp River. It made them thoughtful, and sad, like always.

"Why is that?" she said.

"I'm not sure," Em's father said. "Because our backs are cold. Because you can never really get warm enough."

Streaks of daylight still managed to get down through the trees to where they were, a quarter-turn to the north around Pike's Peak, toward Woodland Park. Still, they had the sense the fire was drawing some kind of nocturnal life out of the woods, tender, lonely animal life that would move in close but never let itself be touched. They could see the shape of a raccoon, as big as a German Shepherd, just beyond the cast light of the fire. The raccoons had come to expect some offering, and Mary Anne knew this, and so brought sugar cubes, apple cores, stale bread, and left them ten yards away. Three raccoons gathered from out of the darkness, and moved roundly, barrel-like, toward the food, puzzled over it for a few seconds, and carried it away.

"They wash everything," Mary Anne said. "If the fire weren't going so loud, we could hear them down in the river."

She was silent.

"It's funny, though," she said after a while. "The sugar cubes. I bet they'll wash them and wash them and wash them till there's nothing left."

But Mary Anne Stanley got away first. Mrs. Stanley woke up in the middle of the night in March and decided that she was dying.

"Mary Anne," Mrs. Stanley called, her voice ringing and high, "it's time. We've got to go now. Seattle. I've got to get to my people."

Mary Anne at first told her mother she'd feel differently in the morning.

"In the morning?" Mrs. Stanley said, the ringing of her voice turned to a caw, the sound of someone trapped. "Look outside. It is the morning. We have to go, I'm telling you."

It took two days to make arrangements. For the whole of one of those days, nobody answered the telephone in Seattle. They wondered if really there were any Seattle relations. They both believed she was dying, couldn't get over how apparent it was, how the texture of her skin and hair changed, softened, even her coloring became high, and like an overexcited child, she imagined all sorts of earthly delights. They watched Mrs. Stanley become the image of her daughter, and Em's mother came to see herself in high relief, her willfulness, the way her course ran parallel to the world's but seemed not to intersect it at any point.

Em's father drove them up to Denver to take the train out to San Francisco, where Mary Anne's cousin would be waiting to drive them north. He tried to find a moment to say some last words, something about how they'd meet up again, and where, but there was never a chance. Even on the steps of the train, when he pulled her aside, meaning to tell her that he'd write to her and she should do the same as soon as she got to Seattle, even then Mary Anne put her arms around him quickly and said, not now.

In California, in January, Em's father received Mary Anne's letter about the birth of the child, and called her. It was the first time they'd spoken since she left Colorado Springs. She told him her mother had died on the train, just outside of Salt Lake City, and so that's where she'd stayed. She let him listen while the baby wailed into the telephone. Em's father felt his throat tighten and tears come into his eyes.

He sent her money over the next eighteen years, but they

thought they should stay out of each other's business as much as was possible or decent, get on with their lives.

When he finished, Em said, "You're my father, aren't you? You're no Uncle Ted. There's no Uncle Ted about it, is there?"

Ted shrugged. "I had a wife later. And kids. It was complicated. And then we just got used to things."

"I have to go to work," Em said, which was true. But all the same, she didn't think she could be in the same room with the man standing in front of her, not right then. She could hardly explain it to herself, as she drove over to dispatch and got in her truck. *I'm inside a big brown bear,* she sometimes thought when she was out making deliveries, like a mantra, *I'm inside a big brown bear.* A customer had told her once that that's what UPS trucks looked like, big brown bears lumbering down the street. That's what you do if you're out in the woods freezing. You kill a big brown bear and crawl inside it. Easy, right? And you just stay there, with the blood and guts and the truth of all that viscera, and you just learn how to stand it.

On top of the First Security Bank building downtown, Salt Lake's female peregrine falcon, widowed a month earlier, seems to have found a new mate. Em heard this on the radio. Peregrine falcons, the news announcer said, may be rare and endangered birds, but they don't seem to have much trouble finding each other. The apparent new mate was a male with slightly different markings and habits from the bird that died earlier. Loss of the previous male forced the female to abandon three eggs she was incubating, and the female was rarely seen in the downtown sky after that, prompting concerns that she might abandon the area. *But Daniel*

Woolf, a biologist for the Utah Division of Wildlife Services, now believes she was out doing a lot of flying to find an available male, and the effort paid off. She has been seen mating with her new partner, and they are spending a lot of time around the First Security Bank nest. Falcons can produce a second clutch of eggs in a season if something happens to the first set of eggs.

"So," Daniel Woolf said, "maybe if we're lucky, they'll pull this thing off."

Em listened in silence to Daniel Woolf's voice. She wondered if it pained him to talk about the death of a spouse, even this way, in the animal world. His voice sounded kind, enthusiastic, hopeful, but not moved. It didn't give anything away. She admired that control, feeling lately that she herself was always on the far edge of it. And somehow her unsteadiness didn't feel like grief, that was the puzzling part of watching her mother die. And now the revelation of Uncle Ted—it was hard to stop calling him that—too. Not sadness or shock but a kind of spin, a sense that her body was moving faster and faster, getting away from her plans, taking on a life of its own. She didn't know, some days, exactly what she was going to do or say. Em thought when she got used to everything, she'd be all right, and then the very idea made her feel shaky, hysterical. *Get used to everything?* How could she possibly, ever?

But on Sunday, in the nursery at St. Mary's, she was calmer, though she felt as if, all her life, she might have been mistaken, duped about everything. Watchful, that's what she'd have to be now, vigilant. Daniel Woolf came in, released Ellen into the swarm of children, and walked over.

"Good morning," he said. "How you doing?"

"Fine," Em told him. "I heard you on the radio the other day. About the peregrine falcons."

"Right. A great story, isn't it?"

Em nodded. She was about to say, getting a new mate is

always a great story, but she wasn't sure how he'd take it, or even how she meant it herself. "Ellen looks cute today."

"Ellen *is* cute today," Daniel Woolf said and laughed. "And she was cute yesterday, and she'll be cute tomorrow."

"She's got some good PR going for her too."

"Would you like to have lunch with us after church? We usually just go for a hamburger. Nothing fancy. Quick. I know you're taking care of your mother now.

"I'd like that," Em said. "My uncle's in town, so I can take a break now and then." She looked at a clutch of children who were beginning to argue over a book. "He and Mother are devoted to each other," she said. "Excuse me. I see trouble brewing."

She began to feel a terrible thirst. She sat by her mother's bed in the living room, drinking glass after glass of water and waiting to hear all about Ted Ames, now that he'd gone back to Bakersfield, the departure from Colorado Springs, what her mother had been thinking all those years. She waited, bent forward in Ted Ames's chair, night after night, waiting for everything to come clear between them. When Em was with her mother in that last month, she felt there was a screen separating them, more substantial than a window screen, like the panel inside a confessional, where the priest and the petitioner see only the dark outlines of each other. When one moves, the other detects a kind of halt and catch, the slow-film stutter of bodies under strobe lights. Em remembered this even though she hadn't been to confession in years. She had wanted to wait, rack up some sins. She felt them coming.

"I thought," her mother said one morning, "I thought, I can get one state over but no more. And then Mother died." After that she was silent for a long time. Em held her hand, petted it. She loved her mother's hands, which were large and strong. She wondered that morning if she loved them beyond reason, if in the throes of grief she would want to have them severed from her mother's dead body so she could keep them in an air-tight bag in a drawer. She'd heard of Vietnam veterans doing that with Vietcong ears and thumbs. A talisman. But that had to do with battle, with enemies. But how could you remember if you didn't have something to hold on to? Em's own hands began to shake then, her teeth chattered. Oh God, she thought. I can't do this. I won't make it through. I'll die too.

A couple of days, she called in to work, said she had to stay home, her mother had taken a turn for the worse. Her manager at UPS was a college student named Rusty Wilson, a nice guy with a shaved head. He was always trying to talk Em into going back to school, telling her she should think seriously about it for the coming fall semester. It fills a person's every waking moment, he said. He told Em she should take a day whenever she felt like it, even if her mother wasn't worse. They could cover for her. So Em didn't have to lie to Rusty Wilson, but she did anyway. She said to herself that she wasn't sure where she ended and truth began. A strange way to put it, but exactly how she felt, that there was nothing true about her. She imagined the day after her mother died, she would go back to work, walk up and kiss Rusty Wilson, and that kiss would bring her back into proper relation with the world. She thought she might have to kiss a lot of people, at work, at church. It was beginning to seem like the only way she'd be able to repay anyone's kindness. She raised her mother's hand to her lips and kissed it. There. Then she turned the hand over and laid the palm against her cheek. Her mother's eyelids fluttered, a beautiful swoon. Everything her mother did these days was beautiful, graceful, the most perfect gestures imaginable.

"Why didn't you ever tell me?" Em whispered, patting her own face with the cool palm of her mother's hand.

"I didn't know how," her mother said.

"Did you think I'd guess?"

Her mother nodded, ran the tip of her tongue over her lips. "And so you did," she said.

The light changed in the room, slowly, from yellow to blue.

"After I go, you'll stay in the house?"

"Of course, Mother. Yes."

"Change things around, though. Be adventurous."

"Like paint, you mean?"

"Anything. Anything you want."

"I was thinking I'd touch up Pedro."

"That old goat."

"No, Pedro the lamp."

Her mother smiled, waved her free hand.

"Mom, what did Ted mean, you got Pedro?"

She waved her hand again, a strange, courtly gesture, which Em had come to understand meant *it's too long a story to tell you now.* She was beginning to have to make things up on her own, fill in the blanks where it appeared her mother would never be able to. She looked over at Pedro, the lamp, the enigmatic smile on his perfect face, the downward angle of his glance.

"He is kind of a goat, isn't he?" Em said. "He's checking out the señoritas, isn't he? He's waiting to make his move. I never noticed it before."

There was a knock at the door, a child selling chocolate bars to make money for her school. As she gave her spiel, Em looked off over her head and down the street. She had the sensation sometimes, standing like that in the front yard, that the entire Wasatch Front was leaning dangerously west, looming like a wave, taking a long time to break. She felt, almost, the great suck of atmosphere that would pull her under the mountains, how she and her mother would lie still together in their cold Pompeii. The girl was saying something about team jerseys, about a trip that she might be able to take.

"Yes," Em said. "Come inside a second. I'll get my purse."

She tried never to say no to these children. Once when she had closed the door and turned to her mother with a Toblerone clutched in each hand, her mother had said, *It's like taking candy from a baby,* and they had laughed together and eaten most of the Toblerones before dinner, washing the candy down with beer.

When Em came back with her purse, the girl was standing at the foot of her mother's bed, gazing down at the candy bar and speaking in a low voice.

"Cocoa butter," she was saying, "chocolate, nonfat milk, milk fat, lactose and soya lecithin, peanuts, sugar, dextrose, salt, citric acid to preserve freshness." She handed the candy bar back to Em's mother.

Em waited.

Then her mother said, "What are you going to do with all this money?" and the girl recited all of it again: jerseys for the girls' softball team, a trip to Lake Powell at the end of the season.

"You're sick," the girl said then, not a question.

"I am," Em's mother said. "But not as bad as I was yesterday. I think candy helps." She was smiling.

"You'll get better," the girl said. "Don't worry." She turned to Em. "That'll be two-fifty," she said.

"Give me two of them then, okay?" Em said. She took out five one-dollar bills.

"I'll give you one for free," the girl said. "Here. For you."

"Thanks. How's your season going?"

"Not too bad. Won one, lost one."

"What do you play?"

"Second base. Third when she makes me."

"She?"

"Coach."

"Third is a lot of pressure."

"I know," the girl said. "It's like you're everybody's last chance. I hate it."

Em's mother turned on the lamp. Then she held the chocolate bar in both hands, turned it over as if she were searching for a way in.

"I don't know," she was saying, "how something so small can take up so much space."

They stood still until the girl looked up at Em and said, "She's right, you know."

A minute later, Em watched the girl walk up the block. She seemed not to be stopping at any other houses, then she turned the corner of E Street and disappeared. Em wondered if there was any such girl on any such softball team, if she was a vision, a sign. She thought of calling Ted in Bakersfield, but felt like there was no room in her head for him. She would get him on the phone, but then not be able to talk, or even to concentrate on anything he might want to say to her. She stepped back into the house and closed the door.

Her mother had fallen asleep, still holding the chocolate in her hands. Em walked over and stood at the foot of the bed, exactly where the girl had been.

"Mom?" she whispered. Her mother stirred but did not wake. "Mom," she said again, "admit it. You're going to miss me."

She remembered later when he answered the door the first time, months before, she had indeed given him a second thought.

"I was just saying to myself," he told her, "'I hope that's the UPS person.'"

"Be honest," Em said. "You said UPS *guy.*"

"No, no. I really said person. I've been having a very feminist day. Just taught my class about the Nineteenth Amendment."

"Which would be?"

"Female suffrage."

Egghead, Em thought, *nerd. Don't mess with me.* Still, she liked the look of him, straight dark hair, longish, that hung gently around his face, brown eyes that gazed at her steadily, impossibly long eyelashes. "This is a little strange," she said, "but do you think I could trouble you for a glass of water?"

"No problem," he'd said.

His name was William Keach, she knew that from the deliveries, one every three or four weeks, a variety of packages but mostly five-by-eight-inch rectangles, videotapes probably. Em wondered vaguely what was on them, but he didn't seem like the porn type. Lately, they'd been coming more often. She asked him for a glass of water every time. Her thirst was astounding and seemed to hit her hardest when she got to William Keach's apartment. She could have carried a water bottle, a thermos, but she kept forgetting.

The sixth or seventh time she delivered one of these small packages to William Keach, he said, "Watch this," and began to unwrap the tape. Em put her water glass down and headed for the door.

"No, wait," he said. "It's not anything weird. It's my niece, and I understand she can say 'Uncle Billy is my favorite.'"

He put the tape into the player and the face of a red-headed baby girl blossomed onto the television screen. In the background was what Em presumed to be the mother's voice: "Say hello to Uncle Billy, Laura. Tell Uncle Billy who your favorite is." Laura gazed into the camera and a smile spread slowly across her face. Em noticed she had a rather adult-looking gap between her front teeth. After another round of prompting, Laura said something that might have been Uncle Billy is my favorite, but sounded much more like Uncle Billy did me a favor, and then, without any prompting at all, baby Laura said, I'm a busy girl, bye, and walked away. William Keach laughed until his eyes filled with tears, and the sight of it made Em feel faint, and then it was as if a bubble had burst in her chest. This is what they mean, she thought, by a breaking heart. All these last months must have worn down the catch that kept it whole, and now in a stranger's house, she was going to fly apart.

"My sister," William Keach was saying, "is the world's most faithful maker of videotapes. She used to send cookies and home-made bread. But it would go bad. You know, no preservatives." He turned to Em. "It's just the two of us, and she's in Boston. But you already know that probably. School's done in three weeks and I can't wait to get back there."

"It's far away," Em said.

"It is." He put his hand on her shoulder. "Are you okay?"

They looked at each other for a long moment.

"I think I'm going to kiss you," Em said.

"All right," William Keach said, and so she did.

Later and always she would remember that kiss as the best of her life, even after years had passed and she was married to Daniel Woolf. At the time, she seemed to know already and so paid close attention to every gesture and touch. She would remember that, as they moved closer to each other, the scent of William Keach was the strange but glorious mixture of Paco Rabane—a cologne she knew from a boyfriend years before—and strawberries. Over his shoulder she saw a silver tin gleaming on the counter, and what she said before he drew his index finger across her lips was *you had pie for lunch.* She thought afterwards he must have done that not to shush her but to get the lay of the land. Then she felt his hand splayed open in the exact middle of her back, guiding her body toward his. She tasted the strawberry pie on his lips and inside his mouth. They were exactly the right height for this kiss: William Keach was maybe four inches taller than she was, Em calculated, and so she was obliged to lean her head back, angle her whole body into a kind of rubbery faint, to float. He held her carefully, lightly, securely. She opened her eyes and watched him, and his long dark eyelashes lying almost on his cheek reminded Em of a sleeping, contented child. His niece Laura probably looked the same way. Every so often, he stopped kissing her and rubbed his cheek against her face. Em felt a faint sandiness. He had not shaved, not yet. He had not been any more prepared for his kiss than she was. She thought about what it would be like to be undressed by William Keach, she tried to remember how many buttons there were on her uniform shirt. She drew his head farther down to hers and, turning her head to kiss his ear, tasted salt. She wondered if he had already been crying, missing his sister, his niece, maybe his parents, lying on his back on the couch so that tears would have run into his ears. With the tip of her tongue, she followed the path these tears might have taken, and kissed his eyes, first right then left, until he opened them. He breathed the word *oh,* like a kind of sob, and tightened his grip on her.

"I'm messing up your schedule, aren't I?" he finally said. "You folks are supposed to do your deliveries in like two and a half minutes."

"They're cutting me some slack these days."

"Because you're so good."

"Because my mother is dying."

William Keach nodded. She could see it made sense of things for him. "I'm really sorry," he said.

"Me too," she said. "Thanks." She took a step back to lean against the wall beside the television. He braced his arms, placed his palms flat against the wall on either side of her face. He dropped his head so that his right temple rested on her left shoulder and the end of his nose touched her neck.

"So how much longer could you stay?" he said.

Em looked at her watch. "About another three minutes."

Later she thought he'd said, *Well then we better make the most of it.*

Nothing like that had ever happened in her life, nor would it again. Amnesia, she thought. I forgot who I was. The kindness of strangers. It's this weather: in an inversion, the air just stays where it is and so there is a reversal in the normal temperature lapse rate, the temperature rising with increased elevation instead of falling. It sounded like magic. It sounded like kissing one of your deliveries. Shouldn't it be the other way around? Shouldn't he be kissing you? Out of gratitude, out of look what you brought me? How wonderful if the parcel delivery business were to become like chimney sweeping and your customers got to kiss you for luck as you were going out the door.

On the third to the last day of her mother's life, Em started to drive her out east into the mountains. Her mother woke up saying she felt stronger than she had in months, she got dressed without any help in what she called her traveling clothes—a skirt and sweater she'd made herself, knee socks and boots—but there was a queer light shining in her face. Em remembered it as the light of a solar eclipse they had seen together, the summer she was fifteen. They'd walked around outside like they were lost or alien, amazed at the planet they'd landed on. It was because the light was so shimmery, everything the slightest bit out of focus and edged with silver. Haloed. Em and her mother felt a little manic. They wanted to touch everything, get that light on their hands, but Em was afraid too. There was something dangerous about it. You wouldn't want to see that kind of light very often. It would make you too tired. After a while you'd do anything to get away from it. Such strange light would show you how dull your life had always been, how safe, how wrong you'd been in your estimation of it. You'd finally see what you'd been missing, and it would be hard to bear.

She was reminded at first of what the girl selling chocolate bars had said to her mother: you'll get better, don't worry. For a second, Em felt her heart open to take in the possibility of her mother's recovery, opened the way doors were opened for her every day: that moment of mystery and expectation before the face appeared, and then hope and delight on that face. But then she knew. This was her mother's last push, the kick at the end. It would all be over very soon.

So they drove east, Em thinking maybe they'd have a nice lunch at Ruth's Diner. But when she was almost to the monument, the This Is The Place, her mother shifted suddenly in her seat.

"No," she said. "Sweetheart. Let's go out to the lake instead."

"Mom," Em said. "To see what?"

"To see? Who said anything about *see?*"

So Em turned the car around. You can do that in Salt Lake City, turn a car around in the middle of the street. In fact, Ted told her when he came to her high school graduation, Brigham Young insisted on wide streets that could accommodate a team of oxen making a U-turn. She got on Interstate 80, and just as she pulled into traffic, it began to snow.

"May 3rd," she said. "And would you look at this?"

"Is it really snow?" her mother said.

"Maybe it's locusts."

For years, this had been a joke between them, snow and locusts, after Em learned in ninth grade history that God had sent a plague of locusts to Salt Lake to ruin the crops and make the Mormons more watchful, more attentive to their faith. And then, in his infinite kindness and mystery, God sent a huge flock of seagulls to eat the locusts. Together Em and her mother had a riddle that began "How can you tell snow from locusts in Utah?" but there wasn't ever any answer. The question was the whole joke. Now, driving west, Em found herself watching for black flakes to hum down and settle over the lake. Her mother bent forward and peered up through the windshield, then sat back and shut her eyes.

When they reached the eastern shore of the lake, Em asked her mother where she wanted to go. "Antelope Island, Mom?" she said, picturing a chance meeting with Daniel Woolf. She thought of him hiking the wildlife refuge looking for widowed animals, trying to get them back into circulation. She thought about kissing him. She thought of Billy Keach, whom she knew she'd never see again.

"Salt Aire," her mother said, meaning the old boardwalk, the arcade, closed for years and all but fallen down.

"There's nothing there, Mom. I don't know if we can even get to it."

But her mother kept silent, so Em pulled off 80 onto an access road, rutted, parts of the right lane drifted over with sand. The snow kept on, falling more lightly as they headed away from the Wasatch. Em stopped by the path leading to the old front entrance of the Salt Aire Palace. She thought there was something dignified and cagey in the building's dilapidation, how it looked all right from the front—in need of just a little new glass, a little paint, some yardwork. But you could see if you looked carefully that it was a shell, there was nothing inside, probably not even floorboards, not even beams to mark off the upper and lower promenades.

"I've always thought," Em's mother said, and then she paused. "I don't know if somebody told me this or what. But I heard an old woman lives in there. And if you knock on the door, she'll answer and say she's Brigham Young's last wife. Susan."

"You want me to go see?" Em said, and her mother nodded.

And Em thought this, running up the stairs to the front door of the old place: All these years and she's never seen me at work. She's never seen how I do it. She's seen me do everything else, from the very beginning, but she's never seen me drive to a specific address, knock on the door of a stranger's house and hand something over.

She felt her mother's eyes, watching, and then she became acutely aware of her own empty hands, realization like sudden pain. What if the door did actually open, and she had nothing to give? What if Susan, or anybody, looked out at her and said *Yes?* Susan with her hair grown blinding white from age and sun, from bathing in salt and disappointment. Sometimes it happened that Em had to knock on a door not to deliver a package but to ask a question, for directions, ask if the person she was looking for still resided at that address. So she would ask Susan if it was true what she'd heard, what her Utah history teacher had told her, how God sent locusts to eat the first harvest and then seagulls to eat the locusts. And why? And why not again, today, right now? How can you tell, Em would ask her, when the clouds rise, piling over Bountiful, when the day darkens so slowly? How do you know it's snow and not the plague with teeth come to chew up your heart and spit it into the lake?

When they got home, Em saw that all the strength, all that fantastic, opalescent light had run out of her mother's face. She undressed her mother carefully, first sitting her down on the edge of the bed to pull off her boots and knee socks. Then she bent and gathered her mother around the waist, took her up like a dance partner or an armful of flowers, gladiolus, iris, something thin, reedy in the middle. She pulled her mother's sweater up over her head, unbuttoned her corduroy skirt at the waist and slipped it down over her mother's hips, held her hand while she stepped free. She turned her mother away from her and unhooked her bra, slid the straps forward and down her arms. She lifted a nightgown from where it lay folded under the bed pillow and eased it down over her mother's head. She helped her mother into bed, covered her and sat down across from her in Ted's chair. She reached over to turn on the lamp, Pedro, but her mother said, "Don't."

"Tell me the true story of it, Mother," she said.

"Not yet."

"When?"

"Later."

Every night through Em's childhood, her mother read to her, always beginning with the words *you know, this could be a true story.* And then Em remembered the look on her face, the one Ted described, emptiness, like the sky before snowfall. The stories seemed to be about her, Em. She thought her mother picked books that her daughter would want to take into herself that way, stories she would willingly confuse, mistake for her own. If there were adults in the story, a mother and a father, Em would of course imagine the mother as her own. But the father. The father was made of smoke or snow, insubstantial, always on his way from one state to another.

Ted Ames said he remembered Mary Anne Stanley in a blue dress, walking ahead of him one spring evening. She must have seemed like a body of water he was coming closer and closer to, an ending he was about to reach. And some days, it must still be that everywhere he looks, she's there, walking away, carrying her child, just ahead of him, a blue dream in the twilight.

Em sat awake all that night in the chair her father made, all night she had the sense she was looking at her mother from the embrace of her father's bones. The moon grew liquid on her mother's traveling clothes. Soon, Em believed, they would both be leaving Salt Lake forever. She listened for her mother's voice, telling her about the great, loveless world, and how she would move through it. How the world buoyed you up and that was a kind of affection, how chance was like love, out there waiting for your arrival, waiting for you to stop, take in the long view and say, this is the place.

Halloween

Marie Shepherd remembers every one of her Halloween costumes, but four of them in particular, the four years when she and her brother Sargent dressed alike. She hardly ever thinks of these years all together because they weren't consecutive, and they weren't all years before she was old enough to choose her own costume. The choices seemed coincidental at the time, though Marie knows better now. She made a joke about it to Sargent long after they'd stopped trick-or-treating; she said, *The ghost you play could be your own.*

She's at work on a Wednesday morning, on the half-time schedule the UC Berkeley Physics Department runs in the summer, and a visiting professor, Dr. Melrose, has brought in pictures of his granddaughter dressed as Peter Pan. He tells Marie this Peter Pan outfit was his granddaughter's Halloween costume last year, and since then she refuses to take it off except to go to bed, to church, or to have it washed, which she supervises. He laughs and makes a joke about little girls not wanting to grow up either, then the smile washes off his face.

"I believe in ghosts," he says, and Marie holds her breath. Her mind works to find the connection to Peter Pan.

"You mean ghosts as in Halloween?" she says. "Ghouls and that kind of thing?"

"All of it," Dr. Melrose says, "the whole shebang."

"Why?" Marie says, hearing the word ring harder and more disbelieving than she wanted it to. "I mean you sound like your mind's been made up for a long time."

"Things happen that you can't explain," he says.

Marie can tell he's thinking of something in particular. He's staring over her head, and his eyes are moving left to right, as if he's reading teletype. She knows that behind her on the wall, there are three photographs of famous physicists. Paul Dirac drinking a cup of tea in someone's garden, his pocket full of pens, his hair blown askew by the wind. Werner Heisenberg thrown off balance by some irresistible force, a single crutch looming in the background. Niels Bohr, seated between a fireplace and a window, turning to speak to someone, gritting his teeth. Another professor once told Marie the person being spoken to was Einstein, but he got cropped out of the picture. Marie loves these photographs, three great scientists trying to act like they weren't, pretending to be anybody, regular guys having a cup of tea.

In that moment of watching him gaze over her head, Marie hopes Dr. Melrose won't go into a long story about the thing that happened to him. And he doesn't. He glances back down at her, shaking off the memory.

"The thing is not to be afraid," he says. "So what were you for Halloween?"

And Marie tells him, briefly and fast because that's how they deal with one another, about herself and Sargent as clowns and mummies, as Batman and Batwoman, as Olympic ice skaters. Dr. Melrose laughs again, and says he certainly thinks of Marie as all of those characters, a clown in the best sense of the word, the wise fool, but then he sees he's only digging himself deeper and laughs again.

"A mummy?" Marie says. "How am I like a mummy?"

"All wrapped up in your work," Dr. Melrose tells her, and disappears into his office.

Marie keeps thinking about Halloween, about those costumes, about ghosts. This is somebody, she says to herself, who knows how and why things work in the real world. He knows all about how it is that matter becomes light. He knows the names of quarks: up, down, strange, charm, truth, beauty. He knows the twelve physical constants and how to make invisible ink, and here he is talking about the supernatural. She tries to remember what in the realm of the inexplicable has ever happened to her. It occurs to her that the answer is either everything or nothing.

What they first were together was clowns. Marie knows this because she's seen it in a photograph. Their masks and costumes were the perfect vision of clownhood: wide white foreheads and bulbous red noses, red-and-white polka-dotted suits with ruffles at the neck, wrists and ankles. In the picture, Sargent's mask is on a little sideways, making him look like a clown who's troubled about something. Maybe his circus act hasn't been going well, or the lovely trapeze artist has let him down pretty hard.

Marie was seven and Sargent was six, but he was already taller than she was. Their mother, Marie senior, bought the two clown costumes the same size, medium, and Sargent's fit perfectly, the elastic at the wrists and ankles slightly higher, so that the ruffles covered half his hands and spread over his shoes but did not touch the ground. Marie's costume was somewhat more baggy, and she looked, her father said, like a "cute little waif." After he said this, he gathered her up in his arms and kissed her. Sargent stood watching, silent, then turned and walked into his bedroom. He took off his clown costume, put on his pants and shirt and sat down on his bed. He said he didn't want to wear his costume, didn't want to go trick-or-treating.

"It's too little for me," he said.

"No, it's not," Marie senior said. "It's perfect. This way you won't trip and fall down in the dark."

But Sargent insisted his costume didn't fit right, that he needed to look like a wife.

"Waif," their mother said.

"Waif." Sargent repeated the word like it was a lesson he had to learn, and stared out the window.

Marie remembers that he didn't cry. There's a picture of this, too: Sargent sitting in his regular clothes, looking blankly at the camera, and Marie hidden behind her happy clown mask, which seems to be smiling down at the rag rug on the floor. After she snapped the picture, Marie's mother led her out into the hallway.

"He just wants to be like you," she said. "Let him try on your costume, okay? They're exactly the same." She propelled Marie back in to Sargent's room and went off to the kitchen.

"You can wear mine," Marie said to Sargent, and he reached over and touched the ruffle on her left sleeve, the one closest to him. He rubbed the material between his thumb and first two fingers.

"I won't trip and fall down in the dark," he said.

Marie got up to go change. She didn't say anything about the two costumes being the same size, and she kept her clown mask on her face, so that when her mother looked at her from the kitchen doorway and raised her eyebrows to make a question, Marie's expression gave nothing away. In her bedroom, she took off the mask, unbuttoned the clown suit all the way down the back, and stepped out of it. She laid it carefully to her right on the bed, so that she would not, for a second, confuse it with Sargent's. She thought that he'd feel it was still warm from her body, so he'd know if she tried to pull a fast one. But why should she? The costumes were just the same, and he knew that, but he wanted hers anyway.

Marie took her costume back into Sargent, and he put it on. She pulled at the legs a little to make the whole outfit look baggier. Then they put on their masks and held hands to walk into the kitchen where their mother was standing at the stove, and their father, Billy, was sitting at the kitchen table watching her, holding his scotch and water in both hands.

"You're going to have to take them out tonight, Marie," he said to Marie senior. "I'm beat."

"I thought so," their mother said. She turned back to the window where pink light from the sunset was zooming in. She had to close her eyes, it was so bright, feel her way through the rest of making supper.

Marie knew her father was sick, in a serious way, though she didn't know how she knew it, just like she didn't know how she knew that babies didn't come from seeds in your stomach and that there was no Santa Claus. It was almost like she'd been born knowing.

"Two little waifs," Billy said, pushing back his chair and turning it so he could put an arm around each child. Marie smelled the scotch on his breath as he bent to kiss them. She thought it was a kind of flower, that's what the scent seemed to her. She reached around for the glass, raised her clown mask so that it sat on top of her head, and took a sip.

"Hey there!" Billy said, and then, seeing her face, her grimace and shudder at the taste, he didn't move to take the glass away from her.

Marie saw that Sargent had also pushed his mask to the top of his head. He was looking at her calmly. She wanted to do what she'd done with the costume, let him have what she had, so she handed him the drink.

"You clowns drink some nasty stuff," Billy said.

"Clown juice," Marie senior said, watching from over by the stove. She was shaking her head, rolling her eyes.

"Mmmmmm," Sargent said, licking his lips. Then he made his first joke ever. "Waif juice," he said.

The next year, Marie and Sargent were mummies. In the twelve months that passed, they had come to understand a number of things, and one of these was that people were easy to scare, in fact almost everybody liked being rattled a little bit by fear, and that was what Halloween was for. It was the night of the living dead, they realized, thinking back to their clown costumes, and not a trip to the circus. So they concentrated on being the kind of spirit that lives between worlds: mummies, vampires, werewolves, zombies. Forget zombies, they said to each other right away, zombies were boring—no costumes and no purpose that Marie and Sargent could think of. Zombies were just tired of being dead, so they got up for a while to see what was going on and generally bother people who had been mean to them in life. The werewolf costume was too complicated and probably itchy. They didn't look good as vampires—at first it was all vanity. They stood together in front of the mirror on the closet door in their parents' bedroom, pulled their hair back off their faces, and drew on widows' peaks with a black eyeliner brush.

"Yuck," Sargent said.

"Yuck is right," Marie said back. "We are two ugly vampires."

The truth was, Marie knew, they scared themselves. The widows' peaks looked natural. The eyeliner brush had drawn what seemed to be tufts of hair with skin showing underneath. And so they were mummies by default.

It took eight rolls of toilet paper to make decent costumes, toilet paper and first-aid tape. Sargent thought that their hands should be bare but all bloody—from scraping away earth to get out, he said. Marie tried to explain to him about the pyramids, but Sargent couldn't really get it straight. If these people were all locked up with all their possessions in stone houses, they'd never be able to get out—and anyway why would they want to? All their stuff was right there, even their dogs and cats.

"Maybe they'd just want to see how things were going," Marie said. "Maybe sometimes they got buried alive."

"Gross," Sargent said. "Don't talk about that." Marie said all right, she wouldn't, but she was sure it could happen.

They were living, then, in Suisun City, a town sixty miles north of San Francisco. There was an artists' colony down the street where Marie senior sometimes helped out, cooking and serving food and cleaning the artists' rooms and changing their linens. There were a lot of artists in the summer, fewer during the fall and winter months, but those who were there got together on Halloween, dressed up as their favorite dead artist and went trick-or-treating in the neighborhood. The neighbors knew to ask for a trick, and then the artist would say something witty or strange, depending on the true history of the artist he or she was supposed to be. Some years, when the artists were especially friendly, they had a party and invited the local children. Other adults, including the children's parents, also received invitations. The artists knew they were generally considered to be distracted and irresponsible, and no parent with half a brain would allow children to be alone in a room full of artists.

This year, there was going to be a party, and Marie's parents thought she and Sargent were probably old enough to go. They, Marie senior and Billy, thought it would be fun too. They liked to see what the artists were up to every year, and there were always impromptu displays and readings and concerts at these Halloween parties. Marie senior always knew one or two of the artists—young men or women she met while serving up *moussaka* or delivering clean linens. The summer before last there had been a young woman poet who hated eggplant, of which there must have been a bumper crop somewhere in the country because the artists' colony was serving it about three times a week. On those nights, Marie senior would make the young poet a cheeseburger or a nice sandwich. In the third week, the poet had a terribly painful ear infection, and Marie senior drove her to the county hospital to have it looked at, and little Marie went along for the ride.

On the way, the poet talked to Marie senior about her child-hood sweetheart who drowned. She was very drunk, she said to Marie senior that she'd been drinking bourbon out of a teacup to kill the pain buzzing in her ear. The poet said she'd never told any-body about this sweetheart, not even the man she was in love with right then. Not even her family knew because she was quite young at the time, and the boy was a few years older and went to a different school. She met him one summer when she was taking a walk by herself, and for a whole year he was her deepest secret. When he drowned, they were in the mountains in North Car-olina, and she left his body and his car and walked to the next town and took a bus home. She sat at the dinner table that night as if nothing had happened. She said to Marie senior that she felt like she'd been sitting at that dinner table, silent, for fifteen years. And now, suddenly, she'd gotten up. She told Marie senior all this because she was drunk, and because she saw the boy's ghost every-where, and she couldn't help talking about it. She'd thought maybe that ghost couldn't get at her in Suisun City, but she'd been wrong, dead wrong. Even as young as Marie was then, she knew the woman poet never should have been so foolish as to think the dead boy's ghost would leave her alone.

Now this poet was back again. She was wearing a crepe party dress under a raincoat, and there was a long scarf wound around her neck. Strapped to her back like a papoose, with the scarf ends braided through it, was a bicycle wheel.

"What's this?" Marie senior said as she tried to hug the poet without getting tangled in the wheel.

"Isadora Duncan," the poet said.

"That's pretty gruesome," Marie's father said, after the poet had explained Isadora Duncan's accidental death by strangulation. The young poet smiled.

"Well, it *is* Halloween," she said. "Where are your kids?"

"Right here," Marie's father said. "They're mummies."

"Scary," the poet said, which made Marie and Sargent very happy.

At the party, there was bobbing for apples, then pin the head on the skeleton, and later a lot of dancing. Marie danced with her father and Sargent danced with his mother. So many people, artists and local Suisun folks, were dancing that after a while, wood inlays the size of a candy bar in the floor began to come loose. One of the artists picked up a couple and clapped them together like percussion instruments, in time to the music.

"These people sure love to dance!" Marie's father shouted down to her, and Marie nodded. When her father wasn't looking, she reached down, picked up a piece of the floor and put it in her pocket. She knew she wanted to save it, though she didn't know exactly why. She thought that a piece of the floor from the artists' colony in Suisun City might mean something to her later on.

She went back to watching her father. She knew he'd tire himself out pretty fast, dancing like this, but he'd never admit it and wouldn't quit until she did. Tonight though, in the middle of this crowd of people, he seemed like someone who'd never been sick a day in his life, a man she almost didn't recognize. Every few minutes, he'd point at one of the artists, bend down and shout to Marie "Oscar Wilde, I think," or "looks like Toulouse-Lautrec," names that didn't mean anything to her. She was happy and scared at the same time, happy that he seemed so well, but a little worried that he'd forgotten her, forgotten that she was eight and that this world was an utter mystery.

He pointed over to Sargent. A lot of the women, the artists and other guests, were asking him to dance with them, and it was easy to see why. He looked adorable, Marie thought, like he could never scare anybody even if he was a real mummy come out of its tomb. It occurred to Marie then that everyone else in the room looked like a person, everyone was a person trying to be another person. She knew a mummy was a person, but it was also a nobody, no costume, no skin, no features on its face. The thought alarmed her distantly, like a flash of light far off on the horizon, leaving no trace of itself and no explanation. She kept watching Sargent and saw, after a while, that he was having trouble with his costume, it was coming apart, unraveling from the head down, and he was trying to keep it together, but getting more and more frustrated. He was dancing with Mrs. Stolz, their neighbor, who taught seventh grade at the junior high school, and then with the young woman poet who hated eggplant. A couple of times the young woman poet reached out to help him with his costume, then she stopped dancing altogether and led him to one side of the room. She looked carefully at Sargent, and conferred with Mrs. Stolz, then whispered something in his ear. Marie watched him nod yes, then stand still with his arms at his sides, waiting. Mrs. Stolz took a cardboard picture off the wall—a cartoon of a black cat that looked electrified. The young woman poet rummaged in a drawer, found a pen and wrote on the back of the cat picture. Then she hung it around Sargent's neck. Marie saw that the sign read MAN WHO HAS BEEN IN A CAR ACCIDENT. Sargent looked happy, and everyone who saw laughed and congratulated the woman poet and Mrs. Stolz on their quick wit.

Marie didn't want to be the only mummy, so she unwrapped her head. Mrs. Stolz made a sign for her that said DOWNHILL SKIER, BEGINNER. That's the beauty of Halloween, the woman poet said, you can ski and fall and nothing happens. Or, she said, pointing to Sargent, you can go from death to life, just like that.

Marie thinks that after the mummies, Halloween went on hold for two, maybe three years. In that time, she learned the name for her father's sickness, Bright's disease, and then he died from it. She can't remember very much about those years, not specifically. Other people took care of her and Sargent, took them everywhere, to school, to church, trick-or-treating. These people were usually their parents' friends, other parents who didn't dress up like anything for Halloween and stayed in the shadows while their children rang doorbells and told the neighbors who they were supposed to be. Mrs. Stolz took them the second year, even though she didn't have any children of her own, and she did dress up, as Peggy Fleming, in a sequined skating costume, wearing roller skates whose wheels were wound with sheets of tinfoil to look like ice skate blades. She had been wearing the same costume at the artists' colony, two years before. She was always Peggy Fleming for Halloween, every year. Her husband owned a skating rink in Fairfield, and so her costume was a kind of quiet advertising, so quiet you hardly knew that's what it was until somebody told you.

They never wanted to be Batman and Batwoman, but their mother had already bought the material, several yards of black velour and some yellow felt.

"It's *Cat*woman anyway," Sargent said. He was so much bigger and looked so much older than Marie now that he sometimes felt he had to speak for her, and she knew this and let him.

"I want to be Catwoman," Marie said, and she saw their mother shoot Sargent a look for putting the idea in Marie's head when she probably would've been perfectly happy as a bat. "I like Catwoman," Marie went on. "You know who I think she is, Mom?"

"Who?"

"I think she's the one who played the oldest daughter in *The Sound of Music,* the sixteen-going-on-seventeen one."

"Really?" Marie senior said. "How can you tell?"

Marie didn't have a good answer so she shrugged her shoulders and turned to look at her reflection in the mirror, trying to see what kind of a Catwoman she'd make.

"Liesel," Sargent said, naming the oldest Von Trapp daughter.

"How did you ever remember that?" their mother said.

"I never forget a face," Sargent said back to her, and there was a pause, then all three of them burst out laughing. Their mother laughed so hard she cried and had to sit down on the bed. She held the bolt of black velour gripped in her hands, then used a corner of the fabric to wipe her eyes, leaving little black pills on her cheeks.

"You should go trick-or-treating with us," Sargent said. "You could be Batmother."

"I'd be afraid for your father to see me."

Batmother is right, Marie thought, and then she felt terrible. Her mother was only saying what Marie herself had been thinking for the past few days. It could happen, she thought. All she wanted was a look at him. Just him standing at the bottom of the driveway or maybe down the street a ways, and she'd tell him, loud in case ghosts were deaf, *it's okay Dad.* The neighbors would probably call the police. Batgirl yelling at ghosts.

It was a cold, clear night and very dark. There were a lot of stars out but no moon, just helpless glittering above their heads. Marie heard only their footsteps, hers and Sargent's and their mother's, and the faraway voices of other children. She wanted to shout *hey Dad!* but before she could, those exact words came out of Sargent's mouth. They all three stopped in their tracks and waited. Marie thought the night got even quieter, and she felt the dark settle more closely around them, holding them securely in place, but that was all.

Then they were Tai Babilonia and Randy Gardner. Ice skating was big that year, a few months before the winter Olympics, so big that all the girls in Marie's class had ice skating parties. They had them at The Igloo, the rink that was owned by Mrs. Stolz's husband. Marie decided Mrs. Stolz really did look like Peggy Fleming, especially when she skated. At school she was teaching Planetary Science, and Marie was completely fascinated by the forces that kept the earth lit up by the sun, and the moon bathed in reflected light, and everything moving around in the heavens. Mrs. Stolz was also teaching them how to diagram sentences. It was hard to square that with the way she looked on the ice. She looked Marie thought, like somebody who'd gotten way past diagramming sentences and would hardly remember how to do it. She looked like paragraphs, like whole novels. She looked like *War and Peace,* which Marie hadn't read yet, but seemed to her the best example of something that had started out with a diagrammed sentence and then worked its way into defying laws of gravity and motion.

Nobody Marie knew had ever actually met Mr. Stolz. There were rumors about him, though, lots of them. Marie senior called him Mrs. Stolz's First Husband Once Removed because they had been married, then divorced, then married again to each other. It had all happened so quietly that nobody knew at the time. For a while he just disappeared and Mrs. Stolz acted like nothing had happened. She went to school and taught her students English and Planetary Science. She went to church and sat by herself in the fourth pew, like always, and she stayed after, shaking the hands of people she knew. This reminded Marie of the woman poet at the artists' colony, the one whose sweetheart had drowned and she never told anybody about it. Mrs. Stolz had her same story, only refracted, bent a little as the light of day passed through it.

Where you could find Mr. Stolz, after he came back, was at The Igloo, mostly wandering around. Marie knew he paid high school kids to handle the skate rentals, the hot chocolate machine and the popcorn machine, which left him with almost nothing to do, except once every two and a half hours. He announced "Clear the ice, please!" and drove the Zamboni machine around and around, resurfacing the ice, getting the nicks out, tamping down the little mounds of powdery crystals the good skaters made when they stopped hard with the sides of their skates. He wore goggles. He was in his own world, alone on the ice, deafened by the roar of the Zamboni's engine, appearing and then disappearing through the wall of The Igloo.

The year Marie was thirteen, the Stolzes decided to have their own Halloween party at The Igloo, a private party for their friends. They wanted their friends to know each other better. When Mr. Stolz was out of the picture, they sort of stopped having friends. Even though Mrs. Stolz was polite, she had kept her distance. They wanted to take up where they left off.

When Marie senior got the invitation, Sargent was trying on last year's winter clothes to see what still fit. He had a pair of dark blue wool pants that were a little too short and tight, and his mother said that with those long legs of his, he looked like a figure skater. That's how Sargent and Marie got the idea to go to the Stolzes' party as Tai Babilonia and Randy Gardner. Their mother sewed gold braid and sequins to the pants. She gave Sargent a shirt of his father's, one that Billy Shepherd had never worn. It had large billowy sleeves and an open neck and a yoke around the chest that made tiny little pleats all down the front. When he put it on, and moved across the room to the mirror, Sargent looked like he was walking inside a cloud.

The morning of the party, Marie's mother gave her a blue skating costume, blue-gray material shot with thin red threads so it shimmered under the light, long-sleeved with a short flared skirt. Marie almost couldn't believe how beautiful she looked in the dress, really just like Tai Babilonia, who they'd seen a lot of recently on TV and in the papers. Marie believed she had that same relieved look on her own face as Tai had. She thought it was the look of someone who, after a lot of back and forth, had just won a long argument. And Marie knew what Tai was thinking, why her face had that absent look: she was remembering that once you get the feel of ice, it will never fight you, never again.

Marie and Sargent and Marie senior drove over to The Igloo early so they could help set up. Mrs. Stolz met them at the door in a sequined skating costume they had never seen before, silver and violet, the new and improved Peggy Fleming, she said. Marie put on her mother's ankle braces, and she and Sargent laced up their skates and skated out to the exact middle of the ice. There was already a constant whir of skaters moving around them in streaks of color and bursts of cold air. Marie pretended she was Tai Babilonia, and she and Randy Gardner were about to start their compulsory routine. She closed her eyes and tried to think of the first few moves, but she couldn't. This was what always happened before any competition or performance, even tests in school: her mind went completely blank, but Marie knew she'd be all right when the time came to move or think or talk. All she needed to know or do would come rushing out of her, as if knowledge and memory weren't in her brain, but in her arms and legs, her muscles and tendons and bones.

When she opened her eyes again, Sargent was pointing to one of the other skaters, a blonde girl, probably two or three years older than Marie. There was something familiar about her, something Marie couldn't account for, and she stood still in the exact middle of the ice trying to figure out what it was. Then she knew: the girl was wearing the same skating costume as Marie, blue, veined with red threads, shimmering under The Igloo's bright lights. But it wasn't just that, people had the same clothes all the time. It was that this girl deserved the costume, and Marie didn't. She was a real skater, she skated as if she were being blown by the wind, or moved by magnets drawn along under the surface of the ice. She never came near the center where little kids struggled knock-kneed on the insides of their skates and older girls and boys practiced short spins or sometimes stood talking to each other. This girl made huge swooping circles around the outermost edge of the rink, far away from the children and the talk, the little inside world. Marie watched her move through her routine and felt utterly lost. She wanted to take hold of this skater in the blue costume and shake her until her teeth rattled in her head, just to make sure she was human.

And then all Marie wanted was to get away, get out of The Igloo before anybody saw how small and clumsy she looked. But of course she couldn't leave. Marie skated over to the rail and walked off the ice. She heard Sargent behind her asking what the matter was, but she couldn't answer him. Marie senior was helping Mrs. Stolz set out cups and napkins, plates of cookies and a big vat of hot chocolate. Marie stood behind her mother and reached her arms around her mother's waist. She pressed her face into the back of her mother's sweater. Marie senior went very still, as if she were listening for a car in the street. Marie knew that her mother and Sargent and Mrs. Stolz were exchanging a certain kind of look, and then Marie heard Mrs. Stolz start to speak.

"I used to get overwhelmed at parties too," she said quietly to Marie's mother. "Sometimes at my brothers' birthdays, at Easter and Christmas, right before the family picture was taken. Then there I'd be, all red-eyed. It wasn't that I was sad, really. Nobody had hurt me. It was just that these occasions were so, I don't know. They were so *moving*. I was easily moved."

"Like everything affects you?" Marie's mother said, trying to help Mrs. Stolz make sense of her girlhood self.

"Yes, that's exactly right," she said. "Like your nerves are on the outside of your skin instead of on the inside, or your skin has fallen off, and the nerves are all just hanging there, exposed." Marie could hear that Mrs. Stolz had gone to sit down on the bench and was unlacing her skates. Marie composed herself and moved to stand next to her mother.

"I'm all right," she said. Sargent brought her a cup of hot chocolate and she took it and held it close to her face so that the steam was like a curtain.

She watched Mrs. Stolz take off her skates and then the wool socks she wore over her tights. The tights were flesh-colored and opaque. Marie looked at Mrs. Stolz's feet, her polished toenails a dulled red through the tights. She saw that Mrs. Stolz had a scar or a bruise around her right ankle, or stitches, Marie thought, like her whole foot had come off and was reattached.

"What's that?" Sargent asked.

"That," Mrs. Stolz said, "is a tattoo. It's an ankle bracelet. I had it done a long time ago when I was young and fearless."

"I like it," Marie said.

Mrs. Stolz warmed her feet by the fire. For a little while she was quiet. Then she said she thought Marie was doing pretty well in the seventh grade, especially in English. She said she loved the sentences Marie made up for her grammar homework, they were very clever. Usually she saved them for last because they gave her a lift, and sometimes she read them out loud to Mr. Stolz.

"Does he know about that?" Sargent pointed to the tattoo.

"Yes he does," Mrs. Stolz said. "But he doesn't mind. He thought it was clever too, to have a piece of jewelry you never took off or had to worry about losing. He likes things that are clever, but not too clever."

Mr. Stolz was walking toward them. He was dressed like a race car driver, in a white jump suit with patches of advertising, Pennzoil and Coca-Cola, Chevy, Ace Hardware, Burger King, Kodak. He had on a motorcycle helmet and his usual Zamboni goggles. Mrs. Stolz made introductions.

"Who are you supposed to be?" Sargent said.

"I'm Andrio Marinetti," Mr. Stolz told them, and they all laughed. "Famous Zamboni racer. And who are you?"

They told him. Tai Babilonia and Randy Gardner, on their way to the Olympics in Lake Placid. Mr. Stolz said they were very good advertising, all of them, Tai and Randy and Peggy come to his rink to skate like regular folks.

After a while, Mrs. Stolz put her skates back on and moved out on the ice. Marie watched her, thinking that her right foot moved differently from her left, as though it was more precious, or maybe stronger because of the tattoo.

Marie did not go back onto the ice. She watched Mrs. Stolz skate all afternoon, right along with the blonde girl with the costume like Marie's. They seemed like ghosts, spirits of one another and somehow of Marie herself, and she did not in the least want to bring them back into this world.

At the end of two and a half hours, Mr. Stolz asked everybody to clear the ice, and then he came roaring through the wall on the Zamboni. He drove his first circuit around the ice faster than anyone had ever seen, making the corners perfectly. No one believed such a big machine could be handled so well, and all the Stolzes' friends cheered. Someone yelled "Trick or treat!" The *William Tell* Overture began playing over the loudspeaker, and Mr. Stolz waved to the cheering crowd. He slowed the Zamboni to its regular speed and drove with one hand, then, standing balanced on the seat, he steered with his left foot, then his right. Mrs.

Stolz dimmed the lights inside The Igloo and turned on the mirrored ball that hung over the rink, so that it began to rotate slowly. Mr. Stolz kept driving, around and around. Squares of light bounced off the Zamboni and the ice and went shooting over the bodies of all the Stolzes' friends, shimmering and trembling on their faces. Afterward they asked him how he did it, how he could make that Zamboni go so fast and not wreck it, and Mrs. Stolz answered for him. She laughed and said that clothes make the man, but beyond that, she couldn't explain. He was just a good driver, and he wasn't afraid. She reached over to turn off the rotating mirrored ball, but Sargent said no, and asked her to leave it on.

Suddenly and undeniably, and in the way that it's happened ever since, Marie believed she could read Sargent's thoughts, and that he was reading hers, listening in as if they were the same person, as if they had crossed some dark road that ran between their bodies. She could see it in the chill and ghost-light of The Igloo, how it is possible for two people to leave themselves behind for an instant. She could see the enormous supernatural force behind it; she felt it as their father's arms lifting her and Sargent, to settle them in close, one on each knee. She felt a pinpoint of light open in her heart, the smallest ease, unstable, almost unnameable: she felt the names physicists had used, charm, truth, beauty, up, down, strange.

Cirque du Soleil

What I like best are inner tubes, "life rings," some people call them, making it sound like jewelry.

Mason Adams will say this to anyone who asks, though no one has, for years, posed the question, "What method of life saving do you prefer?" He used to imagine it's what his patients were trying to ask him while their mouths were propped open wide with a retractor, an instrument resembling a speculum, when in fact they were probably asking, When are you going to be done? or, What was that odd tearing sensation? or, So when does novocaine usually start to kick in? These questions he cannot bear, understandably. He knows he hurts people. He hurts them and then takes money for it. He said this recently—not even fresh out of dental school—to his mother. She raised her glass and told him, "Mason, honey, everybody hurts people. Every day, in every way. You just have found some honest means of doing it."

She was drunk, then, though she would be drunker. She had just buried her third husband, not Mason's father, not even

69

Mason's stepfather. She had buried him and then she was flying from San Francisco to Miami and going on a cruise for Christmas. Mason had invited her to join him for the holidays, but she declined, saying she'd just be sitting over him like a big black crow, her widow's weeds popping up everywhere in his nice garden. She was fond of mixing metaphors. She herself would sail aimlessly around the Caribbean, drink cheap champagne, flirt with the ship's captain and work at getting over Jerry, the third husband. She mentioned throwing his personal effects overboard, one at a time, a cuff link, a lucky buffalo nickel he always carried, his dental floss, cinnamon flavored. She thought she might like to watch his belongings glint in the moonlight, hear them plonk distantly, see if they drew schools of fishy spirits to the sides of the ship.

And she had, in fact, done this. A bolo tie, the golf ball from his only hole-in-one, his pocket calendar, which fluttered like a shot bird, his money clip, his gold-plated bookmark with the initials JL, his fountain pen, the key to his safety deposit box, which was, when Mason's mother opened it, more empty than a harrowed grave. She said, bye-bye Jerry, feeling like those might be the only words she'd say, over and over for the rest of her days. He had been good company for too few years. He doted on her, made her coffee in the morning, and she drank a cup of it while he sat on the side of the bed, and they watched the early sun move over the yard, noticed how the angle of it changed with the seasons, even more minutely than that, changed within the space of a week. Sometimes he held her hand, ran his fingers over her knuckles and whispered, unaccountably, *my, my.* Once he said, *You saved my life.*

Mason could picture it: his mother standing on the deck of *The Princess* or *The Sea Maiden,* or whatever that ship was named, in a floaty dress, probably sleeveless, but with a scarf attachment that would billow out behind her. Looking dreamy and sad, the way she always looked at breakfast when he was a kid, one hand on a box of Wheaties. She stood there, and who should happen along but the Purser, a young guy, twenty-seven, Mason knew his exact age, forty years younger than his mother. And in that moment, Mason imagined, the Purser saw his opportunity. He drifted over to Mason's mother and asked her name. He had an odd accent, crabbed and lilting at the same time, like a good dancer with a bad hip. Norwegian, maybe, but from Canada. "My name is Julia Adams," Mason's mother said. "Cool," the Purser said, Mason is sure, though of course he cannot know. The Purser told her his name was Piers. He took a good long look at her diamond ring, five carats, flashing in the moonlight.

That was the year before. In the next twelve months, Mason's mother saw Piers eight times, flew out to Montego Bay or Miami or down to San Diego to meet his ship. Which is as far as Mason could ever get in his imagining of things. But his mother told his girlfriend, Allegra, some of the details, and she would intimate. That's what they used to call it, laughing together in bed, late at night. "Just let me intimate this," Allegra would say, but Mason refused to listen. As Allegra spoke, he concentrated on her profile in the dim bedroom, or tightened his grasp around her waist and pressed his face into her neck, listening, rather, to the pulse in her carotid artery. But after a while she didn't laugh as much. She said she was worried about his mother and Piers, and then Mason started to worry too. He trusted Allegra, loved her with a deep calm, and also with the pride and satisfaction of someone who's fixed a broken machine and insured that it will run well for eternity. She had been his patient, referred to Mason's periodontic practice for a case of prematurely receding gums. He sliced two small flaps of skin from the roof of her mouth and sewed them over the receding tissue, a gingival graft, it was called. It was a beautiful job, Mason had to admit. He was going down to Stanford to give a lecture on the procedure, and so he took photographs of each stage, before, during and after. "Beautiful," he said, "beautiful," and Allegra told him that wasn't even her best side. She was a good patient, quiet, surprisingly relaxed, even when she could hear the slice of the scalpel through the soft palate, feel the tug of her skin coming away, and taste the blood. She kept her eyes open and watched the whole operation reflected in Mason's Plexiglas face mask. Sometimes she commented on his work. "That looks like sushi," she said as Mason began the graft. He used the word "harvest" to describe the removal of live tissue, and since it was the end of November, they both made a silly joke about Thanksgiving. Mason thought he'd never done better work.

But the swelling in Allegra's face was extraordinary, and three days later, she had two black eyes. When she came back to the office to be examined, she brought her five-year-old son, Sam, who looked at Mason and said, "Did you do that to Mom?" Mason felt like a heel, as well as acutely disappointed. "You have fine, delicate tissue," he said. "This sometimes happens." But when she told him her gums were hurting her a lot less than her divorce, it was as if they'd fallen onto the set of a bad movie: the rest of Mason's office, his assistant and the nurses, became a blur, a dreamy wash of colored light. All he saw clearly was Allegra. He remembered that she had high clifflike cheekbones, but the swelling had rounded out the angles of her face. She looked cute, he thought, though he had sense enough not to say this. Then the wildest notion seized him: *this is how she'll look when she's pregnant.* He snapped to attention and met the eyes of his assistant. She was smiling at him. I'm busted, Mason thought in a southern California vernacular he had never before dreamed of using, and then he gave in.

And now, in a strange conflation of events, Piers and Mason's mother were meeting there, in San Francisco, right there. It was going to happen because Piers's sister was also coming to town. She performed with the Cirque du Soleil, the famous French-Canadian *anti-circus,* Piers called it, and he had tickets for all of them. "She does something with hula hoops," Mason's mother told Allegra. "She can twist her body in two directions at once. Piers says it almost hurts to watch."

"Lord," Mason said when Allegra told him over the telephone.

"And then there's a party backstage," she said. "Sounds like a good time."

"What do you think you say to a contortionist?" Mason wanted to know.

"'Let me get that for you.' I don't know. Or, 'I'll come back later when you're not all tied up.'"

"'Could you just put your elbow over there for a second?'"

"'Is that your leg behind your head or are you just happy to see me?'"

"Do you think he's going to ask to marry her?" Mason said.

"What?"

"Piers. Do you think he's come to town to ask me for Mother's hand in marriage?"

"I hadn't thought of that," Allegra said. "Strange, though, asking the grown son for permission to marry the mother."

"Jerry did that with me. Six years ago is all. We had cigars and cognac and I told him I thought he'd never ask."

"I'm sorry I never knew Jerry," Allegra said. "He sounds sort of too good for this world. Made up almost."

"He was. I can hardly describe it." Mason felt himself close to tears. He knew suddenly that to tell Allegra about Jerry would be like some promise between them, a huge leap into new territory. He looked around his office, tried to read the little yellow notes stuck to his computer screen, stared at the array of photographed mouths on the far wall. He couldn't remember who any of them belonged to, only that Allegra's mouth wasn't up there anymore. It had been in the lineup for several months, until Mason decided there was something obscene or at least kind of odd about it, a strange kind of disembodiment. He wished he could tell Allegra that Jerry knew what you wanted before you knew it yourself, that sometimes Mason would think, "I should ask Jerry about this," and then Jerry would call, or suddenly appear in the waiting room, reaching out to shake Mason's hand.

"But that's the expected gesture, right?" Mason said to Allegra. "To ask the male authority figure for the woman's hand in marriage? Like I should ask your father for your hand, right?"

There was a pause. Mason could hear Allegra's breathing. Then she cleared her throat.

"What are you saying, Mason?"

"You know what I'm saying."

"I have to go now," Allegra said. "God, my break's been over for ten minutes. I got carried away. Got to go. Talk to you later."

She did that, sometimes, on the telephone when the conversation went too deep, too close to the bone, said she was late, had to go, made up a fictitious student knocking on her office door. But Mason was learning to go slow, not to push, not to rush her, keep it light, airy, breezy.

Jerry Ladoucette had been Mason's swim coach when he was a teenager in Long Beach, when his father died and before his mother married Raymond Kennedy and moved to San Francisco. Mason thinks Jerry was probably in love with his mother way back then, but didn't know what to do about it, how to approach a widow and her teenaged son, how to be a comfort to her. He comforted Mason by keeping him in the water, keeping him beyond the reaches of gravity. In the summer after his father died, Mason went to the Long Beach city pool every morning at seven. Up to the middle of June, he had to scale the chain-link fence to get in, until Jerry gave him a key. Then Mason swam, for three hours, until the pool opened at ten o'clock sharp. He would start slow, lengths of crawl, and after a while, he'd stop to rest, and always Jerry would be there, standing between the diving boards, watching. For an hour, he'd coach Mason, but quietly, from the side of the pool, sitting with his legs in the water. At nine the rest of the swim team arrived, about twenty boys and girls, ranging in age from six to fifteen. Mason was a year older than that, and both the star and the loner. The boys tried to be like him, and the girls had crushes on him. He helped Jerry with the coaching, demonstrating strokes, dives, turns. Jerry called him Exhibit A. That summer Long Beach City was the best swim team in Greater Los Angeles. And they were the only team with a slogan, which Jerry made up: So Young, So Fast.

At ten o'clock, the mothers and babies started to arrive, and Mason hung a whistle around his neck and climbed up into one of the lifeguard chairs. Jerry climbed up into the other. They sat like that, high above the water, on opposite sides of the pool. Mason concentrated on the kids in the shallow end, then in the deep end. He counted them, then counted again. He told them to quit running, to take turns on the diving board, to keep tennis balls out of the water. He tried not to be distracted by the college girls who lay on their stomachs and unhooked the tops of their bikinis. He tried not to think about his father, tried not to go over his father's long illness, the cancer that spread slowly and invisibly—Mason always imagined it like moss—stealing small parts of him until it entered his brain precisely on Easter Sunday. After that his father did not recognize either of them, not Mason, not Mason's mother. Mason sometimes prayed that his father would die quickly. He dreamed about it, one image night after night: his father's hand slipping out of Mason's grip. They buried him the weekend before Memorial Day, and Mason did not cry. He did not cry for sixteen years, in fact, until the first night he spent with Allegra.

That summer, when he was not swimming or standing guard over swimming children, Mason thought about teeth. Kids chipped theirs on the side of the pool all the time, or they lost teeth or bit their tongues. He was getting used to the sight of a child's mouth filled with blood—sometimes he thought he was never so calm as when he was pressing a white pool towel to a child's face, then peering in to inspect the damage. The mothers were always hysterical, always they said things like, I told you to watch out for your teeth. They're the only ones you'll have. And Mason thought, what if you could make it so they weren't the only ones? What if you could give people's teeth a second chance?

"Periodontics," Jerry said when Mason asked if this were possible.

Okay, Mason whispered to himself, *okay.* He felt a gigantic sense of relief and of ease, the sensation of a perfectly executed flip turn, when you meet the wall, and it sends you off again in one smooth movement, and faster. He had come up against something hard, and it ended up making him better than he was, in a split second and with no resistance, like falling through air.

Mason and Allegra were supposed to meet Mason's mother and Piers for dinner the night after Piers arrived in San Francisco. Mason made reservations at an Italian restaurant his mother liked, called I Fratelli, in Russian Hill. He arrived early—as usual—and sat by the front window in a space that was given over to small round cocktail tables and the bar. He ordered a glass of wine and settled in for half an hour of letting his mind run down. Happy Hour, said crayoned signs on all the cocktail tables, 5 to 7 P.M. Mason was in the thick of Happy Hour. He tried to hold himself perfectly still and become happy. All around him, other people were happy, or so it seemed. Since it was still a little early for dining, several of the waiters and waitresses, "servers," Mason thought, had tucked their trays up under their arms and come over to lean on the bar. It was the birthday of one of the waitresses, and the others were kidding her about her age, which Mason was unable to determine just by looking. More young people came into I Fratelli and went straight to the bar—from their talk about shifts and managers, Mason could tell that they were all present or former I Fratelli employees, or at least part of that whole subculture of waitpeople. Short, intense attention spans, a kind of shallow friendliness, the ability to look ahead. Mason was jealous. He wished Happy Hour would kick in, send its hazy goodwill into his bloodstream, turning I Fratelli into a silver-toned photograph, pearly at the edges. He began to wonder why he'd come early, to sit and think about his father, Jerry Ladoucette, and his mother and Piers. Allegra. He felt lately that he kept trying to get her attention, but she was pretending not to see him. He'd catch her eye, but then she'd look off just to the left or the right of his face. One of the nurses had told him a story about her daughter, who did the same thing at eighteen months: if her mother or father asked a question she couldn't answer, she'd look over their shoulder and point and say *oooda?* which they had finally translated as *who's that?* So she was changing the subject, his nurse had said, she was learning the woman's prerogative. Mason suddenly knew *he* was the question Allegra couldn't answer, he was the subject she was trying to change. He felt it like a drop in body temperature: his toes went numb, and then the ends of his fingers began to turn white. He took a pen out of his pocket and began to write on his cocktail napkin, to get the circulation going. He wrote *roses are red, violets are blue,* and waited for some sad, ironic rhyme to occur to him.

He thought of the patient he'd been with just before leaving the office, an older man, a poet who'd written fifteen books. Mason had never heard of him until a few days ago, when he was introduced on the radio, on Radio Pacifica. He'd won one of those big prizes, Mason couldn't remember which, but he thought maybe it was the Nobel. Mason wondered briefly if this would affect his own periodontic work, if it would rattle him to work on such celebrated gums.

The poet had been talking about the value of poetry in the world, what it could possibly have to do with people who were just going on, living their lives, all those people who didn't even read poetry. "It's a life-saving device," the poet had said, "the lightest one imaginable. It floats, it flies, it gets to where it's needed." How? the radio host had asked. "Ah," the poet had answered, "that's the secret, isn't it?" Then the two of them, the poet and the radio host, laughed together, conspirators, invisible. Mason felt irritated. The question had not been answered. The poet had been cagey in a way that Mason wouldn't have suspected, at least not from his office demeanor. He had always seemed forthcoming, likable. They talked about boxing and basketball. The poet talked about his wife and kids, asked about Mason's mother, wondered what it would be like to grow up in Long Beach. You can't be cagey, Mason thought, when a guy's fooling with your gums. And then he was ashamed. Periodontics—he shook his head at his own joke—the great equalizer.

So when the poet came in that afternoon, Mason said he'd heard the radio broadcast.

"What did you think?" the poet asked him.

"Interesting," Mason said. "That thing about poetry and the lives of people who don't read it. The life-saving device part. I didn't get it."

"I know," the poet said. "Kind of smug, right?"

"Well," Mason said. "Yes."

"The thing is," the poet said, "not everybody needs his life saved. And, obviously, not everybody *gets* his life saved. And sometimes you don't know it's happening. For instance, what do you do when you think you're at the end of your rope?"

"I think about the last words my father might have said to me."

"Which might have been? If you don't mind my asking."

" 'Take care of your mother.' "

"That's it? Five little words?"

"Yes."

"And that does the trick?"

"Yes."

And then Mason had a flash of memory. Himself, sixteen, alone at the Long Beach city pool, sitting in the high lifeguard chair, a few weeks after his father died. He wanted to get close to the stars, close to where he thought his father, the invisible heat of his father, the radio voice, might be headed. He thought about throwing himself up and out of the chair, arching his body up, like a high jumper, going for heaven feet first. He could do it, hang in the air for a split second, and then fall into the pool, into the deep end. He felt his body tense for the surge forward, he wondered distantly how it was that a body could move of its own accord, how the mind got crowded out sometimes. But then, he started to speak instead. *Take care of your mother, you won't have another,* he said, out loud. He liked the sound of his voice, the rhythm of the words, something about the way they fit exactly into a small space, the space allotted for them. *Below me the pool, luscious and cool.* He looked out over the cinder block building, the locker rooms, the snack bar, up the street, across the roofs of houses, past the trees his father had taught him were named ash, cedar, royal palm. *The cedar like a fat arrow.* He felt the words in his mouth, mingling with teeth and tongue and palate, and the feeling gave him comfort. He spoke and spoke, for many nights after that. He was talking to his father, but not talking to him at the same time, talking *near* him, the words forming a kind of groove between heaven and earth, a soft place for a falling body to land.

"I think I get it," Mason said to the poet.

"Hard to explain."

"It is."

"Hard as teeth."

"Well," Mason said, coming back into the world, "not your teeth. The bad news is, the molars, those old crowns, they're going to have to come out."

"What's the good news?" the poet asked. He hated dental work, Mason remembered, more than most patients. All the color was draining out of his face.

"Insurance will cover it. The whole deal, I think."

"Are you sure?"

"Pretty sure. But we can look it up in the book."

Mason turned away as the poet said something under his breath.

"Sorry?"

"At my age," the poet said, "it's hard to lose anything. You wonder if it might be a jinx. All the rest of my poems might be in those teeth."

"We give them to you, you know. You don't really lose them."

The poet smiled, visibly relieved. "I hadn't thought of that," he said. "You don't really lose them."

"And," Mason said, "the new ones are so much better-looking."

The new ones are so much better-looking. Mason watched his mother and Piers climb down from the Hyde Street cable car and walk toward the entrance of I Fratelli. Allegra would say he was a parody of himself, Piers was, tall and stocky with white blond hair that hung straight around his face, not long hair, but not any regulation cut either. Mason wondered again, and with more reason, if his mother had been fooled. Maybe Piers wasn't a cruise line employee at all, but some rounder who preyed on widows. Maybe he worked in a surf shop in Venice Beach and was good at putting on seductive foreign accents. He was wearing Birkenstocks, Mason noticed—native footwear all right, but whose? He knew his mother was too smart to fall for something so obvious. She liked companionship, but Ray Kennedy and Jerry had been logical choices, men she'd known for a long time. Ray was a golfing buddy of Mason's father. This guy Piers looked more like a caddy.

Then they were in the door. Mason rose slowly, unfolded to his full height. He was aware of the slow threat of the movement, a parody too. He hoped Piers got it. Then he tried to smile, a look that was confident and temporarily indulgent, but he wasn't sure how he was doing, if he was making a mess of it. No mirrors in I Fratelli, he noticed, not that kind of place. Then Mason concentrated on his mother. He could certainly manage a smile for her.

There can come a moment when a child recognizes for the first time that other, private life of his parent, but, Mason thought much later, the child has to be at a loss, the child has to be missing something that the secret life of the parent reveals or—in the luckiest of circumstances—gives back. This recognition is, like everything about children, utterly selfish that way, appalling even in its selfishness. Right then, with the I Fratelli hostess staring and impatient, Mason felt that singular moment wash over and through him like the fog that was at the very same time beginning to tangle itself in the buildings on Market Street, in the guy wires of the Golden Gate and Bay Bridges. His mother was beautiful. She had fine features, a thin nose, high cheekbones, deep-set blue eyes, the kind of face that became more delicate, more "crafted," Mason thought, as the flesh fell away from it. She had kept her hair honey-colored, a shade that looked like it would actually taste good if a few strands of it accidentally flew into your mouth. She wore it coiled into a tight, flat knob at the nape of her neck, which she did, in fact, refer to as a "cookie." She was thin and small and elegant. Mason saw all this when she looked directly into his eyes and smiled. And he knew he could see his mother's most private self, see it clearly now, because he was losing Allegra.

"Mason, this is Piers Hebert," she said, pronouncing the name *a-bear,* like the pro football quarterback. "And Piers, this is Mason."

"Any relation to Bobby?" Mason asked, a test. And Piers passed it.

"We think maybe back in the Dark Ages," he said, "in France. The inventor of the catapult."

"Where's Allegra?" Mason's mother asked.

"Not here yet. But I have a sneaking suspicion she won't be able to make it."

"Why not?"

"I don't know, Mother," Mason said, trying to sound off-hand. "We'll see."

And ten minutes later, their waitress was at Mason's elbow, a message, she said, Allegra got tied up. She'll call you later. The waitress looked sympathetic: here was a grown man being stood up in front of his mother and her—what is he? Mason watched the waitress glance at Piers, then look a little harder. He could see she understood the whole picture, took it all in. She put her hand on Mason's shoulder. She was far too interested, empathetic. She would not last long in this job, he thought.

"She sometimes has to settle fights after school," Mason explained to Piers. "She's a counselor. So she has to get the ice packs, talk to the parents. Get the kids to shake hands. You know."

"Well, I'm sorry," Mason's mother said. "But this is quite nice too." She patted his hand.

"She teaches a course called 'Safety First,'" Mason said, but he was thinking, *I'm going to get shit-faced as fast as I can.* "Lifesaving, Heimlich, CPR. Her students call it 'Air Bags Are Cool But

They're Not My Favorite' because she said that one day in class. They were discussing the most reliable life-saving devices."

"I'm sorry not to get to meet her," Piers said.

"So," Mason said. "Piers. Tell me about yourself." Parody, parody, Mason thought. Why am I doing this?

But Piers was game. He told Mason he and his sister, Elsa, were born and raised in Nova Scotia, a tiny town called Tatamagouche, where there was absolutely nothing to do. His father was among the last of the Acadians, the original French settlers, most of whom had been driven out, and his mother was from Finland. He had an uncle who was an orthodontist in Atlanta, whom they visited in the winters.

"So we have work with teeth in our family too," Piers said.

He told Mason that his parents liked the solitude of Tatamagouche, but Piers and his sister couldn't wait to leave. They went to college in Montreal and never looked back.

"And your sister is with the circus?" Mason had to smile, the way his question sounded as if he'd said *and your sister is part of a prostitution ring?* They were into their second round of drinks, and Mason was beginning to feel a kind of death's head grinning glee that he knew could cover panic and despair. While he listened to Piers talk, he also thought he could hear Allegra's voice, thin, tinny, telling him good-bye.

"Not the circus," Piers said. "The Cirque du Soleil. It's completely different. Well, you'll see for yourself. Tomorrow night? Any night at all I can get the tickets. Wednesday is the last performance, though. So just tell me what is best for you."

That accent, Mason thought, no wonder my mother has fallen for this guy. *Mason,* the way he said that, like the French word for house. You leaned in closer to such an accent, clung on to it in a way. What was that phrase? Hung on every word.

"Mom?" Mason asked.

"Anytime you want. I'm not doing anything. Any day."

"Wednesday then," Mason said. "That's the best for me."

Piers nodded and went on speaking.

"My sister, she calls it the anti-circus, though I am not exactly sure why *anti-*. There are many of the usual, you know, acts. Clowns, acrobatics, movements you cannot believe the body could—"

"Your sister is a contortionist?" Mason said.

"Yes, though she would prefer you to say acrobat." Piers seemed to consider the smoothed cubes of ice in his glass. "What she does is very odd. Sometimes I cannot look." He stared off over Mason's shoulder. "It is all odd. Like a circus in a dream. Frightening."

"But then you wake up," Mason's mother said. Both Piers and Mason turned their heads toward her, as if they'd forgotten she was with them. Mason thought she seemed to be speaking from out of the furthest distance imaginable, from the grave, from the deaths of three husbands, from the memory of what each one, Mason's father and Raymond Kennedy and Jerry Ladoucette, looked like in the moments before he drifted out of her grasp. "But then you wake up," she said again, and the longing in her voice was like a crack in the earth, the ground opening to gather them all in, Mason, Piers, all the diners in I Fratelli, all the winded tourists on Russian Hill, all the people foolish or careless or trusting enough to live in San Francisco, a city that hung famously by its own fault.

They drank wine with dinner, *valpolicella,* which Mason remembered drinking with one particular girlfriend in college. He remembered its color, magenta, unlike any wine he'd seen before, the color of blood in the exact instant that it pulsed out of your veins and came in contact with oxygen. He remembered how it tasted, how the girlfriend's mouth tasted afterward. Why didn't he ever drink valpolicella with Allegra?

Their food arrived—big steaming plates of fettucine, lasagne, rigatoni Amatriciana. Throughout the meal, Piers talked but

Mason wasn't really listening to the words as much as he was thinking about Piers himself. Piers had spent his childhood in a place that was, he said, strange and ugly and silent, caught in the cold Northumberland Strait between Nova Scotia and Prince Edward Island. Then he had been swept into the utter civilization of Montreal. And now I live nowhere, Piers was saying. I live on the move. There is a little too much excitement in his voice, Mason thought. Or everywhere, maybe I live everywhere, he said. The cruise line gave them nice rooms on board, the food was beyond compare, the pay not bad either. He visited interesting places, beautiful, exotic. He made friends all over the world.

"Well, I think it's very sad," Mason's mother said suddenly.

"Yes," Piers said. "It's true." He smiled at Mason's mother and clasped her hand. Then he let go and pushed away his empty plate. He laid his napkin on the table and stood up. "Excuse me please a moment."

"Mother," Mason whispered when he'd gone. "You can't marry him. He doesn't even have a home."

"I know," she began. "Mason, I—"

"No, no, no, no," Mason interrupted. He knew he was drunk. "What would Dad and Ray and Jerry say? You'd live on a *boat*, Mom."

"A *ship*."

"A ship. Or if you didn't, then who knows what would be going on at every port of call."

"Oh Mason," his mother said. She folded her arms across her chest. "Just stop it."

"I mean it. A young guy like that? Strange haircut, but maybe in his uniform. All that ocean. All those parties and duty-free goods, and for crying out loud, Mother, *midnight snacks!* I can't stand the idea. A stepfather who's younger than I am. But it's not that. Not like he'd be giving me my allowance or making me *mind*. It's not that." Mason saw his mother opening her mouth to speak, and he put his finger on her lips. "I don't even care about the age thing. I really, really don't. I don't. It's just that, it's just that I'm all alone."

Mason closed his eyes. He wasn't sure what he'd just said. He felt his mother's hand close over his fist, and he remembered playing paper-scissor-rock. *Paper covers rock,* this would be. She would win. His mother always won because her timing was excellent. She could see in that split second before Mason threw open his hand or jabbed two fingers toward her, or did nothing, what he would do. And she held out her hand accordingly: paper covers rock, scissors cut paper, rock crushes scissors. She never let him win, not once. She could still do it—see where his hand was going to go and get there first.

"I don't want to marry him."

"You don't?"

"I don't want to marry anybody."

"Why didn't you say so before?"

"Why didn't you ask me?"

Then Piers was back, standing behind Mason's mother's chair. She looked up at him, and said "My turn," and left the table. When she was two or three steps away she glanced back and winked at Mason. Piers leaned toward him.

"You think I'm a scoundrel. A gold-digger. Don't you?"

"There's no gold to dig," Mason said.

"Exactly," Piers said, and sat back.

"But I have to say, I don't like the idea of you and my mother."

"You don't know a bit about it."

"I do," Mason said, thinking with a shudder of what Allegra had intimated. "I know more than I want to."

"Well, then. Just forget some of it."

Piers and Mason glared at each other. Mason thought one of them might burst out laughing.

"She doesn't want to marry you."

"I know she doesn't want to marry me."

"Well, don't you want to marry her?"

"No. Not particularly. She's had three—"

"I'm talking about you now. Don't you want to have children? Grow old with somebody?"

"It's a pleasant idea," Piers said.

"Yes. It is a pleasant idea. See? It is a very pleasant idea."

"But it's not for everyone."

"It is, though. It is for everyone," Mason said. "I see everyone. I know. All day long I stare into people's mouths. Gums. All day. Gum's the word. Gums. Hey can I gum a cigarette? Gum me a tune, would ya? The whole is greater than the gum of the parts. I have a gummy ache. This tastes gummy. And what do you stare at? Women in bikinis and no clothes on. The poop deck, whatever that is."

"You're drunk," Piers said.

"So are you, buster."

"Why don't you just let your mother alone? She's a big girl. She can take care of herself."

"She's an *old* girl. She's all I have."

"You're going to make her lonely."

Mason watched his mother thread her way back through the tables. He had to close one eye to keep her in focus. He studied her to see if she looked lonely. He thought maybe she did. But how could she be lonely when she had him, Mason, just twenty minutes away, ready to attend to her every need? Oh Allegra. The name rose without him even thinking, almost to his lips. Allegra, Allegra. Mason shut both eyes and imagined that as his mother moved closer to him through the smoke and heat of I Fratelli, Allegra moved farther away.

* * *

"Mason!"

When Allegra saw who'd knocked on her office door, she stepped back, and her left hand rose to cover her sternum, as if she were afraid. Mason immediately thought the word, *appalled.* "Surprise," he said, half a question. "I didn't know when you'd be home." He looked past her desk, at the empty chair facing it. "Seems like the kids have been pretty troubled the past few days."

"They are," she said. "Full moon. Come on in, though. Sit down. I was just sort of cleaning up for the day." She paused, stared out the window and shook her head. "Actually it's always like this. There's no explaining them, not really."

Allegra's office at Presidio High was just exactly large enough for two people to occupy it without feeling like they had to talk. She had once told Mason that was important; other faculty made snippy remarks about the space she got, the largest office in the school. Sometimes, she said, you just had to sit with a kid. Just be a body near him. Sometimes that was all kids needed: a window to look out of and an adult nearby doing something else, paperwork, making a telephone call. It reassured them, and they could go back to class and at least for a day stop eating paper or cutting their arms with safety pins or beating the hell out of the kid across the aisle.

It was in other ways like a tiny home. Allegra had brought in an old couch and hung photographs on the wall, pictures her brother had taken, mostly in the woods near where they grew up in Pennsylvania. They were all black-and-white, and oddly non-representational, like inkblots. In front of the window there was an old oak gateleg table covered with a lace doily, on which sat a two-burner hotplate and a kettle. Underneath the table was a half-size refrigerator. There were two low bookcases that held college catalogs, SAT test books, safety manuals, a few counseling texts, and copies of the novels and plays students were required to read. There was a wooden file cabinet and a table that served as Allegra's desk. She had her father's desk chair, from his law office in Pittsburgh. He gave it to her when he retired.

Mason sat down on the couch. Allegra settled into her father's chair, directly across from him, and crossed her legs.

"Sorry about dinner last night," she said. "How was Piers?"

"I'm not sure," Mason said. "We got drunk. *I* got drunk. But the upshot is he doesn't want to marry Mother and she doesn't want to marry him. So I guess they're just going to—float in sin."

"Did you like him? I mean as far as you can remember?"

"I guess. I still can't get past the difference in their ages."

"Yeah," Allegra said. "Well it's kind of monumental."

"But," Mason shifted his weight, and the couch made a "ping" sound. "I didn't really want to talk about them. I was worried about you."

"Me? Why were you worried about me?"

Mason pointed his index finger at his own chest and then at Allegra and then back and forth between the two of them. He knew he looked like he was directing traffic. That's how it would have appeared to anyone who passed the window and glanced in. *One of Allegra's crazy boys imitating his arresting officer* is what somebody might have thought. Allegra sighed.

"I know," she said. "I know." Her voice dropped to a whisper, and she leaned forward in her chair as if she were giving Mason some gift of information. She did not take her eyes off his face. "All right. Here's the thing. You know what I'm going to say. I don't think I want to get married again. I don't want to have any more children. I'm not good at it, at either one, probably. I'm too selfish. Or something. I'm too something or not enough something."

"That's not true."

"It is true. And I know what you want."

"Maybe you'll change your mind."

Allegra said she wouldn't. She looked wildly around her

office, as if it were filled with a hundred troubled high school students. Mason knew that was what she was imagining. He tried to tell her that maybe it was just too soon, she was disillusioned, she was thinking that all marriages were the same. He could hear the edge in his voice, the blade of it, trying to wear her down. He watched cedar waxwings land in a clump in the maple outside Allegra's office window, their jaunty little backwards-pointed caps making them look like court jesters. They could hang completely upside down to get at some morsel of food, and not look the least bit uncomfortable. One or two robins had settled in the branches as well, but their movements were halting and ponderous, they had to work so hard to keep their balance. The cedar waxwings kept the whole tree in motion, nipping at the branches, rocking them like a thousand tiny winds. Mason knew cedar waxwings by that pointed tuft of head feathers and also by the yellow band at the end of the tail. They were one of four or five kinds of birds Mason could identify, and for that reason, he always felt grateful in their presence.

He asked Allegra what she thought they ought to do, but he knew what the answer would be. *Cut your losses,* he thought, wondering where the phrase came from, what branch of science or industry or sport.

"Well," he said. It was difficult to get up out of the sunken seat of the couch in one graceful motion. He leaned forward and threw all his weight toward Allegra's office door. "I guess I'll go. One of us has to go."

Allegra tried to smile. "And it's my office."

"It's tiny in here. You can barely turn around. What if a student starts to flail or something?"

"They don't flail. They mostly just hang there on the couch. They just try to hang on."

"Ha," Mason said. "That's a good one. They just hang on."

"Do you think we could try to be friends?"

"No. I can't imagine it. At least not right now."

"Good-bye Mason," Allegra said. She had swiveled her chair to face away from the door, but then she turned back towards him. "Thanks for everything. The teeth, too." She touched her mouth with the tips of her fingers, the ball of her thumb under her jaw. It seemed to Mason the gesture of a woman who had seen something awful, an accident, a disaster, an act of God, and was trying to stifle a cry.

The Cirque du Soleil comes to town like a huge and glorious mushroom, overnight, surprise, surprise. Suddenly, where you have never noticed any structure of any sort, there is a ballooning tent, blue and gold, exotic, alluring. What was there before? In that empty field, beside that sports arena or low-slung office complex? Maybe the tent is covering something, a high school, a church? You become obsessed by the grand failure of your own powers of observation. You swear to do better in the future. It becomes your New Year's resolution, even in July—to notice everything, from this day forward. The creators of the Cirque du Soleil depend on it: that you will come to them wanting to see more than you ever have before. That you will not be afraid to look.

Mason offered to drive his mother and Piers down to the Cow Palace, where the Cirque du Soleil tent had sprung up this year, but they planned to spend the day in Monterey, and so would be coming from the south. Piers told him what seats they had and where to meet, and when Mason got there, Piers and his mother were standing at the opening of the first tent, one on each side, like sentinels. There was something official-looking about the two of them posed that way, and helpful too. Mason decided it was that they were both wearing red, a deep ruby color: Piers had on a red sweater, and Mason's mother wore a red jacket he'd given her two or three Christmases ago. He'd never seen her in it before. Piers was eating sunflower seeds and Mason watched him for a moment, caught by Piers's efficiency. He'd put a seed in his mouth, move his jaw once, to the left, and spit out the seed casing. All the time, his eyes scanned the crowd pressing inside the tent. Mason waved to him, then crossed through the crowd to embrace his mother.

"Wow, Mom," he said, sniffing her hair. "Garlic?"

"We stopped in Gilroy, in a field. Piers wanted to see how it grew." She told him Monterey was wonderful, and that Piers loved the Aquarium.

"Busman's holiday," Mason said, and Piers smiled. He offered his hand and they shook.

"I spoke to my sister," he said. "There's a party for us back-stage. Afterwards. She says they like to celebrate when family comes. And it's the last show."

"They'll be swinging from the chandeliers," Mason's mother said.

Inside the first tent, you could buy popcorn, coffee, tea, beer, and souvenirs. Hats, T-shirts, videotapes and CDs; a denim jacket with the Cirque du Soleil logo handstitched on the back was going for $395. There was a boy standing on a platform selling programs, hawking them in both English and French.

Then, somewhere far off, somewhere inside, a woman began to sing. In French, Mason thought, because he didn't understand the words, but he felt them, deep in his body, echoing inside one of the obscure organs, the pancreas, a coil of the small intestine. He'd never heard or felt anything like it, a musical creature on the loose and ringing his body like a bell. Mason expected to walk out of the hawkers' tent and into the fullness of this woman's voice, but he found they were outside again, in the fog settling around the Cow Palace. The main tent sat hunched before them, heated air humming in through gigantic tubes attached to generator trucks, themselves parked next to two long rows of portable toilets. Mason closed his eyes and listened for the singing. You didn't want to see this part, he thought, the bodily functions of the Cirque du Soleil. There must be a prettier French word for all this. He would ask Piers when they got inside.

Elsa Hebert had reserved seats on the middle aisle in the second row, "so we miss most of the chicken feathers," Piers said and handed Mason their tickets. "You can read those little letters better than I can," he said and smiled. When they were settled, Mason noticed these seats were a kind of axis for the whole tent. Gathered right in front of them were all the tilted planes and angles on the stage, which rose steeply in the back, up to a platform for the musicians, the exact opposite of an orchestra pit. Red lights glowed on an organ, an electric piano, a bass guitar. From this platform, the sides of the stage fell away, curved down and under. Instead of backstage, there must be understage, and Mason thought he could feel that singing rise from beneath his feet. He settled into his seat on the aisle and leaned back. Around him the smells of hot chocolate and popcorn blossomed. A few rows behind, the seats gave way to long wooden benches, which were entirely filled. Mason estimated there must be a thousand people inside the tent, all looking up. Above their heads hung ropes and pulleys and wires. Two rope ladders led from supporting beams to openings in the interior roof of the tent. A figure crouched inside one of the openings adjusting a spotlight.

The singing went on, the voice seeming to come from everywhere, now in a minor key, haunting. Sailors drowned to this music, Mason thought, glancing over at Piers. After a few minutes, the lights dimmed so that the crowd's attention was drawn to a half-dozen torches hung high on the supporting beams. Not torches, Mason could see, but strips of red and orange paper attached to a spotlight and agitated by an air current. The effect was striking, the power of an invention so simple to suggest a time and place, a state of mind: ancient, exotic, forbidden. Mason thought he ought to rig one up for his office. Help his patients forget where they were.

"Isn't this something?" Piers said, and Mason and his mother nodded.

"You never went to the regular circus." Mason's mother put her hand on his arm. "You didn't want to go. Barnum and Bailey or the Shriners or whoever. We'd ask but you always said no."

"I remember," Mason said. "Something about it. I don't know. It made me nervous, the whole idea. It was so big. The greatest show on earth. It sounded like the end of the world."

Someone sat down on the steps beside Mason's seat and began tugging on his sleeve. Mason turned from his mother and found he was looking into the face of a clown. He guessed it was a clown, *she* was a clown. White face, big shoes, a woman under the hobo's clothes. But her hair, strangely modern, Mason thought, a copper color and standing straight up, three inches of copper plateau on the top of her head. She reminded Mason of Grace Jones, but also of his high school math teacher Mrs. Sturgeon. He was delighted and horrified.

"You're in my seat," the clown said.

"You're allowed to talk?" Mason said.

"I'm a clown, not a mime." She spoke with a thick, tangled French accent, like Piers's, only smoky, rougher around the edges. Mason thought of Brigitte Bardot. He imagined leaning over and kissing this clown.

"Let's see your ticket," Mason said, and the clown began a careful search of her pockets. She handed Mason a set of ball and jacks, a banana, a magnifying glass, three pieces of chewing gum, still wrapped in foil, a ring of fifty or so silver keys, a handful of business cards that read *Rustre Extraordinaire,* a deck of playing cards that were all kings, queens and aces, a gold pen and pencil set still in the gift box, ten silk scarves tied together, a cigar and a book of matches, and a picture of a white poodle which she kissed and said the name, Mimi. As she searched, other clowns appeared one by one, until there was a band of them, all playing toy instruments. And then finally Rustre Extraordinaire produced a ticket with Mason's seat number on it.

Mason got up, but then another clown appeared, blowing a whistle. There was a mad chase through the audience, and then the lights went out completely. A voice introduced the Cirque du Soleil in English and in French. The musicians who had been fooling with toy flutes and drums and banjos marched up to their real instruments and began to play.

The woman with the voice was suddenly standing in the middle of the stage dressed in white. She wore a girl's white party dress with puffed sleeves and a wide white sash over white stockings and ballet slippers. She had a large white bow in her hair. But over her skirt hung a kind of white cage, a bell-shaped crinoline. It didn't seem to be heavy, but the effect was unsettling, like the kinds of displacements that happen in dreams. You could not explain it but you could feel it, something amiss, out of context, but—you saw this right away—closer to the truth than in the usual waking incarnation. Like Mason's dreams about people with mouths full of rotting teeth, which he had more often than he'd like to admit. Like this woman's voice. Mason thought there must be something frightening in the words, but the fact that you couldn't understand them saved you from all kinds of nightmares. He leaned across his mother, placed his hand on Piers's forearm.

"What's she saying?"

"Mostly welcome," Piers said. "But there are parts I can't understand. Nonsense or Old French or Cajun."

The acts began then, and followed each other quickly, the high wire, the trapeze, the trampolines, which looked like mattresses dragged out of a hotel and laid on the ground to air. Twelve acrobats ran in from the corners of the stage and flung themselves almost into the arms of the audience, streamed out of the wings one after the other as if they were made of water instead of flesh. A child balanced a ten-foot Y-shaped beam on his head while another smaller child flipped and cartwheeled on a wire stretched between the arms of the Y. Fat-bellied, periwigged clowns juggled and gossiped through it all, preening their pillow-stuffed bodies. They reminded Mason of the crowd of cedar waxwings outside Allegra's office window.

A young man, deeply tanned and dressed in a loincloth, strode onto the stage. He was carrying two firebrands, which he shook at the heavens, then at the crowd before him. He juggled the two fires, swallowed the flame and spit it back into the air, lit his hands and arms on fire without seeming to feel pain. All the while he smiled at the audience, encouraging them to applaud in what Mason thought was a kind of threat. At any moment he might step down from the stage, light someone on fire and stand by with his arms crossed. Mason was reminded of Allegra's students, all those enraged, destructive boys: it was because they couldn't launch themselves into the air, because they were earth-bound. It was the same story with the next act, the strong man, *halterophile,* who did pull a man out of the first row and challenge him to lift the weights. All around these two, from coast to coast, women and children and even other men vaulted and spun and flew, defied gravity while they just stood around watching. Mason wondered if they drove fast cars on their days off, drove them faster and faster, hoping to break through some invisible barrier, the booming, trembling speed of sound, the pure, unimaginable speed of light.

The woman in white continued to sing between the acts, sometimes during. All the songs were different, some even jaunty, or at least, Mason thought, a kind of up-tempo despair. He wished he knew what the words meant—he had this idea they were what he needed to hear. He remembered his patient, the poet who said not everybody gets their life saved. The woman drew her hands up, palms open, toward her throat and then cast her arms wide, out to the audience. Her voice rose and then angled off into a minor key. Calliope, the music of baseball games. Calliope at a funeral. Standing frozen in that gesture, it was the woman singing who seemed to need saving. As her voice eased out of the last note, Mason could hear the man in front of him speaking to his child. "No, no," he was saying, "it's all right. They have wires tied to their waists. They won't ever fall."

At the intermission, Mason's mother and Piers stood up to stretch their legs, get some hot chocolate, but Mason stayed in his seat. He told them he felt a little paralyzed by the sight of all those bodies flinging themselves around. He thanked Piers for getting the tickets, shook his hand again, thinking the bad air between them might melt away. As Piers was putting on his sweater, Mason studied him, wondering about Elsa Hebert. How dangerous could Piers be if he had a sister who was part of all this? He tried to imagine her saying to her parents, in French, Mom, Dad, I want to join the circus. The looks on their faces. How could you explain it? Dad, I have this unusual talent. Mom, I have this saving grace.

He had called Allegra before leaving the house, he wasn't sure why. He had left a few things at her apartment, a toothbrush, a couple of shirts, not much. He wanted to give her a chance to take back what she said to him in her office, and by the time she answered the phone, he'd worked himself into the pure, shining belief that she would have changed her mind, she would say, Mason, I didn't mean it. I momentarily took leave of my senses. I can't live without you.

But when she heard him say her name, her voice went perfectly flat. It was amazing, Mason thought, sitting in his seat at the Cirque du Soleil, examining the hitches and chains, catwalks and ladders, just amazing that the human voice had so much geometry in it. Allegra's voice had become a plane, an angle, smooth, flat, pointed into empty air. He hadn't known she could do that, turn her heart off that way. They seemed to have nothing to talk about. Mason asked about Sam, and Allegra said he was fine. Well, I'll let you go, Mason said, and Allegra told him okay, and then they said good-bye. I'll let you go, I'll let you go. Mason heard the words in his head still, now. Those were, they must be, the exact words being sung by the woman in the white dress. Or no. She was singing I'll never let you go. And it sounded so mournful because it was so untrue, so impossible. Imagine it, the whole idea: *never let you go.*

Never is a long time, Mason's father said that. It was one of his favorite reprimands. I'll never eat cabbage, Mason said, I'll never fall asleep at 8:30, it's too early. I'll never be able to ride a real bicycle, I'll never save enough for skates, for a car. I'll never speak to you again. Easter Sunday, when Mason was sixteen, he walked into the living room to see his father stretched out on the floor. He seemed to be looking under the couch.

"Dad, we didn't hide any eggs this year, remember?" Mason said it with a catch in his voice. He had just that second been thinking he was too old and his mother and father would never hide Easter eggs for him again. When his father didn't answer or move, Mason crossed the room, lifted his father and carried him out to the car. Later, he didn't know how he'd done it—where he'd found such monumental strength. His father was six-foot-five and weighed 270 pounds. Mason was still only about five-ten. He got his height that summer, after his father was no longer able to live at home. Mason got taller and heavier, week after week. Even so, he could swim faster. He could stay underwater longer and longer.

When the lights in the tent began to flash, Mason looked up, past the stage, and saw his mother and Piers making their way down the aisle directly across from him. They held on to each other in an odd way: Piers lowered his head and listened. He seemed as much in need of help as Mason's mother's old bones did. The lights began to dim, and then Mason understood that his mother was telling Piers where the steps were—and that they were lost: he could see them in the uneven light of those false torches, halted at the second row, looking for him. Then Piers felt in his pockets for the tickets, but Mason knew he didn't have them.

The tent was fully dark except for footlights, and the woman in the white dress appeared, materialized out of nothing, not even mist, and began to sing. It was the same unsettling melody they'd heard at first, a kind of theme song. The woman drifted, singing, to her right and began to move around the edge of the stage, singing to the audience, her arms and open palms rowing in that gesture he'd noticed before, imploring. Mason leaned forward and got up out of his seat, made his way as quietly as he could around to where his mother and Piers stood frozen, one of them half-blind. He led them back to their seats, coming face-to-face with the beautiful singer. Not exactly face-to-face. Mason's head was right at her knees, but she looked directly at him. They were close enough for him to see that her eyes were icy blue and her hair was very dark. Strong white light shone full on her face, the kind of light used in movies to show unseen presence, possession, aliens.

She sings this way because she doesn't belong here, Mason thought. That's why this song is so horrifying and sad. She sings this way because she doesn't belong anywhere.

Mason got his mother and Piers settled in their seats, and the rest of the Cirque du Soleil unfolded itself before them: the clown acts, a trampoline board, a long and complicated clown pantomime involving a tearful good-bye, a train in the snow, and then the blizzard of chicken feathers Piers had hinted at. An acrobat hung in the air while his body seemed to liquefy and then began to ooze over and under and through a metal cube. Eight men dressed like characters from those Australian apocalyptic movies strung up a net and tossed each other between two trapezes. And then there was Elsa Hebert.

She was not exactly the grand finale—the trapeze acrobats had been that. She was something else, beyond, and Mason could see right away why she used the term anti-circus. Her act was a quiet, disturbing spectacle. With her toes, she could pick up any number of aluminum hoops, probably three feet in diameter, and with a small, constant undulation of her body, set them spinning, bring them up to knee, hip, waist, chest level. Then she would bend herself over backwards, keeping the hoops going on her ankle, on her leg, her arms, around her waist, then bend farther, so that her head faced the same direction as her toes pointed. Her body was nothing but bone and tendon, all of it, every joint and hollow, outlined beneath a shell-colored one-piece leotard, a shade that hovered between silver and white. What Elsa Hebert was doing seemed beyond private. Mason wasn't sure he'd even seen so much of Allegra's body as he believed he was seeing of Elsa's—and not seeing, that was the dream logic, that covering it made her body more naked. The odd sentence *Now I will have to marry her* wrote itself behind Mason's eyes. Because she was so young and thin, her act felt like something no one ought to be seeing. The delicate, careful way she nudged each hoop with her toe, as if it were an undergarment, drew it onto her ankle and then higher—it was a kind of understanding with every member of the audience. This was a gesture that women recognized from their most private, lonely moments, and men from theirs too. Her body shivered through this impossibly acute, protracted moment of longing. In the end, she stood still, and the singing stopped with a kind of cry. The hoops fell to the ground, and Elsa stepped out of them—just stepped, like a woman changing clothes in a hurry. She picked up the hoops and ran off stage.

Mason looked over at Piers, ready to mouth some words, *wow*, or *she's great*. But Piers had leaned his head back and closed his eyes.

Then the voice was singing that first, familiar song, the theme song, and the performers came out to take their bows. There were many more of them than Mason had thought. He was sure that some of the trampoline and trapeze artists were the same but it wasn't so. The costumes made more sense seen all together—and less sense too: a combination of the French Revolution and the Mad Max movies, everyone diseased and hot and stinking, climbing out of the ruins, amazed to be alive. Elsa Hebert appeared in the same wave of performers as the fire boy and the strong man, all of them the only ones who did not leave the ground. She walked to the very edge of the stage and waved to Piers. Though she wore heavy makeup and the vivid color around her eyes was almost impenetrable, Mason could see the irises move to take stock of him and his mother. There were two more curtain calls, but Elsa did not come back to wave to them.

The party, it turned out, was not backstage but in an administration building adjacent to the Cow Palace. And this too, Mason thought, seemed like part of a dream, maybe the same dream as the one inhabited by the Cirque du Soleil itself. The performers were there, most of them still wearing makeup and dressed in parts of their costumes. They drifted among the other guests, who were family members, arts supporters, francophiles, miscellaneous benefactors. They moved alone, eating from the banquet tables with their fingers and drinking bottles of Canadian beer. They spoke to each other in French, just a word or two, *bien, ce ci c'est delicieux,* or *pas mal, eh?* They seemed like another species, some half-tame animal. A scent rose from their bodies that was part sweat, part a kind of growing impatience. Soon they would be leaving this place too, even if it was San Francisco, soon they would be careening through some other sweet air, over somebody else's town. Portland, Las Vegas, Seattle, where they could cross over into British Columbia, Vancouver. Somebody had relations in Burnaby who would give them a home-cooked meal.

Mason was relieved that Elsa Hebert seemed more substantial in person than on stage. She was wearing a black wool jumper over her leotard and black ballet slippers on her feet. She looked elegant and—Mason knew this was strange, but he couldn't help it—like something out of science fiction. She looked like the future. It appeared that she had silver skin. She was a vision of what everyone would look like someday, what everyone would wear over their bones to guard against heat and cold, wild animals and hard falls from great heights. Mason wondered if her voice would sound hollow when she opened her mouth to speak.

If, maybe he ought to have said, because she stood in front of them for a long time without saying a word. She was listening to Piers tell her something in French—Mason thought it was about their parents—he believed he could recognize the words *maman* and *papa.* Then Piers began to look at Mason's mother as he talked, and so did Elsa. Mason tried to read something in her expression, but her face closed over on itself, her features assumed the same blankness they took on when she performed. It was like seeing a face disappear beneath the surface of a body of water. If you're looking down on the face from above, from the height of a lifeguard's chair, say, and the face is looking up at you, it appears that two folds of water, two waves that parted to make room for this face, draw slowly back together. Then that face is lost to you, though maybe not forever, if you move fast enough.

"Elsa," Mason said, holding out his hand. Piers had made introductions, but it seemed like a long time before. Elsa took his hand and Mason felt her thin fingers, cold from the bottle of beer. "How do you do that? With the hoops?"

Elsa glanced quickly at her brother, as if she needed him to translate. She gave a quick little shrug of her shoulders.

"I am double-jointed," she said, then closed her eyes and shook her head as if she had given the wrong answer and would now correct herself. "It is a God-given talent," she said. "I have never really understood it." Mason must have looked disappointed. He thought so because Elsa was staring at him, furrowing her brow. "It is my way of solving problems," she said finally.

Then she turned to Mason's mother and said how happy she was to meet her, how Piers had spoken of her often. The two women were almost the same build and height, Mason noticed suddenly; there was a quality of opalescence about both, a kind of shimmering. The mirage of Elsa's leotard was very like the dewy, rehydrated look of his mother's skin. It was odd to see them speaking together—eye to eye and toe to toe. It was otherworldly. Mason felt as if he had awakened from the Cirque du Soleil into more of the same dream, the same confusion and conflation of images: his mother as an old woman, but also as a young woman who could bend and move her body in startling, almost erotic ways, the two of them speaking to one another, a kind of echo. What did it mean, this dream? Didn't people have dreams in order to interpret them? In order to be warned by them? Saved by them?

Mason watched Piers, examined his smile. Even in the half-light of the banquet room, he could see that in a few years, Piers would need the same gingival graft that Allegra had had. He would have to tell Piers not to brush so hard when he cleaned his teeth. *I can see this about you,* he began the sentence in his head, *I have taken note.* What on earth was Piers doing in this dream? What on earth were any of them doing? The fire boy passed behind Elsa, eating a miniature quiche, taking small quick bites

with his front teeth. Mason caught his eye, raised his own chin
slightly and smiled in a way he thought would seem to say, Nice
work setting fire to yourself back there. Fire boy glanced at Elsa,
Elsa's back really, trying to decide whether he knew Mason. He
swallowed the rest of the quiche and walked over, pressed his
palm to the curve of Elsa's waist.

Mason believed he felt an unaccountable heat and smelled
gasoline. He thought that there must be something visceral about
juggling, swallowing, playing with fire like that. Elsa turned and
introduced him as Jean.

"*Il fait chaud ici, n'est-ce pas?*" Jean said, and Elsa laughed. So
did Piers.

"He says it's hot in here," she translated. "He says there are
too many bodies and not enough beers. He says he will be lonely
again tonight." Clearly, Jean had not said any of this, but Elsa
went on. "He says he is looking for a nice woman to keep him
cold at night."

They all laughed, and Mason saw his mother lean into Piers,
fit herself perfectly into the space between his shoulder and his
hip. She did it without looking, without any small adjustments of
posture or footing. She did it like she trusted that space was going
to be there. She had found it before, that warm line of bone and
flesh, found it one night, one dark night, months ago, when she
was blind with grief and tottering on the deck of a moon-driven
ship in roughening seas. She found that place and held on.

Mason's sleep that night was littered with such small moments
and little acts. His mother leaning into Piers, Elsa's toe as it nipped
and caught the rim of a silver hoop, a boy on fire, a man who
could lift ten times his own weight, Allegra singing to him in a
language he couldn't understand, the teeth of the prize-winning
poet in a glass of water, words floating up out of them like

bubbles of air. In the dream, Mason was very small and white, and so he could dive into the glass and bring the teeth to the surface, one by one. "Here," he said, handing one tooth to Elsa Hebert, one to Jean the fire boy, and the third to the strong man. Then he was six years old, on Easter Sunday, walking along a dock. This had really happened, and Mason reminded himself of its absolute truth somewhere in the depths of his dream. He had lost his footing and fallen into the water, but he held on to the dock and someone rescued him. A woman he did not know, in a lavender Easter bonnet that kept her face in shadow. She held out her hand and he took hold of it. He could feel the rings on her fingers, a diamond engagement ring. She begged him not to let go, as if she were the one in the water, she asked him to promise, and Mason said he would.

Irradiation

She opened the sea cocks, and my husband died. That's the whole story, all the drama I care to make of it. The head was gone, and so the water would rush in, if the sea cocks were opened. We told them not to, but she did.

She was on our boat for the afternoon, and she went below, a nap, we thought, but she spun the sea cocks open. It happened so slowly. We dropped her off on shore and motored back across the lake, already starting to take on water. After that, everything comes to me in a jumble. He went overboard to survey the damage. The water was too cold for him, the shock of it. A shock to his heart.

Her name was Christine, and I said to him when she got off the boat, I bet she's a handful at home, and he said, distracted, do you think so? His eyes were on the hills at the end of the lake, raised unto the hills, like he'd already got a breath of something. A presence more than himself, more than us. We'd been married for a month. It was hard to believe there could be anything more than us.

Christine had cancer. She was seventeen. We took her and four boys for a sail one afternoon in June. There were twenty-three boats altogether. Why should I remember that detail? The boys didn't have cancer, but they worked at the camp in the Sierra Nevada where Christine and a hundred other bald, rickety children spent part of their summers. The boys were the mess hall crew and the maintenance crew. One of them was afraid of drowning, and stood in the gangway for the entire trip. Another slept. A third kissed Christine in the V-berth. And she opened the sea cocks.

His eyes were on the hills. There was an Air Force flyover my husband had arranged, for the kids. Thundering above us. The blast of it moved strangely through the air, as sound does over water, seeming to come from underneath us, a roaring, furious body trying to rise.

She was a handful. She wanted to dodge the boom, dunk herself in the water when the boat heeled. She moved too fast. She didn't hold on. What did she care? She wanted to be the masthead, facing into the wind, her red hair blowing thickly backwards.

Only the hair wasn't hers. When they got on the boat, I said, anybody need sunscreen? The boys smiled at me, a small young woman, but too old for another kind of notice—to them I was nothing, nobody—and went below. Christine said, will I get burned? She was the only girl. I wanted to take care of her somehow. I'm good with girls. I said, you might, and she said, I don't tan. Yes, I said, too quickly, wanting to seem friendly, motherly, yes, your hair is so fair. She gave me a look then, a glare, theatrical, teenaged. I stared down at my feet, my ridiculous black-bottomed sandals that would surely mark the white fiberglass deck of the boat. I knew instantly what I'd said, that her red hair was a wig. A good wig, the part down the middle the healthy pink of a real false scalp. A good wig. She had parents who loved her. I came to know them well, better than I ever wanted. They were rich. They tried to make it up to me, and I took everything, the checks, the flowers, an urn for his ashes, the warm robe at Christmas. They wanted us all to be friends. Can you imagine?

I wanted Christine. An eye for an eye. I was an Old Testament kind of person. I still am, waiting for the incarnation, for the old story to match up with the new.

She wanted me too, in a way. For a few weeks after, she would call me on the phone and try to explain. She was articulate the way people are when they've spent too much time with psychiatrists. She knew her motives. She could explain everything. I sometimes had the sense of an adult standing quietly by the phone, coaching her, writing little notes: let your voice break now. Let your words run out into a whisper. She was a good little actress. Or maybe she was trying to be honest, but really, what did I care?

"Nothing's important," she said, exploring a new vein. "I'm just going to die anyway."

I was silent.

"Say something. I need you to forgive me."

"I can't," I told her.

"You can't say anything, or you can't forgive me?"

"Both, Christine. Leave me alone."

And for a while, she did. I heard she went into remission. She was going to make it. One day in August, she got into a car with her parents and drove to New York City to college. She never looked back, though she called me first.

"Barnard," she said.

"Good for you, Christine. Isn't that nice."

"I'm sorry," she said. "I'm sorry a thousand times. It'll be better for you to have me gone."

When we hung up, I wept. She was taking him with her, taking my husband, his earthly remains in her bones and viscera.

I didn't understand it. I wanted her, like a lover almost, that frenzied wanting of another body, that communion, eating of flesh and drinking of blood. She killed my husband.

I'd never been to New York.

At first it was going to be a short visit, a week, in the spring. I stayed in midtown, one of the Leona Helmsley places, palaces, in a tiny room. I walked everywhere, all day long, up and down Broadway, across the Village, up to Barnard. I found Christine without much trouble. She seemed surprised to see me, but not shocked. We stood by the statue, wise lady of Columbia, gem of the ocean, in the middle of the campus across from Christine's school. It must have been the first warm day, early April—around us, people sat on the steps, on patches of grass, all acting as if they'd just been set free. Blinking into the sunlight, fresh from the library and their dingy apartments. Christine looked older, thinner. The wig was gone, and her own hair was growing in, also red, or a shade darker, like brown hair with blood mixed in. It was short and spiky, like a man's. Something started to break inside me, an old wound opened under my lungs, soared up in them, the pain of it fresh with each breath. We embraced. Years swept away. There was a certain scent in Christine's hair. Lake water. Ashes.

"Got my own place, couldn't afford it, moved in with a couple and their baby." Christine was telling me this, four years later. "Auditioned, auditioned, auditioned."

"You'll make it," I said. "You will."

"I know. I came back from the dead."

I smiled at her, nodded. An eye for an eye, I reminded myself, a tooth for a tooth.

This time, I would stay in New York for the summer. I could do that, move at will for months or years at a time. I'd come unmoored in this way. I had a few friends I could call on, though I didn't. Not once. Christine was still there. You're going to bury me in this town, she said. I had not seen her since the spring of her freshman year, but we'd kept up. Her parents made sure I heard that their daughter had not come to grief. She was going to be an actress. She was on her way. *That* summer—her father told me this over drinks on my birthday—that summer was the turning point. That sailboat ride cured her, he said, it was a kind of spiritual trade. He was drunk by that time. He was an English professor at the University, and I despised him. His wife nodded. Tears stood in her eyes. They gave me a ticket to New York and a gold watch. So I was retired.

I wanted to be an actress too.

"You have to be a mirage on the highway," Christine said. "Sort of. Some people, you can tell when you watch them. They see emotions as a kind of hysteria. And so, they're pretty good technicians, but they don't feel much. Laurence Olivier, my teacher says. He was perfect. You have to be empty."

"Hmmm," I said.

Earlier, she had taken me to her class at the New School, but we were back up in Morningside Heights. The bar was dark and hushed in the afternoon, full of shadowy men and women. What they whispered to each other was important, earth-shattering. Christine was drinking a Coke, and I was too, only mine had rum in it. She would have to go to work a little while later, waitress at the University Club, serving Nobel Prize winners and their friends, famous academic people no one had ever heard of.

"I'm glad you're here," she said. "So I know where you are. It's like you're my child. You know, I probably can't have children." She looked at my glass. "We have a really weird relationship, don't we?"

"Like a mirage."

"How's that?"

"No. I was thinking about what you just said. Acting like a mirage."

"Oh."

And then she left. We would see each other the next day. I stood up and she kissed me on both cheeks. She said *ciao.*

Like a mirage. You looked, and it seemed like there was a shimmering pool of the most gorgeous, complicated light, just up the road. Most of the time, it wasn't anything when you got up close, but occasionally there was real water. Maybe a real woman. But first, you had to be empty.

I left the bar, The West End, and walked then, from 114th Street to 14th Street, a perfect hundred blocks. On the way downtown, I examined all the people moving past me, and waited to feel the flash of how it was to be them. Or I stared at my reflection in the store windows along Broadway, admiring all the goods and services. Goods and services, to fill you up, so you wouldn't ever have to be empty. Along 23rd Street, there was a delicatessen I got to like, where someone put time into the window displays, someone with a sense of humor: baby's breath growing out from between two halves of a kaiser roll, calmly it seemed, so that you believed such a thing could happen, such a sandwich was possible in this world. And it would taste good. It would fill you up.

Standing in front of that window, I understood why Christine wanted to do what she was doing, transform herself like that ridiculous sandwich, like Laurence Olivier. Her teacher was right—I'd seen all his movies—he could look so different, so not like himself. Think *Richard III,* think *Rebecca.* How could that possibly be the same man? You might keep asking yourself that question, over and over, until finally you believed it wasn't ever Laurence Olivier, not ever—just like it wasn't ever you—but really a man with a terrible secret. Which was that there was no such person, just a body waiting for someone to be.

I enrolled in the class Christine was taking. She encouraged me to do it. Really, she said, you might meet somebody. At first I had no idea what she meant, but then I caught on. I stared up over her head. The subway car we were riding in rocked violently, shaken by large hands.

"Not ready yet?" she said.

I shook my head.

"It's been five years, Alice."

The way she said the words, as if she were not involved, as if she were the director of mourning and kept my husband's body inside of hers and allowed me only so much of it. I felt it again, that urge to carve Christine into a hundred pieces and eat them.

The basics of method acting are, first, that you know you've just been somewhere, which makes you come into a room in a certain way, and second, you know you want something from the people you're playing the scene with. Like life. You had to find new and extravagant ways to say the same things, which always amounted to "I didn't think it would take so long to get here," and "give me that which you have in your hand."

In the first three weeks of class, the teacher, an aging German actress, a child of the war whose name means nothing, told us what she called a great many truths. She wore blue jeans and a black sweater. She smoked constantly, and her voice was full of air raids, men in uniform, battles on foreign soil. She claimed to have known everyone, Lee Strasberg, Marlon Brando, James Dean. She told us that Brando was hard to light, that he always had a hooded look to him, his eyes in shadow so that he seemed to be asleep, sleeping through his parts, delivering lines with his eyes closed. It intrigued me, the notion of a body being hard to light, the idea of acting with your eyes closed. I could imagine that sometimes it was hard for an actor to look at the scenery rushing toward him as he moved through it.

"As an actor," the teacher said, "it's your business to make an audience believe you know a lot of things you really don't. It's your business to get under their skin."

You know how it works: you look at me, but I don't return your looks. I ask questions, but you don't have to answer them, or otherwise admit you're in the same room with me, or compete with my virtues, or resist my irresistible advances.

We learned a speech move called Swan Neck or Double Bend Period, in which there is first a rising inflection to the high point where the comma coincides with the logical pause, then after the turn comes a temporary stop before the voice drops abruptly to the bottom of the pattern. We learned all about pauses and silences, that the pause is the trump card in the actor's hand. We ran the famous wordless scene in Ostrovski's *The Storm.* We learned to wait. Light a cigarette so the audience can see the hand tremble. Pour a drink, pour thousands of them.

We touched each other, all the time. Christine and I were always partners. We leaned into each other, we pressed our fore-heads into each other's palms, in order to know what the other was thinking. Our bones knew, the teacher said, and then there would be a kind of electric exchange. Irradiation, Stanislavski called it, wordless communication, when something streamed out of you, a current from your eyes, from the ends of your fingers, out through your pores.

An underground river, I thought, telephone wires.

It led to *grasp,* that was the term. The teacher defined it, oddly I thought: what a bulldog has in his jaws. We practiced this in class. Getting to grasp.

"But do not do these exercises alone," she said. "Or with an imaginary person. Always use a living object, actually with you and willing to exchange feelings with you. Communion must be mutual."

So we met outside class, in little groups of three or four, for coffee, for lunch, sometimes for dinner. I began to notice that many of us were hurt, or thought so, or had just visited someone who was. I took note of it, this desire to live in close proximity to injury. More so for women than men, but still we all hobbled around on crutches we didn't need, read up on everything terminal, got strange viruses, got over them, got in the way of cars, buses, people wielding sharp objects, callous lovers. I guessed we did it for parts, to learn parts. It appeared that you could enter into the tragic and never want to come out again. It appeared that you ought to.

Christine fell in love then, with a man, really a boy, in class. Named Chad, from California, down south, he said. He was tall, over six foot, and he stared out over people's heads like he was looking for the person you should have been. He liked it that Christine had had cancer. He called her The Cure or Steen. My widowhood made an impression on him too, but only when no one was looking.

I was good. Often better than Christine. I could see the truth of this in Chad's eyes. He looked at us sometimes, swung his big blond surfer's head back and forth between us, trying to decide who was the better investment. He wanted to make it, but not Broadway, not Shakespeare in the Park. He was thinking of westward, ho! Hollywood, television commercials. He had a face that could convince people to buy what they never even knew they wanted.

I liked acting. There was a familiar sensation in it, wakefulness in a part of me that had been sleeping for years. It wasn't that you got to be someone else, it was that you got to be no one, no body. You fed your performances with pieces of flesh from the director, from other actors, from people you knew. You borrowed or stole parts of developed selves and then tried to leave them by the side of the road, but sometimes they stayed with you. And these transactions took a lot of time, hours spent alone, making sure you could be absolutely, perfectly not yourself. You missed things and had to be told about them later. The news, for instance. The weather.

Almost outside my body, I took a job at one of the Helmsley palaces, cleaning. One day when I was staying there, I was going to leave a few bottles of beer for the chambermaids, and then I thought, I'll be one. A chambermaid. My husband always called them that, never just maids. He wondered if the chambermaids ever got drunk on what people leave behind, if they got drunk as skunks and if they ever jumped on the beds before they made them up, or if they read aloud to each other from the Gideon's Bible, if they quoted Luke chapter eleven, verse forty-one: Behold, everything is clean for you.

As its project, the class was going to put together a production of *Dracula*. The teacher had always loved the story, the play. There were a lot of good parts, large and small, male and female. I believed I would play Lucy, "the hapless Lucy," the stage notes always called her. Christine would be Mina. We love each other, and then one of us becomes a vampire. It's Lucy of course, Lucy who is a good girl really. A terrible flirt, but she loves her friend. She's mystified by what's happening to her, but she's empty most of the time, without a will of her own. And then later, her curse is that she can't be still. Every night, she walks through the countryside near Whitby, stealing children for her own, kissing them on the lips, the throat. But she can never get very far away because she wears out her shoes, her little white dancing slippers. Why has Arthur Holmwood, her fiancé, buried her in those flimsy shoes?

To keep her close by? Holmwood is the least inspiring of her three suitors, and in the end, he is the one who puts the stake through her heart, fills her mouth with garlic and cuts off her head, all of which proves he is reasonable, rational, English as they come. You had to think about what their marriage might have been: a nightmare of dull days and awkward nights. The truth about Lucy is that while she's a vampire, she's really interesting. Mysterious, irresistible. What does she say to those children to draw them away from their warm beds, their gentle mothers? What does she promise so that they want to roam the world with her forever? You wanted to know. To play her, you had to know.

There's a moment, though, near the middle of the story, when she reveals something else. In a lightning flash outside her bedroom, you see more—the silenced, frustrated, stubborn part of her. Just this once, before she's buried, before her soul is set free with a stake and her head cut off. It is the whole play, really, the spirit, the ghost of the tragedy.

You learn that every part contains this, a person the character wants to be but can't in order for the tragedy to happen.

There was an American in the Dracula legend, Quincey P. Morris, who kills the Count with his Bowie knife, and has the last word. He says, "Now God be thanked that all this has not been in vain! See! The snow is not more stainless than Mina's forehead. The curse has passed away!" He was in love with Lucy. He was a cowboy. This was the part that Chad wanted, but he wasn't going to get it. He would be cast as Van Helsing, the doctor, the metaphysician who has the temper of an icy brook and understands the widening circle of the Undead.

The way the whole story got started was that years before Lucy's other suitor, Seward, sucked venom from Van Helsing's snakebite, or maybe it was gangrene from a knife wound. A tiny coincidence, that act, someone else's blood and its poison, pressure of lips on skin. Nobody made very much of it.

Because I had nothing much to do all day but clean for strangers, for people I never saw, I read up on vampires, the real history of Count Dracula. I told Chad and Christine about it in a Helmsley Windsor Hotel suite in midtown. They sometimes followed me and my maid's cart from room to room, looking into the still lives of travelers, their opened suitcases, toiletries and unmade beds.

"I bet it isn't pretty," Chad said.

"But it is," I told him. Rising out of all the horror were moments of impossible tenderness, and sadness, parts of the history that seemed unaccountably sweet.

"For instance?" Chad wanted to know. They were standing on one of the beds, holding hands. He began to drag Christine in a circle.

"The excommunicated, suicides, victims of violent death, the stillborn, all more likely to become vampires."

"Ring around the rosy," he was singing, "pocket full of posies, ashes, ashes . . ."

"As if they didn't have it hard enough already, Alice," Christine said, her tone strange, accusing, breathless from their game.

"Also, babies born with teeth," I said, "with a caul, with dark eyes, with clear blue eyes, red hair."

"With red hair, Christine." Chad said this slowly, leering. He pulled her close to him and licked her neck. "We could put on these people's clothes." He stepped off the bed and moved to the closet. "Look." He held up a man's gray suit, neatly pressed, and two dresses. One of them seemed to be made out of tiny mirrors, which caught us all and threw us back into each other's arms.

In these rooms, there had been great sadness or celebration, it was hard to tell which. The trash was filled with empty wine bottles, and dirty glasses stood on the tables, on the carpet. Flowers crowded the sitting room, great, gaudy arrangements of white and yellow roses, tulips beginning to waver on their thin stems, greenish water in the vases. Dust from stargazer lilies streaked our shoulders, our hair. Christine held the glittering dress against my body, and in it appeared a thousand cloying rooms.

In a mirror, vampires are unrecognizable to themselves. They are surrounded by the scent of decaying flowers, an overblown sweetness. We sniffed that heavy air around each other's faces. My lips brushed her ear, his throat.

"The ashes of a vampire should be buried at a crossroads, so he or she won't know what direction to take. Or poppy seeds are strewn in their coffins and all along the roads leading to the cemetery. The vampire would have to gather them, count them."

"Why?" Chad asked.

"Nobody knows. They're obsessed with order. Patterns and numbers."

If you read enough, you saw that vampires are the uninvited guests, the gypsies, the Bolsheviks, sometimes innocent, sometimes not. It was more timing than anything else. It was history.

The remains of breakfast sat on the dining table. Two meals: eggs and sausage, and then, across the table, a sweet roll, untouched. Christine picked it up. "I'm hungry," she said. "Silly rich people are going to feed me."

I let her eat, and then I vacuumed my way out of the room. I sucked everything out and closed the door.

"The Nazis," our teacher said later. "When the crops fail, when the market crashes, suddenly everybody's yelling, there's a vampire in the neighborhood."

There was always a responsible party, she told us, and he had to be found, stopped. There was always some one stranger among us, a shadow, who was incapable of love and ruined it for everyone else. That's what the story tried to say. Someone so alone it was obscene. Someone private, crazy and mean, who spoke to you out of the darkness. Someone beloved and then later despised. Someone who could come to know you better than you knew yourself.

"I've read everything," I told them on the way uptown.

"You're scaring me a little," Christine said. "Why do you want to know all this?"

"For the part."

"It's not like that though. It's out of you. It's for yourself."

"Maybe."

"You're scaring me, too," Chad said. But he held my eyes for a long time.

Christine was still afraid of death, panicked suddenly by nothing. She was twenty-two, still a child, lost in the city. She came to my apartment to run lines and often did not want to go home. I could have let her stay, but most nights, I didn't want her. I'd learned to love solitude, widowhood, my still nights with my husband. At night in New York, I opened the windows and let his body in—I believed it that way—his thin, airy body entered with the breeze, shimmering, a tall sail. His body settled down around me, and the room hushed like deafness. I didn't talk to him—I know some people, particularly women, do that. But there was enough talk in the world for me. It was like making love, the way we'd always done, mostly without words or chatter, except afterwards and not even much then. If Christine was there, he wouldn't come in. Some evenings, I could feel him at the window, a cool, slow scratching, irregular, like the icy fingers of trees. Christine might hear, her eyes would go still in her face, into the middle distance, the fourth wall. I think she knew who it was. I think she knew that something was coming, and not for her.

And then there was a week or two before I returned to California, when he didn't come at all. I was losing him. I'd known this for a long time. Sometimes I could picture his face, but not the eyes, could hear the voice, but not the laugh, not all the words. How tall was he? When we stood together, where did the top of my head go, where did my cheek fit into his chest? I drilled with the old photographs, like flash cards, and still, in the morning, he was half-missing.

After three days of this, Christine asked to stay, and I let her. We went to sleep in the same bed, like sisters, and when I woke in the night, we lay closer, her left arm draped over my chest. The room was lit strangely, by low clouds reflecting the city lights, a bluish glow that in the winter meant snow was already on the ground. I thought then of touching Christine, the small pressure on her back, on her left side, that would cause her to roll over. My hand under her shirt, on her breasts, and then my mouth, the salt taste of her skin, the soft hollow between her hip bones. I felt more surprised than I had after my husband's death, my breath gone out of my body in the same way. I thought suddenly, stormily, of Pompeii, felt it: death by burning, how white heat had come from outside my knowing to entomb me. After a while the day began to take shape in a chair, a table, the closet door. I moved Christine's arm away, felt the coolness of her body in this one limb, saw its porcelain gleam. She rolled away from me, onto her side, and didn't wake for hours. Chad called, but she didn't hear the telephone. I'm leaving today, he said. Let's go.

At the Motel 6 west of Needles, the room was hot and airless, so I turned the air conditioner on high and walked down to the swimming pool, its cool blue rectangle still lit at ten o'clock, still full of people at that late hour. I sat down with my legs in the water at the shallow end, and watched, filled with the gulf and brazenness of traveling. Eight Germans sat behind me, young men, soldiers, judging by the severity of their haircuts, all of them pale as the moon. Jarheads, I thought, *jarkopf,* amusing myself.

Two other women lay on chaise lounges at the other end of the pool, and they offered vodka and Coke to the soldiers, who refused, though they called back to the women, *Where are you from?* and the women answered, *California,* and the Germans said, *The prettiest girls we hear are from California.* The women laughed and turned their attention to two college boys who said they were from California too and accepted their offer of drink. It was duly brought out to them in red plastic cups, the kind people use for keg beer. Slowly into the night the women flirted with the college boys, asking, *So what do you two like to do for fun? Are you married? Would you drive an hour to visit us?* When the boys finally began to ignore them, the women said, *You must be from Chillicothe, where it's always so cold,* pronouncing it Chilly-cothe. One of the Germans called out, *No, they are from California.* Everyone was suddenly surprised to remember the way sound travels across water, how it can carry talk that has nothing to do with you.

That German, the one who wanted to set things straight, sat down near me, nodded his head in greeting, and then looked up at the night sky.

"I will get sunburned even like this," he said.

"Are you guys German?" I said.

"Yes. Very good ear."

"Visiting?"

"From Dayton, Ohio. The Air Force base there. A kind of exchange program. Really we are from Munich." He offered me a beer from their cooler, and I took one. "We are touring your country."

"My husband was in the Air Force for a little while. But he quit."

"Why?"

"I don't really know. He started to prefer water to air, I think."

"Where are you from?"

"New York. Really California. I've been in New York, but I'm moving back."

"You're married," the German said, pointing to my wedding ring. "Yes? Where is your husband? He does not swim?"

"He's in California. He does not travel."

He thought about this a minute, quietly, as if he knew I was lying. "In California," he said. "What do you do in New York?"

"I'm an actress."

"Ah," he said. "Would I know you from the movies?" He leaned in closer to get a good look at my face. "Traveling incognito. Are you Sharon Stone?"

"It would be a pretty good disguise, don't you think?"

"A masterpiece," he said.

"But you think I could pull it off."

"Very truly you could."

A woman traveling alone, a motel, soldiers, night, August. The end of summer a few weeks away, and an invisible highway voice calling *ashes, ashes.* The presence of bad women and college boys to remind us all of opportunities lost. He was thinking all this, my German soldier. I could read his thoughts. Irradiation, Stanislavski called it.

"So if you are an actress, maybe you are acting now, and everything you have told me is not true."

"Maybe."

"May I ask your name?"

"Alice. And you?"

"Ricard, but all Americans call me Sam." He rolled his eyes and shrugged.

We talked about Hollywood, where they had just spent the weekend. I told him where, according to the signs on the highway, I believed they could get tattoos. He told me about a huge cavern of a bar, in town, dark and chilly, and absolutely silent when they went in, except for ghostly shifting at the scarred tables and chairs. It took them a minute to decide there was some kind of acting, a play going on. The bartender was listening, holding himself perfectly still, so when he saw customers out of the corner of his eye, he raised his right hand and put his finger to his lips.

Chad came downstairs then and sat beside us.

Ricard paused, barely, a hairsbreadth, then continued. The actor was a slight young man, probably about my age, he said, in blue jeans and a long-sleeved white dress shirt. He was wearing dark-rimmed glasses that made him look wise, and one knew from the silence that everyone in the bar was thinking the same thing, how wise. He was talking about his father, about what his father says to him from the grave, what his father has left behind. The bodies of the audience leaned toward him, their faces in darkness, waiting for him to tell them the secrets he knew, what, in death, his father had revealed. One thought his voice would break, but it didn't, it rose and fell, perfect hills and valleys. His audience leaned even closer at the moments of falling, farther forward, their bodies defying gravity, hanging on his words. In the dark, their hands were curled into fists.

He told me he would never forget it, those words. How lovely, how infuriating. One thought the pain of it could kill, he said, kill slowly, the pain of someone beloved drifting away. Wished it would kill you. But certainly such a thing would not happen. A waste of time. You, in death, have nothing to reveal. He stopped talking and waited, as if to give me a chance to catch up, and then he said that the audience applauded this young man for a long time. They did not want to let him go.

"You can feel it," I said, "when an audience wants to tell you they know applause isn't enough. That they'd do other things to show their appreciation. Not sure what. They'd tell you later."

"The tables and chairs in this bar were carved and signed by hundreds of people. I thought of this when you said *tattoo.*"

Then one of the others tapped Ricard on the shoulder, told him they were going to their rooms, asked if he would be coming with them. When he turned his head to answer, the spotlights around the pool caught in his hair and made it look gold, liquid and warm, like gold wax running off a candle.

"We should go, too," I said.

Upstairs, ten or twelve soldiers had come outside with cans of beer, and stood against the wall or leaned on the balcony railing. That wing of the motel faced southwest and was on a rise, hanging a little above the Sacramento Mountains. It was an exotic view, foreign, the way the lights shuddered slightly, wavered in the heat. We might have been anywhere.

"Well," I said. "We have a long day tomorrow." Chad reached out to shake hands, but carefully, as if he suspected the German carried something concealed in his palm.

"Yes," Ricard said. "To be reunited with your husband. You should be careful."

"I will. I always am."

And then he bent down and kissed me on each cheek, sweetly, like a brother or an uncle.

"A German farewell," he said.

"I thought that was French."

"They took it from the Germans." He looked at Chad. "French is something else."

There was a moment, a beat through which we all waited to see what would happen next. Then it was over. We said good-night and then, after a shorter pause, we warned each other to drive carefully. Chad unlocked the door to the room, and we went in, closed the door, bolted and chained it. The air conditioner had done its job with a vengeance. I walked into the bathroom and turned on the heat lamp, stood under it, and my skin took on an odd cast, a bloodless blue, the color of skim milk, the color of a corpse. Lucy, I thought. She was a flirt, and look what happened to her. My face in the mirror was a stranger's. Chad's, on the other hand, was startlingly familiar. After a while, some fog cleared. I looked like myself again, but a cheap imitation, slight, like an actress who is so badly lit that her features slide into a kind of froth, a blinding, creamy wash, and you can't see that she has a face at all.

In the morning, I took Chad's car while he slept. I emptied his wallet, left a note that said, *Behold, everything is clean for you.*

At the end, there wasn't anybody around when I took the box of ashes out to the lake and shook it out over the water. There wasn't a crossroads. No cowboy from the West said anything about a curse passing from us. The wind took it away from me, all except one stubborn feather of ash that blew backwards and landed on the sleeve of my jacket. It hung there, high up on my right arm. I ducked my head and pressed my tongue to it, and I could feel the slight grit, taste the shadowy presence of salt. I wondered what it would cause to happen, this taking the remains of my husband's body into mine, this souvenir, this theft, this little meal.

Nothing. It made nothing happen. I auditioned, auditioned, auditioned, and have got a steady, strange sort of job, as an actress in a medical video series. I play women with diseases, with conditions. Cancer, breast and ovarian. Multiple sclerosis. Lupus. Abortions. I do egg donors and pregnancies, plain, multiple and high-risk. Some days, I believe I am the most female woman in America. The last one wrapped yesterday, in Burbank. Infertility. My husband looked like Bob what's-his-name, host of the funniest home videos show. He was a soldier, a kind of Hollywood soldier, off fighting all the time, which was meant partly to explain our failure to conceive a child.

And I'm glad to be done with it because all the time, I felt something inside me, like there should have been a body waiting to be born. The character I played was always drinking coffee and keeping track of her menstrual cycle—she was just wild for it, those rising and falling temperatures, all that blood. I said to the writer, maybe the problem is her caffeine intake, that wine with dinner. She should get off the sauce, give the guy a pair of boxers for Christmas. Everybody thought I was a little crazy. My husband—the guy who played him—didn't ever have much to say. He was away a lot. It's not really his story.

I imagine sometimes that Christine will see this video in her OB-GYN'S office. Her husband will be holding her hand and so be right there when her whole body starts to shake. She'll explain to him or she won't—it doesn't matter. But she'll feel it, finally, that loss, the boat of her body broken open from the inside and dragging her under. We'll be even then, and I can rest in my grave for ten thousand years.

Laramie

You will remember this, never forget it, how the tire blew out along Interstate 80, whoosh to flat, as if it had never had any air in it at all. How you said, get out there and show a little leg so a trucker with a CB will stop and we can call into Laramie, the nearest town, fifteen miles west. You will think you remember that I laughed though I didn't, but I did get out and I did stand on the gravel shoulder beside your car, holding myself close, hands gripping my own biceps, until you made a movement with your arm, a sideways slash that meant, what are you waiting for? go on, *git*. You can probably still see it happening, maybe it comes back to you in dreams and you yell something like my name or *watch out!* or *not now!* and your wife reaches for you in her sleep. You see me letting the cars pass, all of them, every single one, and you swear and start to unbuckle your seatbelt, but then there's a big rig, the shiniest damn truck you've ever seen, and I'm practically in the road, my jacket flying open like wings or a flayed chest. You still hear it at night, the sound of that truck stopping, all eighteen wheels, the scream and gasp of the air brakes. You see the passenger side door open, high above my head. I look up and speak, then glance back once, not at you but at the scablike snow on the field behind me, and climb up in that rig and ride away.

We came back for you though, Al Loudermilk and I, in his tow truck from the shop, with Loudermilk Auto Body painted on both doors. You might have seen us riding east on I-80. There's not much median strip there, and we were going slow. You wouldn't have seen me, though, or not my face because I was turned all the way away, facing the other direction, north, and asking Al so what about this snowfall, and was there likely to be more, and he was saying that there's only two kinds of people who try to predict the weather in Laramie, and that would be new-comers and fools.

"Where are you coming from?" Al said.

"Cheyenne."

"Headed?"

"Yellowstone."

"You could get more weather between here and there. My wife and I lived right outside Yellowstone once, north of Jackson. Town's called Colter Bay. She didn't like it much though. She doesn't care for Laramie either."

You will remember that I told you this later in the motel stuck at the bottom of the shallow bowl that Laramie makes in the state of Wyoming. You stood at the window and laughed like a warning blast, and said, Jesus, what's not to like? I said it seemed like wives were never happy, and you said, watch it. You will not remember how the room we had rented for the night would not get dark enough. You slept right through my getting up to step behind the window curtain and look out, trying to find out where that light was coming from, satisfy myself that it would go out sooner or later: it shone out from a diner or a bar, someplace that would have to close, or else it was the cab light of a trucker checking his maps and receipts. You slept through its eerie three A.M. brightening and you slept on and on, even when I went to the door and flung it open and stood there in my thin white nightgown, ready to scream. If I'd found the source of that light then, I would have thrown my body on it, happily felt shards of glass pass through my skin as the bulb broke and went out, heard the filament inside hiss and wrap itself around my heart, the pliable metal strands knitting themselves into the flesh so that the heart could be bent without coming apart, backwards, forwards, side to side, and snap back into its original position, which is, as you know, slightly askew.

"People live here," Al Loudermilk said, "but they don't mean to. This is pretty much what happens." He pointed to your car, the flat tire. "Or my sister. She writes poetry and she came here to go to school and study with this famous writer, but he left and went to Baltimore. So she's kind of stuck." But, he said, she had this poetry group and people got together and talked about what they were trying to do. And here he pointed out to the highway, and said it kept her and her friends from ripping off their clothes and running out to the Interstate and howling at passing cars. It seemed like there were one or two new people in her group every fall, people writing weird shit about their fathers and their divorces.

"Right now," he said. "October. 'Tis the season. They're out there doing it."

A teacher I had once said there were two kinds of poems, the kind that when you read them, they fill up a space inside you, an empty place that you didn't even know was there. And then there was the kind that when you read them, they made a space that you had to learn to live with, had to carry around until something, some experience filled it in. Hearing that turned me off poetry forever. You will remember me telling you this story, maybe more than once—at the end I know I began to repeat myself. When we were in Laramie, I told you, no, that teacher was wrong: there were indeed two kinds of poems in the world, but they were poems by fools and poems by newcomers to Laramie.

We were on our way to Yellowstone from Cheyenne for a week's vacation. You will remember the rented cabin just outside the park, how cold it was. You will remember doing all the cooking. That we didn't drink, which only seems strange now, that we hiked every day, or drove through the park, or both. You will remember long trips to the pay phone to call your wife, and telling me what to do in case you were killed on the way, and giving me $50 to do it with. You will remember how it was during that week we got tired of each other, but didn't realize for another six months. You will remember being afraid that I would take the car in the middle of the night and leave you high and dry. You will remember saying something as ridiculous and maudlin as I filled an empty space, but what I thought all along was I am new to this and I am a fool.

We met Al's sister that afternoon. She pulled into the shop at 11:45 in a silver Camaro, red interior, "mint condition," Al whispered into my ear, "1976 and still humming along." You will remember her name was Lissa, though as the afternoon went on, and the evening deepened and fogged over, Al started calling her Mel and you did too. She was not quite as tall as her brother, but close, five-foot-seven, maybe, with white blond hair, sun-bleached to straw and badly cut, against the grain, you might be tempted to say, for it had that frayed, hacked-at look. She was wearing tight jeans and work boots and a red denim jacket. In another place you would have looked at me and mouthed the words *hot to go,* but in Laramie, you did none of those things. You walked over and said hello. You told her your name. You said, what kind of poetry do you write?

"Narrative," was what she told you. "Strange little stories."

"That's the understatement of the year," Al said.

I recall thinking at the time: a little while ago, this was just a flat tire, and now I don't know what it is.

"You about ready?" she said to Al.

"Just got to finish up with these folks, and we can go."

"He's taking me out to lunch," Lissa said to you. "I won a bet, and it's pay-up time."

"What was the bet?" you asked her.

"A little family matter," she said. "Nothing worth telling." She winked at Al.

"They're on their way to Yellowstone," Al said.

"Ah," Lissa said, as if it were information she'd been waiting a long time to receive.

"So where would one take somebody to lunch in Laramie?" you asked.

Lissa told us the name of the place, which you will remember exactly, though I don't. I want to say *Circus* or *Something Circus,* even though I know that isn't it. It's in moments like this, I miss you most, your unfailing memory, the way you could hear every word I said, the very intonation of the words, days, weeks, months after I'd said them.

She was giving you directions while Al talked to me about the new tire, the spare, tire rotation. In the middle of it all, the phone rang, and he stopped to answer. Just by the way he said hello the second time, I knew it was his wife. I'd developed an ear for that conspiratorial lowering of the voice, how men talking to their wives never stare off into space the way they do if it's business. They look down, and they concentrate on a part of their bodies or their clothing, thumbnail, forearm, shirt button, belt loop. You will remember my pointing this out to you, though you may or may not recall what you said in reply, which was *bullshit.*

"Liss," Al said, "Mary wants to know what's up for Columbus Day. You got the day off?"

"Oh," Lissa said. "Right. No. I mean yes, but it's poetry group night."

"Okay," Al said, and relayed this to Mary, telling her, well, they'd go anyway, just them. "You too," he said and smiled into the receiver. His wife had just said she loved him. I could almost hear her. There in his body shop in Laramie, Wyoming, hungry, cold, still a little dazed from the flat and the fifteen-mile ride in an oil rig and the ride back to your car in Al's wrecker, I almost thought I *was* Al's wife, saying *we'll go anyway, just the two of us,* and then *love you, honey* and then nothing.

When I got back to myself, you and Lissa had decided we should all have lunch together, at Something Circus, when the car was ready to go. You two were talking like a couple of old friends, about poetry. I may not be remembering this correctly. She was saying you wouldn't think Laramie, Wyoming, would be a big town for poetry, but just look around, she said, and we did, all four of us, around the inside of her brother's shop and then out through the open bay where your car was held up over our heads, toward the Interstate, up out of the bottom of the trough of Laramie.

"People get here," she said, "and they write poems like they never have even dreamed of before. Like it's automatic. Like it has nothing to do with them. It's shocking. It's weird. Spontaneous overflow of powerful feeling recollected in the middle of nowhere." She shook her head and nodded over at Al. "And the family is here too. You know how that is."

We followed them to Something Circus. I tried to think of what to say to you in the car, but every single sentence that came into my head seemed petty or mean, or worse, likely to provoke you. We were going to lose a day at the cabin, or most of one. I didn't want to stay in Laramie any longer than was necessary. I don't know why you didn't get it: everyone, it seemed, was telling us that people who landed by mistake in this town got sucked in—they lost the will to leave and then started writing poetry to fill up the place where the will used to be. But we went anyway.

Something Circus was a dark bar with a restaurant attached to it. Everyone there seemed to know Lissa. People hailed her on the way in, waved from their tables, reached out for her hand as she walked by. Most of them said congratulations. A woman told her she sounded great, different from her usual self, but great. Once we sat down, a man and a woman came over to the table. The man squatted so that he and Lissa were face-to-face; the woman stood behind and put her hands on Lissa's shoulders. The man called her Mel.

"We were driving home," he said, "and, hot damn, there you were on the radio. I almost wrecked the truck."

"It was just getting dark," the woman said. "It was perfect."

You raised your eyebrows, and Al leaned across me to tell us both that last Friday Lissa read some of her poems on National Public Radio.

"You're with a celebrity," he said to me. "You and your husband. And I bet you didn't even know it."

"I did, sort of," I said, and you will remember looking at me, a little surprised. Then you patted my hand and nodded to Al.

"Woman's intuition," you said.

We had cheeseburgers and beer. And then more beer, until you decided there was no going on toward Yellowstone, and left the table to make a motel reservation.

"So can I ask what the bet was?" I said, emboldened by beer, and wanting to know something you didn't know by the time you came back, wanting to have a secret with Lissa and Al.

"Our father," Al said. "It's kind of a long story."

"He's not in his right mind," Lissa said.

"Pretty much in his *wrong* mind," Al said, and they smiled at each other, sadly, a little, but not tragically.

"He thinks everybody's somebody else," Lissa said. "Well, maybe not everybody. He knows us." She looked at Al. "I guess he knows us, right? But newcomers are the problem. So when somebody comes over to the house and he hasn't met them before—we make bets about it. What he'll come up with."

"It's just a silly game we have," Al said. "Making bets about stuff. Some people say to their brothers and sisters, hello, how are you? Instead of that, we say, I'll bet you lunch."

"I'll bet you," Lissa said, "if we brought these guys over, he'd think they were Aunt Hattie and Uncle Bill."

"Too old," Al said.

"Is it always relatives?" I said.

"Usually," Al told me, "but not always."

"Some repairman," Lissa said. "A few months ago. The furnace guy. Remember that one?" She looked at me and made her eyes go wide. "Spiro Agnew."

"The resemblance was striking," Al said. "Remember, Mel? Haunting."

How do such things happen? How did it happen that we stayed in Something Circus or Circus Something with Al Loudermilk and his sister Lissa, who was becoming more and more Mel, for another two hours, drinking beer, and then shots of tequila. You will remember how it happened. You will remember that they asked us no questions, not a single one, about ourselves, our lives in Cheyenne, our trip before the tire blew out. They asked us about Yellowstone, though, where we would be staying, how we planned to drive the rest of the distance from Laramie. It was as if, for them, we had begun to exist with the flat tire, and the *pop!* it made was the two of us bursting fully grown, and fully expected, into the world. You will think now how oddly true it was—you will use the word *odd* in a detached, musing way—that just moments before, we had been unformed, indecisive, hesitant. You will remember what we had been saying, whispering to each other like a vow, *whispering*—it kills me now—even though no one was in the car with us, and the road was practically empty and the sullen landscape around Laramie was too busy worrying its patchy snowfall to pay any attention to us. We had just said to each other, this time we might not be able to return to the people we were married or otherwise beholden to. They'd snap back, we said; they'd carry on. Then we named them, each one, out loud, across the dashboard, as if that were a way to love them, the best way, to get them all jammed into the car with us, crowded in up front, to let them look down the road too, and see what was coming.

When we came out into daylight, it was 3:30 in the afternoon, and we were going to pay a call on Lissa's and Al's father. We had to see him, they said, the most forgetful man in Laramie, the namer of repairmen, the reassigner of parts. By that hour, the sun was dropping quickly out of the sky, racing to get away from the sight of Laramie, Wyoming, the sight of us. There is a kind of abandonment about a winter—even early winter—afternoon, in unfamiliar landscape, where you don't know what the sun will actually *do*. It made me think that part of the romance of a sunset is knowing exactly what will happen: the great red ball of heat will drop behind a certain mountain or flash along a predictable edge of a body of water and then fall beneath it. People know these things about celestial habit, and so they are free to concentrate on their beloved. When you don't know, when there's no habit, the two of you must hold yourselves apart, hold your breath, and wait.

Between this fact of nature and the tequila, the senior Loudermilk had grown to be an oracle. You will remember calling him that, The Oracle. We were, in some strange sense, going to him to find out who we had become and what we should do about it.

"I'll bet you he thinks they're Fred and Ginger," Lissa said, laughing. "Jesus! I bet he thinks they're Elvis and Priscilla."

"I bet," Al said, all seriousness, "he thinks they're friends of yours, people from your group."

"I bet he thinks they're friends of *yours*," Lissa said.

"And so he'll try to kill them."

Old Man Loudermilk lived alone in a small blue house on the western end of Laramie. The neighborhood seemed down-at-heel but plucky: houses were painted in not-for-house colors, pink, bright yellow, a sort of undersea green, yards were mowed, front stoops and porches decorated with plants and wicker furniture. The sea-green house had one of those iron jockeys in the front yard, holding up a lantern, trying to get a good look at us as we drove by. The owners had put a deerslayer's cap on the jockey's head. We parked at the curb and got out, and Lissa went to the mailbox, collected her father's mail. Something about her expression when she bent her knees to peer into the box—the way the shadow of its inside fell across her face—it looked grim, satisfied. She was bringing her father the gift of us. Newcomers who would confuse him. That was it. I didn't know until that moment, and you won't remember at all because I never told you.

And then she would write a poem about it. I saw that too. With startling clarity. We would become one of her strange little stories.

You waited for her at the end of the driveway while Al and I walked up to the front door and rang the bell. I looked back to see you pat her on the back, put your arm across her shoulders and whisper something into her ear. You will remember what it was, but I will never know. I thought for a second that you already knew Lissa, from some other part of your life, maybe you'd been to Laramie dozens of times, you knew the town, in fact, like the back of your hand, and this visit to Old Mr. Loudermilk was all a joke. He would know you because he'd seen you in the company of his daughter, and when you came in the door, he'd nod and smile and shake your hand, say your name, ask you what's cooking at Wyoming Power and Light. He would know what you had become because he knew what you were before. Then he would look at me, and his eyes would cloud over, go blank and gray like patches of snow in the hollows of earth around Laramie. He would take me for his sister, his mother, his other daughter who died of influenza at the age of two.

You will remember how my thoughts could run like this. You will remember the sickness of my imagining your wife everywhere, hearing her voice in the basement of my house one night, or behind the pyracantha bushes in the backyard, on the telephone, saying *who's there, who's there, who's there,* like the wise old bird she was.

But what Old Man Loudermilk called you was "George." Then he said hello to Mel, but did not acknowledge Al at all.

"I kept all your letters," he said to you. "Every single one. I knew you'd be back. They told me you'd be back. They told me you'd run off to the war. Then they told me you'd died, but I knew that wasn't right. And it isn't, is it?"

"No," you said. Lissa had given you the sign to play along. "It's not. Here I am."

"Mel," Mr. Loudermilk said, "I heard you on the radio the other evening."

"Wasn't she great?" Al said. He put one hand on his father's shoulder.

"Just hush," he said to Al. "And get your big meat hooks off me. You know I can't stand it. I don't know why you keep after me that way."

"Sorry," Al told him. He didn't look at us when he said, "Everything means something else to him now."

"You sounded funny, you know," Mr. Loudermilk said to his daughter. "What was it? Was it the Bible?"

"No, Daddy. It was poetry. Poems that I wrote."

Mr. Loudermilk opened his eyes wide and let his jaw drop in a perfect imitation of surprise.

"Mel," he said, "since when do you write poetry?"

"Pretty much all my life, Daddy."

"Well, it's news to me."

"Shit," Al said. "Not again."

"You watch your language. You kids. The way you speak to your elders. You try to get all tough-guy with me. Talking that trash. John Wayne. Well, howdy pardner to you too."

"Remember that one I wrote for your birthday?" Lissa said.

"Sure don't."

"Oh come on, Daddy. You remember that's why we came out to Laramie in the first place."

"Mel," Al said quietly, "he really *can't* remember."

"I've been meaning to talk to you about that," Mr. Loudermilk said. "Why do you keep moving me to hell and back again?"

"You didn't like Colter Bay anyhow," Al said.

"It's just so everybody will think, there's good kids doing right by their old Dad." Old man Loudermilk turned to Lissa. "You're just the big noise all over this town, aren't you?" And then he shifted to get a look at Al. "And you fix the getaway vehicles."

"Mel," Al said. "Don't get worked up over it."

But it was too late. You will remember what was in her face right then. What we all saw. It was plain as day, a map of all the roads leading out of Laramie and all the ways they got snowed on, ploughed under, washed out, sunbaked to dust before anybody could get over them. Weather and geography and what they made together in these parts, which was prison. You will remember how, in the space of a few seconds, the atmosphere in the house thickened and then thinned out and cooled down to nothing, like space. You shivered. I remember that, watching it, a tremor running through your body, your body which I so loved and could never get enough of. The Loudermilks were going over old ugly ground. You could see it in their eyes, the three of them, looking for their footing in this familiar, hideous terrain. Mel went into the kitchen, and you started after her.

"George," the old man barked, "get back here." Then he turned to his son. "Boy," he said in a gentle voice, "come listen to me a minute."

You will remember this change, what we thought was a transformation. You will remember that Al walked over to his father's chair, shoving his hands in his pockets.

"Your mother," Mr. Loudermilk said, "she thinks it's time you moved out. Found a place of your own. She doesn't care for all the noise. That baby screaming at all hours."

"I will," Al said, clearly shocked by something you and I will never understand. When he tried to say the words a second time, his voice broke. His mouth hung open. Something in him had once been ruined, smashed to bits, and here it was happening all over again.

"She wants you to go tonight. Take all your things. All of it. That kid too."

"He wasn't hurting anybody," Al whispered. "He was *two*. He never hurt a flea."

"He was," Old Man Loudermilk said. "He was hurting everybody. Why can't you *see* that for once?" He struck his fist on the arm of the chair. "It was a blessing in disguise. It was just a goddamn blessing."

You looked at me. We realized then that it had gotten dark. Someone needed to turn on a lamp or an overhead fixture. Mr. Loudermilk had become a squat shadow in his chair, the last light catching on moisture around his lips, a gleam from inside his mouth when he spoke. The sun shifted into a low space between two trees and came barreling in the window around the upright figure of Al Loudermilk. He was all in shadow. He looked like a charred spike of pine after a forest fire.

"I think we need to go," I said, and at the sound of my voice, Mr. Loudermilk turned toward me. Light shook in the whites of his eyes.

"Penny," he said. "We've been married for forty-seven years, and in all that time, did you ever hear of Mel writing a single solitary poem?"

"Fifty-seven," I said. You will remember that often I did not think before speaking. "But who's counting?"

"Fifty-seven," he said quietly, awed. "Fifty-seven." His hands moved as if the number were an object that had to be turned over and over before the person holding it could get any sense of what it was. And then he got it. His hands folded together and fell back into his lap. "So where were you all the time?"

"I was away on business," I said. "I was working late." You will remember that I did not look at you. You will remember that even if our eyes had met, it would have been too dark for us to see each other.

"Yes," Mr. Loudermilk said. "I remember now. That's what you told me."

Mel was still in the kitchen when we left. The house seemed to be growing darker and darker, far more so than the night falling around it, drowning in shadow. And then, when we were almost to the car, someone flipped on a light inside, and we could see them all through the picture window, Old Man Loudermilk in his Barcalounger, Al still standing with his back to the window, a flash of Lissa's red jacket crossing between them. You stood for a moment next to the driver's side door, waiting, I guess, to see if anyone would rush out and beg us to stay, or come to their rescue or get the hell off their property. But no one did.

I waited a little longer than you did, standing in the street, at the right fender. I was thinking I might have to be sick right there in the street—I tasted a hint of lime and salt at the back of my throat. So I did not realize you'd gotten into the car. I swear I did not hear the engine turn over. I was trying to steady myself, take in the cold Laramie night air, keep my body from spinning out of control right then and there. And when you inched the car forward so that the front bumper nudged my knee, I thought, *Go ahead.* I thought, *I feel like I'm about to die anyway.*

You may remember how that little metal touch was a kind of sign between us. And you may not. You may remember one night, months before, driving my car around and around me on your lawn, making tracks in the wet grass. How the moon was an empty eye above us. We'd gouged it out so it wouldn't see, wouldn't tell our sad story, the story of fools, a story that was never new in this world, never would be new in this world again. I have to get home, I said, while you kept driving those crazy circles, ellipses, veering off towards the woods at the edge of your property, coming back in close enough to graze my leg. I have to get home, I said again, but you pretended not to hear. Go ahead then, I said, go on. I was laughing, and then I dropped everything I held in my arms, a hat, a pair of gloves, a box of books. I almost said, run me over, run me down. I remember now that in fact I did say it. I remember because it comes back to me now, how I felt like one of those toys on a spring that would snap back, keep standing up no matter how many times it got knocked over.

You will remember the next morning, not too far west out of Laramie. You will remember which exit off the Interstate, you would be able to say its name, even now. You will remember it was around nine or ten, and each of us held a Styrofoam cup of coffee. You will remember, still, how I take mine, cream but no sugar. You will remember that when we saw them, the family, we tried to hand each other the cup we held, we did, in identical flinging gestures, as if looking at the scene before us required both hands. They were standing outside their car, which was an old sedan, copper-colored, all three of them, man, woman, girl-child, their trailer straddling the railroad crossing, but flung on its side, all their earthly possessions strewn over the tracks, and two hundred yards down, the single white eye of a train opening towards them. We stopped close by, and I will never forget the look on the man's face, like he might throw himself down in front of the train, under its wheels. And how the woman stood clutching the laundry, towels and sheets, how at her feet toys spilled out of their boxes. What we saw then was the moment of its not happening: there must have been a warning, a radio message some miles back. The train stopped in time and waited.

You wanted to get out and help them. I said no, thinking of the flat tire and Laramie and poems where you didn't think there could be any, and the way the lives of strangers can haunt you worse than your own most treacherous acts. But we did. We parked your car well away from the tracks and got out and tried to talk to the woman. But you could tell that oncoming train still roared loud in her ears. She shook her head and yelled at us, even though the morning had become calm and silent and cold again.

"I asked him not to do it," she yelled. She shook one red fist at the train. "I asked him not to go. He can't work." Then she turned to me. "It's like he's hearing something else in there. A radio. Like everything goes too fast for him to keep up."

All this time she watched her husband, who staggered on the tracks like a drunk, kicking at a carton of dishes. You will remember. I know you, know your heart, even after all this time, and you will remember walking after him and what you were thinking then. I watched the little girl reach into a box and pull out a doll, undressed, its chest caved in from the weight of some other, heavier toy. It was a big doll, half the girl's height, probably one of those you could lead by the hand and it would follow in a halting, businesslike way. She lifted it and went over to sit on the curb, and laid it across her knees. She pushed then, at its belly, where the doll's last ribs would be, and the chest sprang back out. I could almost hear the invisible heart sputter and start up again.

Then the man was yelling at you, *Son of a bitch, leave me alone.* You pretended not to hear, though you would not, after that, turn your back to him. You kept on picking up their things, stuffing clothes and linens into your arms like it was yours for free if you worked fast enough. The strangest idea flashed into my head: I thought you were taking their things, stealing them. We were going to take their things to Yellowstone and begin our life with these spilled possessions. I thought you were taking advantage. That's how little I knew you. Then the man sighted me, like a hungry animal, he pushed past you, and came at me, shook his fist right in my face.

"Your husband," he roared, "your husband says this ain't no big thing. He says we can just pick it all up."

I must have looked at him strangely. "He's not my husband," I said.

"Well, lucky lucky for you."

I do not remember whether you were close enough to hear. I don't know. I didn't want to know then either.

It seems to me now much, much later that we finished helping them gather their belongings. It seems to me the light changed drastically and permanently, that I felt the air become electrified and clean the way it will in the evening before snowfall. A tow truck that was not Al Loudermilk's arrived and hauled the trailer off the tracks, the train went lumbering past us, west. I thought we could get into your car and do the same, but that when we did, it would be like going over a cliff. We carried a last box over to the car, and there was the other child, the little boy, still belted in. You will remember how thin and pale he was, and that there seemed to be something wrong with his eyes—we could not tell what—or his neck because he rolled his head like it was loose.

"Where's the train?" he called out, over and over. He strained against his harness, furious. "Let me out! Let me *see!*"

For some reason, through all these years, I have had to convince myself that this child wasn't blind. You will remember that we argued about it almost all the way to Yellowstone, until I turned my head away and watched the landscape of central Wyoming fly by, sinister landscape, the juttings and declivities of bodies under a blanket.

And you, you will remember saying the word *no* and then *no no no*, all in one breath, through northwest Wyoming, when you thought I was asleep, through unpredictable bouts of snowfall and blue sky and then the strange horizontal afternoon light that seemed to be coming from behind us, from Laramie, from the place where Laramie met the horizon, the place that seemed the end of possibility, the end of poetry because all the poets there suck up the air like too many people in a small car. A place you might like to, but will never, forget. Then only rank and weedy roadside darkness, and still you believed I was sleeping, and you cursed me for letting you drive, and then whispered your wife's name, just once. A moment passed, a mile of highway, and you shook my shoulder, hard, and I opened my eyes.

"Don't ever do that again," you said. "Don't ever leave me alone that way."

"No," I said. "I won't. I promise."

But all that time, I wasn't anywhere near asleep, I tell you, I was wide awake. I was thinking about the woman at the train tracks.

"I wish we were back home," she said. And then maybe half a minute later, she added, "wherever that is."

"Laramie?" I said.

"We were there," she said. "But he never could get used to it. He never could learn how to find his way around."

She sat still then, bent over, caved in, then jumped up like a shot and ran off towards the woods, away from the wreckage. She stopped, stood for a while at the edge of the trees, then turned and came back.

"I wish I was another person," she said. "And not this one here now."

Anybody could tell she was about to get her wish. Anybody could see this was one of those moments in life when something crosses over.

When we got to Yellowstone, we said to each other that it had all been a strange little story, like one of Lissa's poems. And then we never spoke of most of it again, never of Old Man Loudermilk or the family on the train tracks, nothing of that. I cannot tell you whether or not we had a good time that week, or five days—it was less than a week by the time we arrived. I see images in my head, Mammoth Hot Springs, the Petrified Tree, Artists Point, Inspiration Point, Old Faithful. I see us hiking and cooking. I see us in each other's arms. I see us sitting still in the evenings with nothing in our hands, not a drink or a book. You will remember that we had a radio, for news and weather, we were crazy to know what the weather was going to be, sometimes for music, but we got tired of Chris Ledoux and all the rest of them. You will remember listening to National Public Radio and hearing the host introduce her segment about local poets in far-flung places. You will recall how quickly I reached over to turn it off.

"Why did you do that?" you wanted to know.

"I was afraid," I said.

"Jesus. Afraid of what?"

"Of Lissa Loudermilk. Or Mel. Whatever her damn name is."

"Why?"

"I don't know."

You let it drop. You just let it go.

But of course I did know. I knew perfectly well. And by now you do too. That open space, that part of you a poem carves away. Where does it go, that bloody piece of flesh you lose at times like this, that walking wound? Where does it go? Where did it go, the part of me that loved you? Don't you know? Don't you *see?* It all goes to Laramie, hightails out to Laramie, Wyoming. Staggers on into town like the big noise, says, howdy pardner, I got a flat, got a wicked thirst, got a strange little story to tell. Looking for somewhere to tell it. Been driving for hours and got a little doll here beside me with a caved-in heart. This looks like just the place for us, like the highway at sundown, a little familiar, a little foreign. Like we've been here before. Have we? Do you remember?

Gray's Anatomy

I.

"All I ever did was almost invent nylon," I was saying to some-body at one of the wakes. I was drunk, of course. "But sheesh. These guys. Shamus figured how to get the seven dwarves to go to work. And Ray, he kept us warm, gave us those little coffee cups you can take a bite out of, and saved us from drowning. And they got the girls too." I don't know where that last part came from, not exactly. It was killing me to have to bury them, a week apart. I might have been a little out of my mind.

We met for the first time just last year, in an emergency room, in Cambria, California. My kid and their grandkids were sick. We were all spending the summer there with our families, or parts of them, and we got to talking. Ray's granddaughter had an ear infection. Shamus's grandson had broken his leg in three places—that was the wild one, Kevin. My little girl, not so little, really—we didn't know what the matter was then. Our kids were hurt, and so we met. Can you beat that? Three old guys, tired of the beach and the sun. Just minding our own business. It was the summer of 1994. We were all at least fifty years past our best work.

Shamus was looking at a copy of *Gray's Anatomy*.

"The leg bone connected to the hip bone," he was saying quietlike to himself and Kevin. Kevin was greenish with pain, the color of the Pacific Ocean on a cloudy day, which there had been only few of the whole month of July.

"How'd he do that?" Ray asked, gritting his teeth, his head trembling like it did sometimes, and then always, of its own accord.

"Bike," Shamus said. "Meeting of bike, boy and seawall. Over the beachhead and into the surf."

"Heigh-ho," Kevin said without opening his eyes.

"Not a friendly meeting," I said.

Shamus smiled and went on sketching something with a pencil in the margin of the anatomy book.

"Shamus Culhane," he said and glanced up, nodding at Ray, at me. He held our eyes a moment to see if we recognized the name. "Sorry to meet you under these circumstances."

"Ray McIntire," Ray said.

"My dad's name is Lewellen," my little Patricia said. She would do this whenever she had the chance, make this preemptive strike. She told me when she was much younger that I had a name kids made fun of, Lewellen for a boy, so it was better to get introductions out of the way quick. She really had it, that sensitive nature you watch lying heavy upon dying kids in the movies. It usually makes me furious to see them now, made a spectacle, a cliché, but Patty really was that way.

"Lewellen O'Malley," I said and then went for the gracious lie. "Wish we were all back out on the beach." We looked at our sick kids, nodded.

We didn't know who we were then. I like to say it that way

because it's more true. We were men into old age, two of us a year before death, responsible for teenaged children, and we had no idea who we were. I think of that afternoon now, and I wonder if Shamus was drawing Dopey and Doc for the millionth time, if Ray was imagining some unholy marriage of dry ice and Styrofoam. I myself was thinking about nylon. As usual. Pantyhose.

I didn't know where my wife was, not exactly. My second wife. I hadn't known for some time, thirteen months. I could still see her legs, the backs of them, walking away from me, down the steps of our old house in Newark, the left leg with a camel-colored seam, the calf, the soleus muscle, the Achilles tendon, her still-slim ankle disappearing into the car. She was too young for me, really, forty. She had just said, "When will you ever get over this, Lew? Why can't you just forget? It's been more than sixty years." We wanted to hit each other and then she went out and got in the car. I can imagine her foot's stamp on the accelerator. I know how the ankle bone and the surrounding muscles allow the foot to perform that action. Like the punch that waits inside your fist, but less so. I didn't need any illustrated text showing me how women walked. Sometimes I got myself to believe that *shimmer, flex, hop* was actually my gift to womankind.

And then there was Patty coming apart at the seams, and me running around trying to put her back together, my hands full of her hair, fingers, teeth. That was in dreams, working to piece her together, once opening my hand to find that inside was her heart. How to put *that* back? And her tiny still voice whispering, no, Daddy, that's *your* heart. You keep it. No, no. Someday you'll need it. Yes you will.

That day on the central coast was the beginning of something I'm only just now starting to understand. The world has just given up those two, Shamus Culhane, pioneer film animator, and Ray McIntire, inventor of Styrofoam. I won't outlive them by much, I feel sure. And the world has also just lost Julian Hill, the inventor of nylon, my old lab partner at Dupont, who, at precisely the wrong moment, said, "No, here Lew, I'll do it." Then he introduced a thin heated surface, a glass rod, into a polymer. We expected a shiny, hard material, but instead he got that famous elastic, named for New York City—NYlon, hoopla, celebration, the World's Fair in '34. Looking back, it seems like that moment was always coming at me. Just like it doesn't surprise me that Shamus and Ray and the kids should have met and for a little while had our lives mixed up together. It's destiny. It's *grace,* that beautiful electric kiss. There's a part of the human anatomy that has it for a name, grace: the most superficial muscle on the inner side of the thigh, thin and flat, broad above and tapering below like an exclamation point of flesh. You can forget this grace muscle, *gracilis,* is there until somebody runs a cool finger along it.

"Nothing worse than a sick kid," I said then, back in the waiting room in Cambria. I was just making conversation. Nobody was asking about Patty because you could see the problem was something unspeakable. Shamus was over there, across the sea of false cheer in that waiting room, maybe reading about it in *Gray's Anatomy,* how her bone marrow was supposed to work, but didn't, filling up the shafts of the long bones, but also extending into the canals that contain the blood vessels, how normal marrow cells look like the olives in your martini.

"In the summer, especially," Shamus said, and rubbed the tip of his index finger lightly on the back of Kevin's hand. It was a gesture unbelievably acute in its tenderness. Ray watched and then his shoulders contracted inward, a kind of wince, the scapula shoveling forward to protect the tender heart.

"Great weather we've had," Ray said. "Good for swimming."

"Nice for them, especially," I said, nodding at the kids.

"Not really a kid town, though, is it?" Shamus said. "Kind of too quiet."

We agreed the place appeared to be a sleepy secret, a dream.

Shamus said he'd just come up from Los Angeles, and this sure wasn't like the rest of California.

"Maine-ish," he said. "What you're doing here is your own business. Even in a motel with thin walls. Privacy." He laughed. "I sound like I'm doing some shady deal, don't I?" He shook his head. "It was supposed to be a nice vacation for my grandson. And look at him."

"You renting here?" Ray said, nodding at both of us. We said yes, long-term at the Best Western, the Blue Dolphin, good to be out of Manhattan for Shamus, out of Delaware for me, Michigan for Ray. He and his wife had a little apartment. We were all just down the street from each other, on Moonstone Beach. Somehow that was a relief. I could feel it, there in the room, a relaxation of tensed muscles, a slowing of hearts that had been clacking away ever since we came in the door. I think, at our age, you're drawn to people whose pulse rates are exactly the same as yours. I think it's that simple. We smiled and looked at our kids, all of whom had their heads back against the mint-colored walls and their eyes closed. Patty and Ellie McIntire were actually snoring. A thin line of drool ran out of Ellie's mouth. Ray reached over to wipe her chin.

"Tylenol and a big Margarita," he said, meaning the sleeping potion he'd concocted for Ellie. We waited a second to be appalled, for the police, child protective services, to walk in right then. We laughed. Shamus shot his eyes left and right, then leaned forward.

"How about we make a deal?" he said. "First one through here has the other two in for drinks." It was three in the afternoon. "Nothing fancy."

"Unless there's an emergency," I said.

"Of course," Shamus said. Once again we all looked at Patty. Do I remember now that we heard a faint ticking inside her bones? A rhythmic scratching, ghostly? I remember that we were all deeply tanned. It was the end of June, and for four weeks, the weather had been perfect, not too hot in the afternoons. Women on the beach were practically drunk with coconut oil and Coppertone, and with the color of their own skin. You would see them glance at themselves in store mirrors, car mirrors, the corner chrome on the freezer case in the ice cream parlor. And it seemed the darker they got, the more impermeable they became, all those deeper tissues the skin protects growing safer and safer. All of us, I thought, in our darkening fortresses.

Ray got through first. Ellie's ear infection was obvious to treat—swabbing, a dose of penicillin. The doctor also removed a tiny pebble from her middle ear canal.

"Her ears are beautiful," Ray called to us on his way out. "So we'll see you when we see you." He gave us his telephone number.

"She ought to quit keeping stuff in there, though," Shamus said. He looked at Ellie. "That's what drawers and closets are for, honey."

Ray stopped with his hand on the door knob. "Have you ever seen the inside of an ear? I got to look, just now. God, it's beautiful. There's this little triangle of light that sits at the bottom of the whatever it is."

"Membrana timpani," Shamus said, raising *Gray's* up to show us the source of his knowledge.

Patty and Kevin took a little longer to finish up. The break in Kevin's leg was monstrous. The *breaks,* I should say, three of them. A transverse fracture of the patella and both tibia and fibula, and an odd dislocation of the ankle. Shamus later told us the doctor said Kevin's leg looked like it had been through a mangle. He studied Shamus for a long time. "But it was a bike accident. Is that right?" he said to Kevin, and Kevin, who seems to have arrived at full-throttle manhood at that precise moment, told the doctor to stop thinking like a suspicious jerk and get on with it. When they left, Shamus said he glanced back to look for Kevin's

childhood kicked away into a corner of the examination room—
so he could maybe retrieve it— but it was gone for good.

Patty had a fever and a cough that wouldn't go away. She was
impossibly tired, run-down. The examining physician asked us
some questions about where we were from, how long we were
staying, pleasantries, I thought. Then he asked me to go back out
to the waiting room. I didn't like that much, but Patty said it was
okay, so I went. *Gray's Anatomy* was sitting on the low table where
Shamus had left it, along with a white tennis sweater. I picked up
the book, took a quick look at the female organs of generation, as
Dr. Henry Gray would have it, then the brain. I love the brain. I
love Henry Gray's drawings of the four lobes: frontal, temporal,
parietal and occipital. Not so much the drawings themselves, but
the colors he assigns them, those grade school geography book
map colors: sky blue, buttery yellow, a green like sage, and the
pink that's the peculiar shade of pencil erasers. Not the primary
colors, but something far more elemental. Colors that will make
you panicky for the rest of your life.

So when the examining physician came back out, I was
already shaken. He wanted to run more tests. He wanted to know
where Patty's mother was. I saw it happening all over again, her
back out the door, her left leg folding itself into the car, the way
she said, I can't take this anymore, and made her arms swoop to
mean all of it, all of our life. I wanted to reach for *Gray's* to explain
it to him—all that ridiculous Latin: fibula, tibia, dorsalis pedis
artery, soleus flapping under the skin like the fish it's named for,
tendo achillus, the thickest, strongest tendon in the body. There
were illustrations. This is how she walked out, I would say. Look,
I can explain everything. It was all very scientific. But even in science, the unexpected could happen. You might be asked to step
aside. You'd tense up for brittleness, a crack like a hand across your
cheek, and all of a sudden, the substance would get like taffy,
stretch and pull, evanesce, liquefy. You'd stand there watching,

your fists in your pockets. You'd stand there maybe all night, staring at the blue glow from the burner.

At Ray's later that afternoon and into the evening, we drank a lot of gin, always with lime, mostly with tonic. We met Elizabeth, Ray's wife, who is blind. We met the college student from Washington, D.C., who was house-sitting next door, whom everyone later came to hope I would fall for, even at my age. Which I did. Her name, in the dreamy, besotted coincidence that summer became, was Shayla Gray. We discovered, grandmother and father and grandfathers and Shayla Gray alike, that we had come to Cambria with one suitcase and one child, though all of us—except Shayla—had at least two children or grandchildren. The others were off at camp or visiting friends, and we missed them, truly we did, but what we confessed to each other that evening as the sun fell headlong into the Pacific, was that the child we'd brought with us was the favorite.

"You're kidding," Shayla said. "You can't have a favorite. It's not allowed." God, she was young and beautiful and demanding.

"Yes, it's true," we told her, glancing wildly around to see if the other children might have crept into town, into the room at just that unfortunate instant.

"And look," Shayla went on. "They're all sick. How about that? The favorites, and they're all just broken and infected and . . ." She looked at me. "What's wrong with Patty, did you say?"

"Exhaustion," I said.

"It's hard work being the favorite, isn't it?" Shamus said. "Jesus Christ."

After that, I think I recall the women going into the kitchen to make clam chowder or clam sauce for spaghetti. I don't quite remember. I don't even know if I ate it. By that time, we knew who we were. Shamus and Ray talked about royalties and patents and investments, and I told the story of Julian Hill and the invention of nylon. We were talking in the dark, which I mean in every possible way. We were all that summer looking for something to carry us blazing into the future. Shamus was writing his memoirs. He was also fascinated by human anatomy. He thought there was something happening in the motion picture industry, some fond alliance of the human body and animation, like in the *Terminator* movies, a discovery that would relieve the world of stunt men forever. He knew a few who'd been hurt, paralyzed, one who'd died. Ray was experimenting with insulation, dreaming up problems and solving them, casting off old ideas with the *no, no, no, no* of his shaking head. I was mulling over the sheerest, strongest nylon stocking possible. We were at the edge of ourselves then, at the edge of the world, and the sun was falling over it. It was dark, and our favorite children were sick, and the women had abandoned us.

What we did next was very strange. We got up and walked out onto the porch, down the backstairs, and over to Shayla Gray's house, not her house, of course, but her uncle's. We let ourselves in the kitchen door. We snooped around the place, which was immense: five bedrooms, three and a half baths, living room, dining room, kitchen, screened porch. Not *snooped* really. We didn't open any drawers or peek into any closets. We simply took stock, like prospective buyers. Then we went back to Ray's apartment, the downstairs bedroom, hauled our sleeping children awake and took them over to Shayla Gray's uncle's house, installed them in two of the five bedrooms, Kevin in one, Ellie and Patty in the other, though naturally they got up right away to look around. We brought the gin with us. And then Ray called Elizabeth and Shayla and told them where we were.

It was all my idea. I can say that now, though I have even less of a clue why. Years ago, I might have said it had something to do with Julian Hill getting credit for the invention, when the truth is I was standing right there holding the glass rod. I wanted to say that sentence: *It was all my idea.* I loved Julian though, I really did. I loved it when he said he was something better than a good scientist. He said later, in his retirement speech, that he was lucky. I knew he was talking about that moment in the lab. He *was* lucky.

The women came over.

"I don't understand this," Elizabeth said.

"Ask him," Ray told her. "Ask Lew."

"We're occupying these premises," I said. "Shayla, my dear, we're moving in. We all have one suitcase and one sick child, and you have this big house." That's as far as I got.

"The kids are lonely," Ray suggested. "We'll help with the rent."

"I'm not paying rent," Shayla said.

"Great," I said. "Better. Perfect."

Shayla touched Elizabeth's arm. "What do you think?" she said.

"Well," Elizabeth said, "maybe we should eat first. We can eat here. Is anybody even hungry?" We allowed that we were. So I guess I do remember this part. The two of them went back to Ray and Elizabeth's apartment. I noticed that we could see them through the kitchen window, talking. Shayla was lifting the big pot off the stove. Then Elizabeth picked up the phone, and it rang in Shayla's house.

"It's for me," Ray said. He lifted the receiver. "Hi, Liz. Okay. I'll ask her." He called over his shoulder, "Ellie, Grandma wants to know if you need to be in your own bed."

"Not really," Ellie said. Ray got back on the phone.

"She says no. She says it's not her bed anyway. It's some rental bed full of rental sand."

We could see Elizabeth shake her head in the kitchen next door. She hung up the telephone. Then she tucked a loaf of French bread under her arm and let Shayla lead her back to us. At her uncle's house, Shayla got out some bowls, white like moons.

She found a shaker of Parmesan cheese, stink in a can, Shamus called it, and the kids broke up laughing. It was good to hear.

We ate without saying much. By this time it was 10:30. Then Shayla assigned rooms.

"I'll sleep on the couch," I said when it was my turn. "Somebody might need something. Something might happen."

"All right." She looked at me, I like to think wondering about the possibilities, about my old bones, wondering what they might still be capable of. One of the hardest structures of the animal body, bones, tough and elastic both, thin plates of tissue circling central canals that look like the eyes of owls. And all you got left at the bitter end.

II.

In the beginning, Betty Boop was a kind of puppy dog, Shamus told us the next evening. We were all sitting in the living room, eight of us. Dogs got to be his specialty, in a way. Pluto, for example.

"He was the perfect specimen of doghood," Shamus said. "Smart enough, but not too smart. And a real Romeo."

"Why'd you call him Pluto?" Ray said.

"Because he's out there?" Shayla Gray suggested. "I mean, jeeze, his master's named *Goofy.*"

"Is Goofy Pluto's master?" Elizabeth wanted to know.

"Pluto was always his own master," Shamus said. "But he was Mickey's dog."

"What do you think about all those new cartoons, *Aladdin, Pocahontas,* that whole crew?" I said. "Do you think of them as, I don't know, pretenders?"

"Sort of. They're so pretty. Well-dressed."

"Well, Shamus, remember Goofy. How come you dressed him that way?" I said.

"Goofy wasn't my doing," Shamus said. "Krazy Kat, Popeye, Woody Woodpecker, I did those guys. The fringe personalities, you could say."

"No offense," Shayla said, "but it seems a funny thing to want to do. Animate. Like I always wondered why guys who make mobiles do that. How do you explain it in your book?"

"I can't," Shamus said. "I never could."

Shamus looked at Shayla, and his eyes seemed to move farther back in his skull. It was an odd effect—it seemed like an effect rather than a physical possibility. It occurred to me then how large and still and full this room was in Shayla Gray's uncle's house. And how strange a thing it was that we had done. I couldn't at that moment even remember why it had been so imperative to me that we change houses, move in together. Or why everyone else had agreed. There were eight of us in various stages of sickness, health and the cocktail hour. Everyone had slept well, even me, on the couch, half waiting for the door to Shayla's bedroom to open and admit me. We all woke up early and had stayed inside most of the day. Shayla had a part-time job at the Cambria paper, and so she went into town to work and brought back a few groceries. Now she was in the kitchen cutting up beef for a stew. She was wearing a tank top with thin straps, cut low in front and behind. I liked the way the muscles of her arms and back worked as she sawed the knife into the meat, tricep, deltoid, trapezius. Gray's anatomy, Jesus, it took me long enough to think of that one. I wondered if there was any relation.

"Maybe it's like acting, only it isn't you?" Shayla said.

"Exactly," Shamus said.

He got his start, it seems, when a veteran animator showed up drunk to work. Shamus covered for him in the production of an odd little scene, a monkey with a hot towel.

"A stolen towel?" Elizabeth said.

"A *hot* towel. You know. Like a Turkish towel."

"A *monkey?*"

Behind us, the children were laughing. Kevin had rolled his shoulders forward so that his arms dragged low to the ground. Then he was batting a napkin in the air as if it were too hot to touch. For a moment, we all watched him. He was almost seventeen that year, and his body was just coming into its real power. He wasn't wearing a shirt—it seems like he never did for the whole month we stayed in Shayla's uncle's house. Partly, it was the extraordinary heat, but also Kevin's fascination with the man he was turning into. He didn't move much, but when he got up to go to the bathroom or to his room and passed the mirrors in the hall and then on the bathroom door, he looked. He usually found some excuse to stop, to rest, to try to get at an itch down inside his cast. It thrilled me a little that he didn't ever, not that I saw, look at his own face. And he was a good-looking young man. But he seemed much more interested in the cut of his shoulders and chest, all of it named in the book that came with us and sat on the coffee table: pectorals, biceps, triceps, the obliques, the transversals. He watched himself move in these small, limited ways, eagerly tracking the spread and gather of all that fibrous tissue lying secretly under the skin. When I go to the gym these days, I see other young men—though older than Kevin—peering at themselves in the mirror in just the same way. It interests me that the women never do this. The few women who work with weights in that part of the gym almost never even look in the mirror at all. If the mirror suddenly surprises them, they drop their gaze. Patty and Ellie never looked at themselves publicly, not that I saw.

Shayla Gray didn't much admire herself either. Though she ought to have more. She had a sort of native, charming modesty so that no matter how little she wore out on the beach, if ever one of us joined her, or when she came up to the house, she put on a T-shirt and shorts. I have made her into a kind of vision here, I know, a strange, passive presence, a woman who would let the rickety circus of us take over her house, her solitude. So to make her active, imagine a woman of medium height with light brown hair and blue eyes, shockingly, piercingly blue in the depths of her face. She was intensely muscular, from running, it seemed, which she did every morning without fail and for a long time, over an hour. And she was tanned, of course, we all were, but I have never seen such thoroughly freckled skin—small, soft brown freckles and then larger black ones, moles I guess, but somehow oddly attractive, not at all witchlike or contagious-looking. I should say here that while I admire women's bodies and always have, there is something frightening about them. It often seems a death-defying act to touch them. It's hardly surprising then that I should have only nearly invented nylon, and justice that I didn't get any credit for it.

For some time, four days, we didn't leave the house, except to walk across the street to the beach. We didn't speak much either, until evening, when we convened for cocktails and sunset on the front porch. We moved about the house, I think, like dancers, good dancers, who know there must be a sacred space preserved between their bodies, an equidistance. And that if they do touch, it must be lightly, with grace, and full of longing. No one seemed to know this better than Patty. As I sat reading, she would drift up behind the chair, lean down and lay her cheek on my shoulder, though only for a moment. Then she would come around and sit on the footstool in front of me.

"Why are you still reading that book, Poppy?" she asked me more than once. "It's reference."

"For the pictures," I said. I had taken to Shamus's copy of *Gray's Anatomy* like it was a thriller, a real page-turner. I was stunned by what I never knew about the body, and by what was known 140 years ago, how much. It did in fact seem like a mystery novel, and at the end, if I understood the human body, I'd finally have the truth about the heart, its troubles, about who did what to whom.

"You should get out and get some fresh air," Patty said. "See what's going on." She gave me a kiss and drifted away.

Our news of the world came from Shayla. She went into town to *The Cambrian* and the post office. She also worked for the Motion Picture Association of America in what seemed to us a very unusual capacity. Every few days, she would receive copies of European cable television listings: from France and Italy, the Netherlands, Sweden and Spain. Her job was to translate the movie titles and blurbs for anything that appeared to be an American movie. Often European television ran American movies without paying the cable fees, and Shayla Gray's job was to compile a list of who had shown what when and send it back to the MPAA.

"Translation is weird," she said. "And sometimes European TV producers are tricky. They like to yank our chains a little. For years, *The Graduate* ran on Swedish television as *The Dropout*. The French too. *Gone with the Wind* ran as *Plus Jamais Faim*, roughly, *Never Hungry Again*. Sometimes all you have to go on is the name of an actor, but they don't usually list them unless it's somebody way famous."

So, she said, it made her one of those people you liked to be standing next to in the video store when you're saying to your date, what's that one with Mickey Rourke and all the food. She won't even look at you when she says *9½ Weeks*.

"The French love that guy," Shayla told me. "I don't get it. He always seems like he's just ordered a pizza. That lazy, hungry, I'm-going-to-let-the-empty-pizza-box-lie-around-the-house-for-a-while look."

Okay, I was. I was falling for Shayla Gray. It was her uncle's beautiful house, too, and the Pacific Ocean out in front of us all day long, whispering, the sun's setting on you, Lew. There was a kind of momentum at work. Something dragging all of us forward out of the bedrooms to stand alone and look at the horizon, and then sending us back in to each other's company at night.

"So isn't there anyone waiting for you back home?" I said to her one day, about the end of the first week.

She shook her head no in that way women can do it, where they shake their heads and roll their eyes at the same time. I think it's physiologically impossible for a man to do: the recti muscles in the eye of a man cannot operate in tandem with the sternomastoid muscle. I do not know why this is. Dr. Henry Gray is mute on the subject.

"So why did you come to California?"

Shayla glanced around the room, to check, I presumed, and see whether there were children present. "I heard you could get laid here," she said. Then she laughed. "Not really. D.C. is a swamp in the summer. It was the free house. You know, *there's no such thing as a free house.*"

"You couldn't say no."

"I couldn't say no." She looked past me, out the window, then back. "So where's Patty's mother?"

"She left about a year ago." For a moment we watched Ray lead Elizabeth up the path to the road. They waited to cross. "I'm hard to live with, I guess."

"Shoot. We're all hard to live with."

"No. I've been hard to live with since the early nineteen thirties."

"Since Julian Hill and his polymers?"

"So you heard?" I said.

"Elizabeth told me."

"You just can't imagine."

"Sure I can," Shayla said. "I'm a woman. Of course I can

imagine what it's like to be standing right there and not get any credit."

Ray and Elizabeth stopped trying to cross the street. They turned back in the direction of the ocean. I knew at once someone had called out to them, or up to them, rather, from the beach. It always stuns me how you can get the most profound information just from how far the head turns. I resisted the impulse to consult *Gray's* about it. And sure enough, the children came scrambling over the rise behind them, Kevin limping without his crutches—he'd given up using them after two days. He managed to pull Patty up with him. Ellie followed a ways behind. Kevin and Patty had in five days become devoted friends. Just to look at them, you could see how the one needed the other: Kevin's bullish, hardening body needed the china shop of Patty. Her frailty made him more careful, and his energy seemed to make her less tired. They had embarked together on the project of getting rid of Patty's cough, trying every remedy they could think of: honey, salt, steam, lemon, boiled water from the Pacific.

And Ellie did not want them. Ray joked that Ellie's ear infection had left her a little bit deaf. And it was true. Much of the time, she seemed not to hear us when we spoke to her, or even near her. It appeared to me sometimes that she was counting. Her lips moved and her chin rose and fell just slightly, almost imperceptibly, the way it looks when you're working with numbers, determined not to be interrupted by the telephone ringing or an idle question. Ellie was a little overweight, "round," her grandparents called it, and this seemed to make her conscious of her body, alive to its present and future betrayals. I could see Ellie assess Patty's thinness. Her face would stay almost blank, almost completely empty, but then there was a flickering around her eyes that I recognized from other women I'd known. It said, *Hmm, that's interesting. What if I looked like that?* Men don't do this—it's all those years naked together in locker rooms, getting used to the variety of shapes and sizes that bodies come in. Women are more modest. I think they are anyway.

Ellie was alone in her body, with her body in a way that was, to me, awe-inspiring. There was power in her solitary gawk, her stride over the ice plant, past the low, wind-blasted cedars. I'd never seen such a fierce unsteadiness, and I said this to Shayla Gray as we watched her that afternoon.

"You know what she's doing all the time, don't you?" Shayla said. "While she's stalking around here?"

I told her I thought it might be math.

"Nope. She's praying."

"Praying? How do you figure that?"

"I don't figure. I asked her."

"What's she praying for?"

"You. Me. Her parents. All of us. And especially—and these were her exact words—*for Patty's body.*"

I didn't understand, and Shayla said she wasn't sure she did either, but the gist of it was Ellie believed that Patty's body was in revolt. That the soul of Patty was A-OK, but its accommodations had been poorly constructed, poorly maintained.

"So what does Ellie think we can do?" I said, trembling, feeling myself to be on the brink of some wisdom I wouldn't be able to understand.

"Nothing," Shayla said. "Pray."

At night, while the kids were watching television and Shayla was translating or at the newspaper, the adults sat outside and talked. Talked about the children. It felt as if we were hungry for them, starving, even though they were right there. Talking about them was something like touching them the way we could when they were babies, when we could put their tiny, perfect fingers in our mouths and stroke their satiny bottoms and kiss every inch of their little faces. We talked about them with that same pleasure and desire, all innocence. We talked about how bad they used to be.

Kevin, Shamus said, had until just this year loved to run away. Most of the time, he never went far, Central Park, the Empire State Building. A kid in New York City almost couldn't get beyond the Hudson or the East River. And usually, Kevin left a note saying he'd lit out because of some punishment or restriction. He liked to make sure everybody understood what he was doing.

"And then he'd tell us what time to expect him back," Shamus said. "Once he went up to his aunt's when she was living in the Bronx, but she made him call."

But the last time, he said, was Kevin's *tour de force*. It was the morning of a day when Shamus was throwing a big reunion bash for Disney animators and muckety-mucks. Like a meeting of the wheat and the chaff, he said. It was quite an affair: caterers, a pianist, young women swishing around with trays of canapes, the works. And Kevin had slept over, but wouldn't get out of bed.

"I looked in on him a couple of times," Shamus said, "and shook his shoulder and he'd groan or something, but he wouldn't get up. I had to go rushing around, and I was out most of the afternoon. When I got home at five or so, he was still asleep. I was mad then, so I went into his room and threw back the covers, and there were pillows and clothes plumped up to look like a body, and one of my ex-wife's wigs on the pillow and some old stuffed cow that mooed whenever it was shaken."

And no note. Shamus said he was furious and scared and about to host a party for fifty people. He finally tracked Kevin down at a friend's house, Shamus making phone calls while Michael Eisner was scarfing caviar and making deals Shamus wished he was in on.

"I wanted to put that kid on ice for a year," Shamus said, "but

I was so impressed with his decoy. I had trouble not slapping him on the back and getting him to tell me all about how he thought it up."

Ray and Elizabeth talked about Ellie. Ray did most of the talking, his trembling head seeming to deny every word he said, while Elizabeth sat with her body turned away from us, but her face inclined toward the candlelight. In the middle of his story, the candle blew out, and I think we were all glad. There was something in Ray's face you didn't want to see. He was telling us that Ellie sucked on her left index finger until she was about ten. He could see it was messing up her teeth, and the finger itself was growing crooked and pointed, like a crone's.

"I came up with these Byzantine contraptions and punishments and ointments, stuff I cooked up in the lab so it tasted really terrible. Wrapped her finger with first-aid tape. I watched her one night carefully slip off the entire mummy case of tape and fall asleep with that finger in her mouth and a smile on her face."

"It was awful," Elizabeth said.

I could hear the ice in her glass, the catch of gin in her throat. We were all a little drunk. We had important things to tell each other before it was too late.

"For a little while, I slapped her," Ray said. "God, that was the worst." He took a drink too. We all did. "Tough love," he said with some derision.

"As if it wasn't already tough enough," Shamus said.

I say we talked about our children, but the truth is, I didn't say a word about Patty. I couldn't think of one single story to tell about her. Not one anecdote about her charm, her cleverness, her willful nature, her little tricks and traps and turns of phrase. I just couldn't. I needed to keep her to myself, keep her inside my body like a secret notion, like an idea whose time has not yet come.

* * *

On Sunday, a week after we'd begun the occupation of Shayla Gray's uncle's house, we all went to church. Except for Shayla, it was everybody's first outing since the separate trips to Community Hospital that brought us all together. Most of anybody who practiced anything was Catholic, so we piled into two cars and drove five minutes to Santa Rosa Church on the west end of Main Street in Cambria.

To go into church as a visitor has always struck me as entering another life, someone else's life, but in the middle of it, say at age forty. A little like the way amnesia gets portrayed on television, but not exactly. Conversations are already going on; there's a bake sale, but you've brought nothing to the table. Still, everything looks vaguely familiar. Men and women you've never seen before shake your hand, smile, and say welcome. When they hand you food, the cup of wine, your name is on their lips. They seem not to notice the infirmity of your corporeal self; they pay no attention to your deep, even tan, your blue eyes, as if they've been seeing you every week, all their lives.

At Santa Rosa Church, everyone was elderly, our age, maybe a handful of people under fifty. There were two babies in the arms of a man and a woman who looked much too old to be their parents, the teenaged son and daughter of the guitarist, *guitarist,* for this was the folk mass, and our crew of hurt kids. All around us were stooping and crouching and aching, shattered hips, walkers, the gnarl of arthritis, the flash of bifocals. You could smell the Bengay, the wheaty breath of Metamucil, hear the dry-bean rattle of nitroglycerine pills, and Doan's and melatonin. I think we sat Shayla and Kevin and Patty in the middle of the pew for safety—their youth was in danger here. Ellie McIntire wanted to be on the aisle, and I sat next to her.

For reasons I did not understand we had what's called a silent entrance, a practice most often reserved for the penitential season of Lent. There was the usual procession, but no music: an altar boy and girl, two lay ministers, and the priest, who seemed in his walk up the aisle to be trying to get a sticky substance off the bottom of his shoes. I realized when he got to the first row of pews that there was something wrong. He had a clubfoot, maybe two—the bones of the tarsus become altered in shape and size and displaced from their proper positions—and the movement of his arms and hands, his refusal to look out at the congregation seemed to betray profound embarrassment. I glanced over at Ellie and saw that she was clutching her hands together—from across the room, they might have appeared to be folded in the attitude of prayer, but I could see that the ends of her fingers were flushed where they pushed on the knucklebones of the opposite hand. Her face was still and rapt and utterly sad. She was the very picture of empathy—it was there in the tensed muscles around her eyes, the *orbicularis palpebrarum, levator labii superioris.* Here was another body in revolt. In that first glance, I wondered if I would have to keep Ellie from running into the aisle and up to the altar and throwing her arms around this priest.

Which surely would have knocked him down. I don't believe I have ever seen a human body more unmoored than—I looked at the church bulletin for his name—the body of Father David Holmes. It was partly a matter of balance. The feet are placed at right angles to the legs in order to keep us standing upright and still, and so, because Father David Holmes had to walk on the insides of his feet, the rest of his body moved in a constant sway. He looked like an anchored ship in a rough port. His body seemed to surprise him by being everywhere at once. And he appeared to move more than was necessary. He knocked into both the lectern and the altar as he passed between them. It did not help matters that he was tall, over six feet. When it came time for the little altar girl to hold the Missal, she had to balance it on top of her head. And I felt quite afraid for her. I could see Ellie was thinking it too: what if one of those windmilling arms fell suddenly and mightily on the open book. It could break the child's neck.

The voice of Father David Holmes, however, seemed to come from some other, perfect, magnificent body. It was low and rich, not merely deep. You would say it had breadth, it had atmosphere, the luminous aftershock of thunder, but it was also a little thick, as if he were just recovering from a cold. There was the ghost of an accent too, British, Father David Holmes sounded British to me, but he'd left his native land long ago, and the not-quite-clipped quality of his speech made the words he said seem to roll away from us, disappear, like a face in a dream. But even as he spoke, he was unable to meet the eyes of his congregation. You wanted to help him out, put your eyes before him, like Saint Lucy even, in a dish. As the couple in front of her shifted, Ellie continually repositioned herself to be able to see Father Holmes's face, try to meet his gaze somehow. I could tell that's what she was doing because I was doing it myself.

Even his glorious voice betrayed him, though. He staggered over words, made mistakes, apologized for beginning a sentence with the word "thesis" when he meant to say "This Jesus," and he began the reading again. He had his homily written out, but stumbled there too. His body would halt him in any way it could. He told a story of teaching a catechism class in Monterey, and having the children draw Adam and Eve, and how one of them drew Adam and Eve in a stretch limo driven by God, cruising down Highway 101, at the end of which was the Garden of Eden. Adam and Eve were on their way, and God was at the helm. I don't remember his point, the link between this anecdote and scripture. What I remember is how Ellie leaned forward to listen to him, and how when he told the story about the child's picture, she laughed more heartily than anyone else in the church. She laughed with pure pleasure, with relief. Her whole body shook.

When it came time for the exchange of the peace, Father

Holmes came off the altar and made his tortuous way down the center aisle, to the very last pew and up again, clasping the hands of everyone he could reach. Sometimes priests do that, but not usually past the first few rows. When he shook Ellie's hand, I could see that his left eye, so blue it was almost violet, rolled off at will. It seemed to spin slowly in its socket, unmoored from the rectus muscles that stretch backward like a ready slingshot.

He hates this, I thought, every second of it, the publicity of his failure of a body. But here he is. Ellie knew it too and Patty would learn it, how the body will go to wrack and ruin, and so would Kevin, though for a while in his late teens and twenties, he would forget. In the seconds before he invented nylon Julian Hill had gently moved me out of his way. Suddenly there in Santa Rosa Church I remembered it, his gentleness. I had just burned the back of his hand with a heated glass rod. I was twenty-one. The lab was too dark. It was late in the afternoon in December, and we hadn't turned on the lights. I was clumsy and in a rush. He said I ought to step aside and take a deep breath. He said, now just watch.

We drove home in absolute silence, and then, it seemed, everyone disappeared, to the beach, I thought, or Shayla may have driven back into town. I didn't know where Patty was. It was lunchtime, but no one came in to make a sandwich, boil an egg, scoop out some leftovers from the casseroles in the refrigerator. I stood in the kitchen, trying to decide what I wanted myself, and happened to look up out the window and into the kitchen of Ray and Elizabeth's old place. Shayla and Kevin were there together, Shayla leaning against the counter. They were talking, it seemed, and then Kevin took a step closer, and Shayla began to unbutton her blouse. He kissed her then, and she kissed him back. They moved a little ways apart and she held his elbows while he moved his hands, the tips of his fingers, over her breasts. He took off his own shirt then, dropped his hands to her waist and lifted her onto the counter, pushing her blouse all the way off her shoulders, and kissed her beautiful white chest, white like plumage against the tan of her arms and throat and belly. Shayla looked down at the top of Kevin's head and laid her cheek there and smoothed his hair and ran the fingers of her left hand along the side of her neck. Then she raised his chin and brought her mouth down to his. He lifted her off the counter and, limping, carried her out of sight.

A few minutes later when I heard their voices outside, I was still breathless, not with my own longing, but with surprise at their tenderness, their warm, brown bodies coming to know each other slowly and gently. The silence of it too, the vortical quiet of held breath. Then they were standing in the kitchen doorway looking at me.

"Where is everybody?" Kevin said.

"Well, we're all right here," Shayla told him, watching my face. I tried to make my expression mirror hers, which was oracular, her skin flushed beneath her tan, bathed in the noon light, and her eyes not blue at all, but darker than any I'd ever seen.

III.

In the next week, Cambria was shaken by a horrible crime. It happened in three parts, disconnected-seeming, like in slow motion. First, on Wednesday, a two-year-old girl disappeared from her parents' motel room. They were visiting from Visalia, a town three hours east, in the San Joaquin Valley. The parents worked for almond growers and had saved all year, maybe for years, to take this vacation. It was in the paper and on the local news, broadcast back to us from San Luis Obispo, an hour away. The motel was about a mile down the road from Shayla Gray's uncle's place, and so the police eventually came to us during their house-to-house search. They found our arrangement very suspicious, and then just

plain odd. They wanted to call in the missing spouses for ques-
tioning. Where were the mothers of Kevin and Patty and Ellie?
How did Kevin break his leg? Why did Patty look so ill? What was
Ellie saying? *Speak up, honey*, they kept telling her.

"It's the breakup of the nuclear family," Shayla said, making a
stab at levity, but the investigating officer didn't like it one bit.

"Miss," he said. "You need to produce some parents."

It struck us all as a bizarre reversal, hilarious even, under different circumstances. But Shayla held on. "Do you know who
you have here?" she said. And then she introduced us, Shamus
Culhane, pioneer in the field of animation, Ray McIntire, the
man who gave us Styrofoam, she said, tapping her finger on the
policeman's fast food coffee cup. And Lew O'Malley, she said,
taking me by the hand, the man who invented nylon. My whole
body started. I couldn't look at anyone in the room. It must have
been too much for the police, too, because they left us alone. I
wanted to say something to Shayla, but what? Thanks for the
rewrite of history, thanks for making me what I should have been,
what I never could be. But she wasn't waiting around. Shayla
Gray's exquisite anatomy followed the police out the door, peeled
off from their huddle by the side of the road, and headed down
to the beach to help look for the body of Araceli Torrez.

The beachhead in Cambria is already roped off in several
places up on top of the bluff, mostly to the north toward the
motel where Araceli Torrez and her parents were staying. Police
were trying to keep bystanders away from these areas, and there
was an officer stationed at the bottom of each of the plank stair-
ways that led down to the water. When I caught up with Shayla
Gray, one of these officers was asking why she needed to be on the
beach, what she knew that could possibly help. I drew her back
and we stood there watching police and dogs scrabble over the
sand. I remembered an afternoon ten years ago when Patty was
missing on the beach at Jekyll Island. When we found her, she

said that from the back, everybody looked like her mother. She said, a few years later, that she was sure somebody would find her if she kept walking. She knew not to go near the water, but the · sand was hot, and her feet burned, and so she moved down to the water's edge, where the sand was kept wet by the farthest fingers of each wave. Finally she sat down, then lay down, then fell asleep. For a while everyone thought she belonged to everyone else, but then as the tide began to come in, and Patty kept sleeping, a woman gathered her in her arms and headed up the beach towards the lifeguard's tall chair. That's where we found her a few minutes later. She was so bad to have walked away from us. We said that to her over and over.

I was telling Shayla Gray this story and then I was weeping and then I was holding her in my arms. That was all. That was all that ever happened between us, but as long as I live I will never forget the feel of her, the bones of her spine, vertebrae, cervical, dorsal, and lumbar. What your hand feels is the centrum or body of each vertebra; the pedicles and luminae reach inward toward the vital organs. Sometimes in *Gray's* they look like crossed fingers, reminding you that the strength and duration of the body is a false promise. I felt the muscles, trapezius and latissimus dorsi, and I thought of the weight machines at the gym, where that perfect specimen of the body is depicted, stripped of its skin. Those illustrations always turned my stomach, the body dissected that way. Dr. Henry Gray gives instructions about how to do it—at the beginning of every chapter: place the body in a prone position with the arms extended over the sides of the table, and the chest and abdomen supported by several blocks, so as to make the muscles tense. The illustrations that accompanied these instructions disturbed me too: the body incised along straight lines, corners of skin folded back like marked book pages, and inside revealed a darkness, a blank mystery that threatened to cancel out all of Dr. Gray's careful work of knowing.

* * *

Araceli Torrez's small body was found face down on the beach a day later, bloated with salt water. At the press conference, Shayla heard one of the investigators say that her eyes were open and her head was turned seaward so that she appeared to be watching the horizon. Her legs and dark hair were tangled in kelp, so that she looked, he said, like the little mermaid. He was beside himself, he had small children of his own, "the goddamn little mermaid," he said, two or three times before someone led him out of the room.

He said it because that was, at first, what everyone thought: Araceli Torrez was playing out the mermaid story, believing anyone, any girl especially, could swim to the bottom of the ocean and befriend the fishes, grow new lungs and marry the prince. But there was an autopsy and an inquest, and it turned out that the little girl died of internal injuries, inflicted most likely by heavy blows to the abdomen. The bruising on her belly and lower back, her thighs, was extraordinary. The parents were questioned, and what the father said was, "I never meant to kill her." As we watched all this on television, read about it in the paper, Elizabeth McIntire sat in that peculiar pose of hers, her body canted in one direction, her head turned toward sunlight coming through the front window, which she swore she could see on the insides of her eyelids.

"Sometimes I'm glad to be blind," she said.

It is a strange thing to watch a blind person cry. The tears are somehow even more private than those of a sighted person. Dr. Henry Gray has nothing at all to say on this subject. Not a word.

We stayed in Shayla Gray's uncle's house for another two weeks, until the end of August. Shayla went into town, to the paper, the post office, to buy groceries, and occasionally one of us went with her, but not often. Usually it was Ellie, who would be dropped off to pay a visit to Father David Holmes. Santa Rosa Church is almost directly across the street from Cambria's one supermarket, and sometimes Ellie and Father Holmes would walk over to pick up a few things for the cook, butter, milk, apples for pies, fish on Fridays, all year. Father Holmes insisted on walking. He was trying to give his body to the world, he said.

Despite the eight people living in it, Shayla Gray's uncle's house was always very quiet, the patient, half-alert quiet of bodies waiting to fall asleep. Shamus kept working on his autobiography, "my *mem wahs*," he said, and then, "as if anybody's going to give a damn." He sat for hours drawing the old characters. Once he said out loud, surprising even himself, "What the hell did I ever see in Betty Boop?" and Ray and I laughed because we'd spent some time, many, many years ago, wondering the same thing. Most of the drawings never got finished. Kevin tried to save them for a while, for the archives, he told me, but then we'd be short of paper, and on the back of Pluto someone would have to write *eggs, sugar, coffee, ground beef.*

Elizabeth and Ray took long walks together on the beach, sometimes three times a day. They moved slowly, with their heads down, so that they seemed to be looking for something. In the afternoon, they went swimming together. Ray led Elizabeth into the surf, keeping up a running commentary about the height of the waves, the angle, the pitch. When they crashed against her body, Elizabeth never seemed surprised—she never jumped or cried out. She and Ray would wade out to where the water was chest-deep, past the breakers, and then Elizabeth would stretch out on her back, and Ray would raise his arms, and she would float in them, buoyed up. They seemed impervious to riptides, the moods of the current. Sometimes he would swim her up the coast a little ways, north towards San Simeon, but mostly they stayed in one place, gazing out to sea.

The children grew, in those last two weeks, to be like nest mates, puppies or kittens. They often read or watched television leaned against each other, Ellie too, with Patty resting on her chest, her own back against a pillow propped on Kevin's outstretched legs. His cast made a good backrest. And they wrote messages on it, to each other, or quotations from their reading. Ellie wrote the beginning of Hamlet's famous speech, only she changed the words to "to knee or not to knee." They noted the days passing and the weather, which sometimes they invented or romanticized: "Sunday 8/20 morning squalls." Patty found a book of poems by Lorca and down at Kevin's ankle, she wrote, "The children observe a point far far away." Patty did not get better, and Kevin's cough remedies underwent a change. At the end some of them were three of the new blue M&Ms, a sip of Coke, followed by a sip of beer, then a sip of vodka. A mark on Patty's throat made with the ashes of a burned Taco Bell wrapper.

Whatever I had witnessed unfolding between Kevin and Shayla Gray did not seem to continue—or if it did, perhaps I simply did not notice. I had room in my thoughts only for Patty, for the details of her steady decline. As her body weakened, there came to be a great distance in her face. My impulse was often to hold out my hand to her and say, no, what's your hurry, you just got here, didn't you? And yet, I want to think of Shayla and Kevin together. I want to think that the subtle language I saw their bodies learning came to be a gentle and generous idiom. I want to believe in that kind of knowledge. I sometimes imagine such thoughts are the last consciousness we have before there is nothing and darkness and mystery. I imagine that the body's last breath is visceral that way, the deep, blooming gasp and clutch, our last and best lover's fingers moving along the grace muscle, before the spirit makes use of it to get up and walk away.

Five miles down the coast from Cambria on Highway 101 is a place called Harmony, an artisans' colony. *Population 18,* the sign reads, and you can hear the cartoonish voice of the whole little town—amused and proud, booming out its isolation, insulation. When we all drove down there at the end of August, we decided Harmony would be a good place to be buried, remote and beautiful, quiet, near enough to hear the Pacific Ocean without being worn away by it. We asked one of the artisans, the glassblower, if there was a cemetery in town, and when he said no, Shayla wondered out loud what happened to the dead. He pointed to his furnace and smiled. We all laughed.

"What?" Elizabeth wanted to know. "What did he say?"

"Light," Ellie told her.

"Of course," Elizabeth said. "Light."

I should have turned on the light, in December 1931, in the Dupont lab. Then I would not have burned Julian Hill's hand, and he would not have gently moved me out of his way. The last time Patty called out to me, it was three in the morning, and I threw on my bathrobe and went into her room, and though she did not like me to do it, I turned on the lamp by her bed. At the end, she did not want me to see her, the waste of her body, the round moon of her face rising out of the blankets. She closed her eyes, as if this could make her invisible. "Poppy," she said, and that was all. I lay down beside her, holding her long, still bones that had rotted from the inside out, and watched more than felt the warmth flow out of her. It should not have been me, there, then, like that. It should have been a husband, children, and at least eighty years later. It should not have been me there. It should not have been Patty. We ought to have traded places, her damaged body for my good one. Hers that was not big enough to heal itself, for mine that was so large and empty on the inside, and like all bodies, so utterly dark and unknowable.

The Loop, The Snow,
Their Daughters, The Rain

Their daughters say Grandma. Their daughters say door, chair, spoon. Their daughters say no. Their daughters say cut my hair with a raisin. They once said, Let's play orchestra, and they will soon say, Everybody here has a chair except I have a step stool. They say, Because I might not be able to get out. The snow is coming down loud. They say, I want to do it all by myself.

They are not yet forty, and their daughters are not quite three. They are sisters, Louise and Lana, and their daughters are cousins, Hannah and Sarah. Their husbands, who work together, are about to go on a business trip to Chicago and take their daughters. At the airport, their daughters say bye-bye plane, and at the last minute, Louise and Lana decide they will not be able to bear the silence in the house, and so they go too.

In Chicago, the forecast says rain. It's Saturday in the Loop. On the plane their fathers taught Hannah and Sarah to say loop, and now their mothers prompt them. Loop. They say, Where's Daddy, and their mothers say, At his meeting. Hannah and Sarah have learned to say the last three words of any sentence they hear. *Sentence they hear.* All morning long, it has been *back soon dear, back soon dear,* like a species of forest animal, their mothers think, white-tailed and always just departed. The husbands said, Don't forget your umbrellas, and so their daughters point at the umbrellas everyone carries so unwillingly: *forget your umbrellas.* Then they just say ella. The sky over Lake Michigan is glowering and restless, full of clouds that can't seem to get away fast enough. In Marshall Field's there are checked umbrellas, lost umbrellas, cheap and expensive umbrellas, umbrellas swinging from wrists and elbows like odd useless appendages. Ellas everywhere.

Their mothers take them upstairs to see the dolls, the ones with complete wardrobes and trousseaux, with glittering eyes that open and shut: Mary Poppins, Scarlet O'Hara, Sleeping Beauty, whose green eyes are set with tiny lead weights and so are particularly slow to open. Of all dolls, their daughters say *Ella,* as in Cinder——, the girl who starts out as a silent scullery maid and then gets to marry the prince. In odd, still moments, their mothers have wondered about that. What would you say to a prince? Nice coat. Hey, you're a real good dancer.

Outside again, their daughters say lake. Michigan is too much to ask. Their daughters say *swimming?* And so against their better judgment, the mothers wheel them, carry them down to the beach at Grant Park. Chilly water, their mothers say, about lake water the color of cold. If they could open up this wind blasting their faces, peel it down to the center, the color of chilly water is what they would find. From out of their backpacks and their strollers their daughters look east across the lake and their eyes deepen into black. Their mothers notice but keep silent. How would you say to a daughter, I see you becoming bottomless, so you can be filled up. Stop it before you go too far. Plenty of time for that later. If the fathers were here, they would put a stop to it, they would be able to say no, come back up to the

Loop. Loop, they would say, loop their daughters would say, not really frightened at all, like a French child crying wolf. *Loup.* A false alarm. Like rain that never comes when it is expected, like a child talking. Their mothers look up, and it is raining, their daughters are talking, and no one can say how or when it began.

On Sunday, they all go to church, where because it is so quiet, their daughters say everything that comes into their heads. An unfamiliar church, somewhere on the South Side. The lake is still not far away, and their daughters can hear its beating against the shore, its playacting, *I am an ocean, I am the sea,* over and over, its wet shoulders falling forward onto the sand.

St. Philip Neri, it's his church. Their daughters say Flip and then they laugh. They can see him on one side of the altar. It's his church, their mothers say. Their daughters say *house?* At communion they watch their mothers chew the communion host and say *have some?* Holding out their tiny hands. When their mothers grow quiet and drop their faces into their open palms, their daughters watch without moving. They don't blink their long eyelashes. There is an old woman in the pew behind them, so old she is wearing a lace veil like a skullcap, the kind of veil no woman has worn into St. Philip Neri in twenty years. She believes the daughters are contemplating the nature of the soul. She trusts that small children can do this, believes hers did it before they started to grow up, her children who have now moved far away. If they can't, she asks her husband in her prayers that night, who can? She believes he answers *you.*

Outside St. Philip Neri, it begins to snow. Their daughters, in their still-infant wisdom, feel this before they see it. They see the statues in the church pull their stone cloaks closer. They touch the knees of their tights, glad for covering, not yet knowing anything of pantyhose. Outside the snow announces itself with a few flakes blown in over Lake Michigan like feathers from some wintering gull. On Lake Shore Drive, people are dazzled. It's only

September, some say, and check their pocket calendars. It's too early, some say, close to tears, the easily betrayed. No, some say. No, their daughters say. Global warming, some say, the armchair meteorologists. Falling, the sidewalk acrobats say. Each one is different, some say, tourists coming out of the Art Institute.

Their daughters say no, which of course means snow. The snow comes harder, and their fathers pack them into their car seats. Why don't they cry when we do this? the mothers wonder as they help pull the harness over their daughters' soft, small heads, pull their tiny arms up from under the padded bar, unbend the stick legs. Their daughters say *Go! Go now!* Their daughters say *Costco,* which is what a car trip often means. The snow comes at the car windshield in heavy, white blots. Their mothers point and say cotton. Like cotton. Next week, their daughters will say cotton and wowder, when they are discovered cleaning the floor with talcum powder, cotton, water. Now they say wowder, which means both thunder and water.

Their daughters look out at snow falling on Calumet Park and Riverdale and Blue Island. No, no, no, they say over and over, refusing weather, refusing southward travel, all travel. But no, the fathers have driven in the wrong direction, they don't have the map, and so it's back up north through Cicero, Schiller Park, Des Plaines, all those new languages, and the snow like a blanket over them, over all language. Binkie, they say, for blanket. Look! their mothers say. Can you say snow like a blanket? Their fathers glance in the rearview mirror, watch the disappearance of the sooty Loop, and they ask, Can you say heavy industry? Their daughters think their fathers are silly and miraculous. They cannot bear to lose them. They know this even now but will never be able to say it.

Their daughters say Grandma, which is where they are driving now, to Grandmother's house we go, west from the Loop, out to Hoffman Estates. They will have lunch, their daughters' foods brought in glass jars, glowing, and lustrous like the windows at

St. Philip Neri. Their mothers will leave several of these jars for dinner, *foof*, they say, for food, as if eating were magic, *foof!* And then they will drive back to Chicago with their husbands and go out to dinner and disappear into their hotel rooms early, into each other's arms. Already they are dreaming of a night, a whole long night during which their daughters will say nothing. That is how they look forward to it: silence. Their daughters will, for one night, stop learning the language at this alarming rate, stop pulling words out of their mothers' bodies they way they once did breast milk. Their daughters will forget Ernie, whom they love beyond reason, and far more than Bert. They will forget babba and chilly water. They will forget no, and the mysterious *Ada,* the goddess of used-upedness, whose name must mean *all done.* For one night, they will be too shy to ask anyone to take them outside into the front yard to look for the moon. They'll forget to cry *balloom, balloom,* and point into the heavens and wait.

Their mothers are thinking of the silent night of the body, what they have never had words for. They know some women have words for it, they've read such words in books, heard them spoken, remember a few of them, water, heat, blossom, open. They have a shardlike memory of a woman saying, *It feels like you were born there.* From the movies, they think, maybe. Translated in a subtitle. For themselves, though, the point is no talk, casting themselves adrift and going back so far that they come to a time before words, before that kind of need. To speak is to need, they think. To speak is to admit how lonely a place the world is. They wish they could save their daughters from it, hush them up tight against loneliness. They wish it with the part of themselves that is fierce and aboriginal and always silent.

At Grandma's the television is on. One of the cousins does this, turns the television on and leaves the room, gets the sound going so he can hear it all over the house. All of the young cousins do it, mostly for the channels that play music. Like the radio.

Their daughters stand in front of the television and rock their tiny hips from side to side. They say *dance?* and when nobody will, they say *help?* When any group of four musicians appears—three guitars, one drum kit—their daughters say *Hootie.* An old clip of the Beatles runs, and they pause to count and then they say *Hootie.* All the young cousins laugh. These cousins have come to the age of first sly thoughts, and so they want to teach Hannah and Sarah how to say, *Mom, could you get me a beer? A pack of Marlboro reds please.* The young cousins want to teach them to say *firetruck,* hoping that the whole shiny long word will prove too much for their little mouths and collapse into obscenity. The cousins have come to a place that might as well be across the whole world from Hannah and Sarah. They know all the words for what they want to say, these young cousins do, and they know what the words mean and this knowledge has made them mute.

Their daughters say *outside,* and Louise and Lana put them into the arms of the college-aged cousins. The snow has stopped falling, gathered behind clouds and held its breath. There is in the afternoon air north of Hoffman Estates toward South Barrington the sense that something or someone has asked a question of great moment and is waiting for an answer to be spoken. From Grandma's they walk, the mothers, their daughters and the college-aged cousins, beside Poplar Creek. Sometimes there are deer nosing the deadfall at the water's edge, and the college-aged cousins would love to see Hannah and Sarah get their first glimpse of deer. They walk all the way out to the lake, a pond really, drying up smaller every year, not big enough to name, and so everyone has, privately, like wishing. Louise and Lana ask the cousins what they are learning, and the cousins tell them, the words for business, the words for economics, anthropology, genetics, literature. They ask, so what do you do for fun, and then their daughters repeat the cousins' words, catch them up in the thin nets of their voices so they will not fall into the lake and be lost, or roll away into Poplar Creek. Their daughters repeat, *lover, field hockey,* they say *glee club,* and the sound rises and drops over the lake like a shiny penny to wish on, *glee, glee, glee.*

The wind blows in a strange, aching gust, like a scratch, like a tear in fabric, and it begins to snow again. Their daughters recognize it now—they say *no* and then they say *Daddy.* The six women walk back to Grandma's, two cousins, the mothers and their daughters. The older four say to each other, It's so good to see you. It's so long between visits. The oldest two say, Next thing we know, you'll have daughters of your own. The snow makes them speak this way, as if through the window of a departing vehicle, with the breathlessness of departure. They feel this hurry but they don't know why. There are no words for it, this quality of snow, snow too early, in the suburbs, their backs to the nameless lake, water of wishes and promises, so dark below the surface.

The fathers and husbands, and the lovers, watch from the picture window, thinking also without words, how beautiful the women are, with their chapped faces and their dark hair struck with snow. They say nothing, each alone with his breaking heart. Something about those flecks of snow—the word *proximity,* the word *ease*—how the women let snow rest in their eyelashes, in the fine hairs in front of their ears, places they hardly ever let the husbands and lovers touch, something feels like it will drive them into a fury. A fine needle of anger rises up through their bodies. They wonder why a woman would take a baby out into the snow without a hat.

Meanwhile, the snow turns to rain, and then after a time, the temperature drops again. The west suburbs will be trussed up in ice, then covered again with snow. In September. Even among the real meteorologists, there are no words for what is happening.

The mothers know they must say good-bye to their daughters

so they can drive back to Chicago in time for dinner. There are reservations, but first the ritual of dressing, and talk, drinks sent up from the hotel bar. It is an hour more private than any other, more inviolable, a word the husbands love, but would never say, a word outdated, a word that not much is anymore.

And so the mothers look all over Grandma's house for their daughters, find them in a corner of the big cousin-filled room, playing with a bicycle pump. Their daughters take turns with the needle of the pump, one pressing it gently into her navel while the other works the pump's plunger. The mothers stand still and watch and wonder what it is their daughters want from their game, how they remember this old connection site. When they kiss their daughters good-bye, the game is barely interrupted. The daughters look up at their mothers with a great unfathomable knowledge in their eyes. The blue seas of iris swim. Their mothers have the sense of being seen through, seen beyond. Their daughters say *bye-bye,* they say *nigh-night, see you in the morning time.*

On the way back to Chicago, the husbands talk business, they say *investment,* they say *securities,* they say *prime rate,* they say *Greenspan.* They talk about the World Series, *underdog, Atlanta in six, Wohlers,* and the wives look up at that, a beautiful name, mysterious, a word for something warm and smooth-edged. *Don't know what that is, don't know what you'd use them for, but wohlers would be nice to have around. Like Justice.* Sometimes the mothers, the wives feel this way, that when people talk, they don't understand the language, don't know where they are. Suddenly now they're wives again. What do the words mean? How should they act, like wives and not like mothers? They sneak looks at their husbands, the fathers, twenty minutes ago they were the fathers, but now they're the husbands, and it doesn't seem to confuse them at all. The mothers think about the car seats in the trunk, lying on their sides, looking vaguely prosthetic that way, and dangerous. They are driving east around the northern rim of O'Hare Airport, where the atmosphere trembles full of air traffic, the frenzy of de-icing, the spew of it, and inside the splintering of families. *Bye-bye.* A grown daughter and her parents in the airport bar. They saw this once, pieced together the story. She had a layover, the grown daughter did. She was catching a flight to Los Angeles. A couple of beers apiece. Her father bought her a new carry-on bag. She and her mother talked. Louise and Lana watched them, then without discussion, got up and followed them to the departure gate. At the last moment, embracing her mother, the daughter began to weep. The mother said, *Don't worry, you'll get your . . .* and then murmured something they couldn't hear. The father wiped his eyes. The daughter got in line with the other passengers and then when she turned to look again, she saw that her parents had gone. This made her weep more; she reached into her bag, found her sunglasses and put them on. Louise and Lana clasped hands. Each wondered, privately, why the whole world did not fall apart, did not drown in tears like this, sadness that could never be soothed, only diminished for a time by a cocktail, an in-flight movie, distance, time, speed, weather.

Now they are mothers missing their daughters in a darkening landscape made even more insubstantial by snow. They wish it could happen somehow that their husbands would pull the car off the road and, there behind the cover of evening and snowfall and increasing fog on the inside of the windows, make love to them. It has happened before, once coming home from a funeral, once after a long, mean, smoldering argument. It is a place to go when words fail, a capitulation, a bargain, truce, condolence, code, sign, shorthand. And of course impossible now, surrounded by the husbands, the fathers, the wives, the mothers, this car crowded with people who, like everyone all over the world, cannot put even their smallest griefs into words.

At Grandma's their daughters say, *The snow is coming down loud.* The young cousins argue, telling them that the point of snow is quiet, that it never makes any noise, never. Their daughters shake their heads in the young cousins' reddening, bulge-eyed faces. *Loud,* they say, and the young cousins, who cannot disagree with anyone else in this house, and win, take Hannah and Sarah by the shoulders and shake them, hard. They know this will make for a huge outcry, and an adult will come running into the room, and there will be trouble, but they cannot help themselves. What are these babies doing here anyway, the young cousins think, they are ruining everything, and it's all because they were wrong about snow and we were right, and it always happens like this. Why would anyone think snow is coming down loud? At that instant, the young cousins' mothers hurry into the room. What on earth have you done, they are saying, can't you see they're just babies? And precisely in that moment, the young cousins hear it, in the silence after their mothers' question, in the gesture of a mother bending to pick up a child, their mothers bending to pick up someone else's children and not them. They hear the snow loud on leaves, creaking the invisible hinges of tree limbs, snow clumping like shoes on the walkway, *ding ding* loud on the slate roof, snow sorrowing itself into the wind. What have you done? these mothers say, and the young cousins want to tell them, *Oh Mother, we have grown too big for you to carry. That's what we have done. We have grown up.*

And in that same moment, everyone looks outside to see that darkness has fallen. Everyone has a word for it: *dinner, porchlight, 60-Minutes-is-on, make-Zachy's-lunch,* for tomorrow is Monday, a school day. Hannah and Sarah twist out of their rescuers' arms and go to the picture window. *Balloom,* they say, *balloom.* But all they see are their own faces, and then far in the distance, a secret glittering, all the wishes in the nameless lake risen to carry the weight of the snow. Behind them, aunts and uncles and cousins pass back and forth carrying plates to the table, silverware and cups that catch the light and fling images against the darkened window. The prongs of a fork, the bevel of a drinking glass make stars; the curve of a white plate makes a gibbous moon.

Their daughters have come to expect that the heavenly bodies are not visible some nights, and some nights they are, and then these bodies stay still while their mothers lift them up and say *look, balloom.* But it is never this way, a flash, then gone, an idea, an image half-remembered. Never this close. Hannah and Sarah can feel some force building in the room behind them, a loud noise growing even louder, an insistence. *Yes,* the warm air presses against their backs, *yes,* the smells of roast chicken, garlic; they smell without seeing the buttery ooze of mashed potatoes. *Louise forgot to leave it,* they hear. *Oh well. They can eat what we're having. They're big girls. Aren't you big girls?* Grandma says.

Yes. In the dark window, they are big girls. The wind is blowing huge wet snowflakes in at them. *No,* they say, pointing. They could say *snow,* but they like the baby word, the economy of it. *Aren't you big girls?* The fire in the fireplace says *yesss;* the spit from a pot on the stove says it too. What is that gleam on the lake, snow piling at its edge, ice creeping toward its dark, nameless heart? *No.* Where are their mothers? *No.* Grandma tries to draw them away from the window. *No.* Oh yes, she says, come away from there. *No.* If they turn from the window, they will understand that their mothers have gone and left them here. They will realize. If they could only get out to the lake. *Glee club,* they remember, *glee, glee, glee.* If they could only get to the lake. Their mothers would be there, saying *no like a blanket.*

Snow on the fields between Hoffman Estates and the Loop. Snow on the highway. On the broken backs of corn, on the planes at O'Hare, on the ten o'clock news. Unaccountable, unbelievable, in September.

Somewhere, their daughters are inconsolable. Their mothers can feel it. In the Palmer House, on the fourth floor, they sit up in bed, they loose themselves from the tangle of their husbands' arms. They listen. There is a streetlamp outside the window, and snow falling inside the yellow tent of light it casts down to the sidewalk. Someone is calling. A man by himself, a failed meteorologist, is whistling. He has lost his job tonight because he stood before his maps and charts and blowing clouds and couldn't say a word. Dead air. Snow in September? the sportscaster prompted. The producer snapped his fingers, cursed under his breath. The pretty news anchor, who knew people whispered she was a bubblehead, she said, Bill? But the meteorologist couldn't think what to say. Somewhere there was a teleprompter, he knew that much, the words running down like a waterfall. Somewhere. Snow in September? Absolute silence in the studio, inside a million homes. And then, finally, he turned to camera one and said, *Do you people know there really aren't any maps up here next to me? There aren't any maps. I just sweep my arms around and pretend.* He thought about his years of training, weather school, clouds and patterns. Natural disasters. Unspeakable, all of it. And then he walked right off the set, walked off through the curtain of snow, walked until he came to the Palmer House and went into the bar. There was a trio playing jazz. He watched two couples having brandy, jewel-like after-dinner drinks, saw the sleepy drift of each woman toward her husband. He sat down at a table next to them. Tourists, he believed, who would not recognize him, would not have seen what just happened on the ten o'clock news. He listened to them talk about two women, Hannah and Sarah, who were not there, and gradually he realized those two women were their young daughters. Their mothers said, The boys tried to get them to say fuck. And the meteorologist thought of telling them, You try to keep it at bay, but you can't. The unspeakable. The truth. That there aren't any maps. He had children, out in the great wide world. A CPA, a carpenter, a jazz singer. He would go hear her, the next time he was in St. Paul, sit in the dark and listen to her tremble through all those nonsense syllables. *It will rain,* he said out loud, but to no one in particular. *It will turn to rain, all of it.*

Now, hours later, he is leaving the Palmer House and whistling, and the mothers hear him, and they think, unaccountably, those old sayings, *whistling in the dark, whistling past the graveyard.* They think of their daughters, and it feels like a million miles between this room and Grandma's house in Hoffman Estates. Their daughters may be frightened, and they haven't yet learned how to whistle. Their daughters may be inconsolable. And like a shot, the telephone rings, like a whistle driven out of a man by a hard fall on ice.

It's Grandma, sputtering, tired out, at the end of her rope. There's crying in the background, wailing, long choking sobs. Their daughters won't go to sleep. They've been crying for hours. At first it was words, *go home now? Where's Mommy? Where's Daddy and the car?* The college-aged cousins tried to put them to sleep, in the back room, together in the bottom bunk. *No no no,* they said, and the cousins asked, Why not? and Hannah and Sarah pointed to the top bunk looming above them and said *because we might not be able to get out.*

You can hear them, Grandma says, listen. For two hours, wailing, like this, no words. We ask what they want, and they can't tell us. We just asked if they want to talk to you, and they cried harder. Then one of the college-aged cousins comes on the extension. She says, they can't talk. We don't know what happened. They were looking for the moon and then they just lost it.

The mothers put their palms over the phone's mouthpiece. They explain to the husbands. Do you think they'll just quiet down and go to sleep? But the husbands, fathers again, say no, let's go. Already, they're out of bed, switching on the bathroom light. Already they're into their clothes, out the door, down to the front desk, the parking garage, revving the engine, blasting the heat. All ready, already. The husbands say that all the time, in all situations, all tones of voice. The fathers say it even more, constantly, like the breath that's behind words, all words, every single one.

And so they drive out from the Palmer House, out from between Wabash and State, past Monroe, Madison, snow slices like wedding cake balanced an inch high on top of the street signs. But in this preseason emergency, the authorities have come through, that's what the radio says. And truly. The streets are newly ploughed so that the just-now dusting of snow looks like sugar, and the car rides sweetly over it. The fathers drive. The mothers are in the backseat, leaning into each other, the warm line where their bodies meet like a language, but better. *What a relief,* it says. *Of course,* it says. *We knew all along.*

The fathers are tired but jovial, their voices low, murmurous, back and forth, signal and return. The mothers don't listen, and then they do, and they hear the fathers saying lines from movies, from old television, back and forth, each finishing the other's sentences, lines about driving, lines about snow, lines about darkness, lines about nothing. In the fathers' voices, it all becomes a song, the radio going on low, like an orchestra, under the words. *Let's play orchestra,* their daughters said, just last week. The mothers shut their eyes. Close around them are machinery, darkness, men, all the places where words are said to fail, but really almost never do.

The snow is coming down as it always has, its inescapable erasure of language, all language, the words we need and the spaces between them. This is what the mothers see behind their closed eyes, spaces between themselves and their daughters growing greater tonight and every night to come. This is what the mothers hear, half asleep, traveling toward their daughters: their daughters say, *I want to do it all by myself,* and their mothers must let them. Their daughters will say *bye-bye.* The nonsense syllables of Ella Fitzgerald crackle on the radio, like the sound a body makes when it is standing still, trying to decide which way to turn, where to go next. When it is waiting for the heartbreak which will surely come and from which no mother can save it.

Up ahead, ten more miles now, is Grandma's house, the house these daughters turned mothers grew up in, before they met their husbands and went so far away with them. Inside their own daughters will be sleeping, finally. But their mothers will lift them gently out of the bottom bunk, and their fathers will follow with yellow and pink canvas bags and toys. The mothers will carry their daughters out to the car and hold them in their laps, rolled in blankets, belted in awkwardly to their bodies. This kind of carrying is dangerous in snow, Grandma says, dangerous in any weather. Not dangerous, the fathers say, just not lawful. Remember how we rode like this as children, without any kind of special seat, and worse, entirely unbelted, punching each other, all talking at once into the driver's ear?

Their daughters whimper, but do not awaken. Though maybe they have. Maybe they are listening with their eyes shut tight, listening to their parents talk about tomorrow and breakfast and the airplane home. How the snow may cause delays. Their lips move obscurely against their mothers' coats. They are dreaming the sentences they will say in the morning. They are naming the lake out behind Grandma's house. The little breaths out of their mouths sound like *wish.* The mothers say, So much for our big night, and the fathers smile a little and shake their heads. From out of the roadside darkness, a deer driven in by the snow steps onto the highway, concludes who knows what, but wisely, and steps back. The mothers and fathers see it all, thrill and calm in nearly the same instant. Their daughters feel the big highway lights on their faces, then the interval of darkness between, like heaves of storm. In their sleep, their daughters say *wowder,* then with an exhale and the last sob, they say *rain.*

You Can Sleep While I Drive

I.

He was telling himself the story of his own father, the way he would tell it to his son. *I don't want to say he was a drunk, but there it is. My mother, his wife, sent him away after he lost all her money, three apartment buildings, a farm in Montana. Drank it up, like wood and glass and pastureland—Bitterroot, that was the Montana place, and a good name for it—like wood and glass and land was just a thin mixture you could pour down your throat. I was three, then I was five, then I was the man of the house. Then it seems like the next thing I knew, I was sixteen and he was asking me for a nickel on the street, showing up at Mass and graduations, places where you think the only vision from hell is going to be you. How he died was starvation, how drunks die, if you really get down to brass tacks. He forgot to eat and wasted away. At the end, he was like four sticks bound together with string and rags. You'd think he'd have gone "clack, clack" against the sidewalk when he moved from one street corner to the next. And he wouldn't have moved at all if he hadn't been looking for me, waiting for me to show up and give him his next drink. "MacKenzie," that's my real name of course, "MacKenzie," he'd caw that name, and his body would shake all over like the body of an exhausted child that's forgotten why he's screaming.*

You're never going to be lucky, not ever, he said once, after a high school track meet, when I came in second, not even close to the school record everybody knew I could break. What got in my way was a bird, I remember it as a crow, a sleek black ghost, suddenly dipped low out of nowhere, and blossomed close to my face, wings flapping. It happened in the space of probably two seconds, but it cost the race, and my father took it as an omen. I wash my hands of it, he said, a black bird like that, right at you. No way to get past that kind of thing.

Mack Reinhart recognized this part of the story, the fever of his father's turning away, a history of signs, foreknowledge, the idea that the future was all mapped out, and in the right kind of light anybody who had the guts to look could see it. Still, he had loved his father's strange ways, his view of the world in a sidelong glance, from the corner of an eye, the vision skewed into darkness. He thought his father was right about everything. He made up his father's wisdom, invented it out of a few mysterious words, the way all children do. *So I'd hear him calling my old name, the name nobody ever called me, and I followed the sound of his voice and found him and took him someplace warm to eat soup or drink coffee, then back to his mother's apartment, where she was always getting ready to go somewhere. It was like I was bringing in a cat or a dog, some small part of the household that was expected to have spent the day wandering the neighborhood, baying at strangers.*

But I'm getting ahead of myself here. All those afternoons when I was sixteen and seventeen, I'd sit across from him in a coffee shop and say, "Dad, how did you get this way? Tell me, tell me now, so I can fix it or make it up to you." I always thought I could do one or the other for him, but he would only look at me, and his shoulders would go up once in a shrug—it wasn't even really his shoulders, more like his back would rise slightly, like he was trying to get out from under an unbearable, impossible weight, and he knew he couldn't escape it. Then his eyes would arc off my face, not just move off, but roll up slightly and back down to the right or the left. It was like he was trying, once again, for the millionth time, trying to die, but he just couldn't do it.

He drove on in the dark, past Central City, Georgetown, and Silver Plume, a town named, he felt sure, by dance hall girls watching the steam engines pull away in the night. Dillon, Vail, Glenwood Springs, the road swinging like a rope ladder up above the whole country, over ravines that hid tiny glistening rivers at the bottom. Williams Fork, the Blue and the Colorado Rivers. Years before, he might have stopped to fish, like he used to the Hoosic and the Batten Kill outside Saratoga Springs. But no, he sped on, eyes raised to the stars that were so close, he half expected them to hit the roof of the truck, make sparks fall on the pavement behind. In a convertible, he would have been burned by the stars, blinded, cast off the highway, all his possessions spilled out into the ravines and deep canyons below. He drove and the full moon hung over the highway like an opening in the heavens, through which God might look down and chart his progress.

I had this picture of him, with me all the time, one I stole out of a pile of photographs he was sorting through. I saw it and was struck by the way a photograph taken of him at age five could be a clue to the rest of his life. I guessed he was about five, five or six. There's no date, just "Charlevoix, Mich." written on the back in pencil, the name of a town on the lower peninsula, right at the tip of the ring-finger, the chewed-off part of the mitten that is Grand Traverse Bay. He's not quite knee-deep in water, either Lake Michigan or Lake Charlevoix. There must have been sun because he's casting a shadow, but the age of the photograph, the quality, gives you the impression he's surrounded by fog. He's squinting at whoever is taking the picture. His left hand is clenched in a fist, but his right hand is open and graceful as a dancer's.

*But he looks cold, unhappy, a little annoyed or puzzled. His head is
turned to the left like he's listening, maybe for someone to call him back
to shore. But he doesn't want to go back because he likes it out there by
himself. He's comfortable, alone with his wavering shadow, a shadow
that, on closer inspection, looks like the sharp lines on an EKG or a
seismograph. In the act of registering huge disturbance.*

   *When I showed this picture to your mother, I said, "Here's my dad
in his moral universe." Your mother nodded her head and said, "Fine
upstanding young man." But she didn't really get it. It wasn't that my
father was perfect, or had cornered the market on morals. That wasn't
what I meant. It was that he was all by himself. The face that looked
out of that picture was the face of someone wondering why no one else
was out there in the haze, in the cold water, where he had gotten to.*

   Mack Reinhart thought about his father in the bus station in
St. Louis, saw him sitting in a blue plastic chair, watching twenty-
five-cent television. He thought about his son's mother, suddenly
missed her, and heard again her voice on the telephone: *I thought
I was through with this.* But you're never through, is what he had
told her. Something about missing her made him want to keep
going. It came into his mind, Zen-like, that the way through is
the way back. If he had looked over his shoulder right then, he
would have seen the Rocky Mountains behind him, the back
range—they'd pretty much fallen down to hills past Parachute
River and the turnoff for Plateau City. There was a strange comfort in knowing the mountains were there, and that he'd crossed
over. He was past the mountains now, and couldn't turn around.

He left Grand Junction at first light, heading west and slightly
south on I-70, across the great sandy sea of Utah, and north to
Salt Lake City. He was going to hurry right along, try to make the
eastern shore of Nevada by evening. He thought of heading
straight west on Highway 50, but who wants to travel a route that

calls itself The Loneliest Road in America? *My father hated the desert, its inhuman thirst. He said, it sucks all the water out of your body. Invisibly, out through your pores. You have to drink gallons to put it all back. Gallons. Drink first as a preventative measure. Drink to keep drought at bay, my father said. And he should know. He drank up an entire fortune, an entire city block of real estate, the blood of his family. Drank it neat.*

But then the desert transforms itself northward, rises right up into the mountains and forests, Uintah and Wasatch. There's the glint of water off to the left, Utah Lake, and then Provo, Orem, Salt Lake City, towns a traveler could stop in. But he didn't stop, except for gas in Grantville, west of Salt Lake. He had wanted to see the Mormon Tabernacle, but now he shook his head and set his jaw against the idea. His father once told him Mormons were just like Catholics. *You know. Breeders and missionaries.*

And both living on the doorstep of Hell, he thought when he saw the beginning of the salt flats, the great salt desert, a half-hour later. Not desert though—something far more terrifying. Absence. The literal absence of Lake Bonneville, which covered a third of Utah twenty thousand years ago. But there were other absences too. He'd joined the track of the old Donner Party, four days and four nights of hard driving in 1846 over broken sagebrush, dazzling snow-white salt, the sharp chill of desert nights and the heat of late summer days, volcanic rocks, too much light, ashlike sand, sinks in the salt crust where wagons and oxen and horses had to make their way through an ooze of salt water, mirages in which a man saw himself times twenty, where really there was no one. The further mirage of greasewood, looking green and water-laden from a distance. But for Mack Reinhart, it was just 123 miles of salt and sky and speed. What would the Donners, the Reeds, the Eddys, the Breens and the Murphys think if they knew the stretch of trail that had cost them the most time was now being used to achieve record-breaking land speeds?

The absence of landscape on the salt flats is the presence of the
Donners and all their unhappy party. That white heat is their
flesh, commingled and chewed up, and the sky at evening, the red
bowl of it, is a cauldron of their blood, that dark, infectious soup
about to be poured over the earth.

Wendover, Nevada, had a long time ago resigned itself to being
not anyone's destination. A man could gamble, he could eat, he
could sleep and then he could leave, and no one would ever miss
him. It seemed like the kind of place a man would run to to get
over some woman. He'd blow into town, swearing to drink every
drink, break every heart, but what would happen was he'd sit at a
corner table in the first saloon he came to, order two beers and
not finish the second. He wouldn't gamble, believing he'd done
enough of that already.

He kept saying her name. Brenda. And wondering, why
won't she just go away? The only string of words he'd said out
loud in days, and it was her name. Like inhaling salt, that's how
it felt.

He remembered a scene, right then, as if glimpsed sidelong,
in Philadelphia, before he took off on his own. He was talking to
the tour guide in Independence Hall, a Park Service ranger who
looked strangely like Benjamin Franklin. He was showing the
ranger his tattoos. Brenda pushed their baby in his carriage.

"I heard a story once," he was telling the park ranger, "and I
wonder if you can confirm it. I heard that George Washington
had a tattoo, a small one, just words, over his heart. It said, 'Live
Free Or Pie.' He got it when he was elected first president of the
United States. The 'Live Free' part is obvious, but the 'Pie' was a
private reference to all the cherry pies his mother had to make the
day he cut down that tree. Have you ever heard that one?"

"Never," the ranger said, "but I lead kind of a sheltered life in here."

He was still talking to the ranger when she told him she was going across the street to see the Liberty Bell. He said yes but after that he'd meet her in Atlanta. Just like that, it bubbled up out of him. He wanted to do a little traveling on his own, it just came over him. They were outside then, crossing the street that runs between Independence Hall and the glass house where they keep the Liberty Bell. She had a terrible look on her face, and he watched her glance at an oncoming car and then step off the curb right in front of it. He yanked her out of the way at the very last second, and she turned to him and said, See what will happen if you go. And then she kissed him, hard, on the mouth. He said, I can't help it. He looked away, and he'd been looking away ever since. This was the true story: an afternoon in Philadelphia. Tommy was a baby. You were just a baby, he would say. I'm not going to lie to you. I just had to get away.

How many lies do fathers and sons tell each other over the years? Probably not all that many. The son says, those aren't my cigarettes. No, I didn't dent the car. The father says, Santa Claus won't come if you do that again. He says, there's nothing to be afraid of. One asks if ghosts are real and the other says no. One says really, really, really promise? And the other says really promise. And husbands and wives. How many lies do they tell?

His son would ask him if it was too long a story, maybe say it straight out, a statement: "I know it's too long a story." It would take too long to get through. Yes. And then they would have to go on asking and telling until somebody drove a stake through one of their hearts, his or his son's. That's what it would take. Neither one of them would be able to get up from the chair, the bed, leave the room, the parking lot, the goddamned state of

California. They would have to stay right there, feeding on little bits and pieces of each other.

He opened the road atlas and looked again, a town called Emeryville, just across the bay from San Francisco. He had an address on an envelope, a return address. There was a letter inside, dated twenty-one days ago. It started *Dear Dad,* and ended *Tommy Loftis.* It said, *If you're coming, do it quick.*

So he drove on the next morning, thinking about this son he'd not seen in thirty-five years, in the steady white light of the highway. The word *blood.* As if in explanation. Blood running in the family. But this Tommy Loftis. Now there was some blood.

And Tommy's mother. Brenda. After that day in Philadelphia, she wanted everything, wanted it all to be hers, by sheer force of will. She wanted to eat him alive. Even before that: his mother baptized him, the baby Tommy Loftis, in the kitchen, with tap water. It was called baptism by desire, she said to Mack Reinhart, the will of the child's mother makes it true baptism, the tiny clause in the webwork of theology that saved babies from Limbo. She told one of the parish priests she had baptized her own child, and he was furious, tried to explain how she'd done something that sounded like plagiarism, taken the words right out of his mouth. False sacraments could cause a person to lose his soul, she knew, and in this world, his shadow.

Tommy and Brenda and himself. They had worked at their strange, ungentle family for two years, playing it out silently, like movies before sound, growing more quiet and more adept. When they spoke, it was always momentous, like they had been saving up the words. White-faced, moving slowly, feeling their separate, same ways, palms open flat, moving against the imaginary walls inside which they lived. Buster Keaton. The mime outside the big museum in New York, on Saturdays. The difference is words.

Because they can't talk, mimes have to do the same tricks over and over, they have to discover day after day the glass room that gets smaller and smaller. And then sometimes they find a door and let themselves through. And it was because they couldn't make themselves disappear and couldn't use words.

He reached up and pushed at the roof of the truck, placed both palms flat against the cloth interior, pushed it away from his face like it was too close, like he needed more room to breathe.

It was also Brenda's idea to cut bamboo for breathing tubes and use swimming goggles to see to the bottom of a deep hole in the creek out behind the house in Saratoga. See it clearly, at its deepest, where she believed it must be spilling down to the white hot center of the earth. She went in first, surfaced once, and looked right at him, though he knew she wasn't seeing him or the woods around them or anything. Then she let herself sink again, slowly. It seemed like he waited a long time for her to come back, then the bamboo straw floated up by itself and lay flat on top of the water. And then just before he would have had to go in after her, she shot to the surface. Like light over the edge of the world. She said she saw everything, moonstones, scuttling albino creatures. And then she said that there wasn't any bottom. She brought up a pale stone, opaque really, almost perfectly round and flat. He could see partway through it. And then she cleaned it off with moss, winked it into her eye like a monocle and laughed. It looks like you have a halo, she said, then handed the stone to him. Here, she said, you make me have a halo too.

She told him something once. She said that when she was in love, she saw beauty in the world. She said it was like the way a person feels in front of any kind of harsh landscape, walking through it: cut to the quick, but exhilarated. She said it was private, it was like her body was chalk, pure white and about to blow away. He wanted to say, well, leave me a goddamn message on the sidewalk when you go, would you please? But he'd look at her sometimes when she'd be explaining herself this way, and she looked like somebody who'd just done something bad. Or was about to.

She walked every day for hours, all over the neighborhood. She always looked ragged around the edges from no sleep or too much sleep or sleep when the rest of the world was awake. Her face was its own shadow, like she was wearing a big-brimmed hat pushed all the way forward, but of course she wasn't. And he thought at these times she was like a perfect picture of the modern world, turned inside out, trying to make something nice where there was only meanness and grief. That was the last time he loved her.

He wondered if he'd fallen asleep. Dreaming trackless through northern Nevada, no guide or landmark. Going off to see his son when everybody knew he had no son. Except that now he did. Dreaming through broad, treeless valleys, rocky hills, one or two mountain sheep, then broken sagebrush, desert ridges, the warm and stagnant Humboldt River lined with bushes and scrubby willows. Naked mountains of rock, sharp-edged, brown, yellow, red and green, bore down on him. He drove in silence, too stunned for radio talk. The truck had got covered with gray dust, he saw when he stopped to buy gas in Winnemucca, his chalky barge. There was a woman, young and pretty, walking along the road in front of the gas station. All of a sudden, she stopped and tilted her head back and looked up at the sky. She opened her mouth and closed her eyes like a person who's drinking in drops of rain. But it also looked like something else, a cry, a woman yelling in a dream, a woman who can't make a sound. Or can't think of what sound to make.

"Still Nevada." He was talking to himself. "It's so flat. I wonder what happens around here in the winter. When it snows. Gets pretty white. Empty white. Empty. I think I'd hate living around here. Especially in the winter. You know what Brenda would think about that? I don't know whether she's a genius or crazy. Brenda would say emptiness is the way of the world."

She would say you don't need to hate it. You don't need to hate emptiness. In fact, if everything was empty, if you were always empty, nothing could be taken away from you. That's what Brenda would say.

The landscape lay rusting in the midafternoon light, like fields of blood, what grass there was grown tussocky and uneven as if it was there against its own will. At every point, he was within sight of the edge of the world, feeling the air changing, growing drier and hotter, then thinner. He wished whatever was about to happen to him would hurry up and do so. Heat moved with him across the country and he hoped it would get so hot out there in the middle of Nevada that rocks would crack open, split with a sound like thunder and turn the world back into dust. Signs along the highway read Do Not Drive Into Smoke, but it already was much too late for any such warning.

You don't know him, Mack Reinhart feared this, about his son. Also, *you won't know him.*

Yet he drove on: *So there I'd sit, getting to know my father long after it happened for most people. It teaches you something about affection, and that is you don't have to know somebody to love them. You know that saying—to know him is to love him. I hear it in some woman country-and-western singer's voice, to know, know, know him is to love, love, love him, but it's a lie. I didn't know my father, not ever, not even at the end, but I loved him. I kept trying to do otherwise, to look at him, consider him like he was just another guy, a stranger, but there was no way. So when he died, I felt so peculiar, but also relieved, and not in the way you think, either. I felt glad that I could show grief, mourn, finally, like I'd been doing for years. I was glad there could be a shape to my being sorry, a vessel, a place to put it, and a place that the world understood.*

He died outside, in the snow, at the foot of the steps leading up to his mother's apartment building. He was leaning against the brick-work. My grandmother said that she saw him when she was leaving, on her way to a party, and called out to him, hello son, she said, but half the time he never answered her anyhow, so she just went on her way.

I think somehow this is only the beginning of the story, or it's the kind of story you have to tell the end of first. Or maybe the person who tells it is the only one who can't—I mean my father should be telling this story, how he died, what his last thoughts were, how he came to be on that snowy step at that hour, that broken down and used up. I have the same feeling right now that I had when I was sixteen: I don't know you, but I love you, all the wrack and ruin of you standing here in front of me.

He was still following the Donner Party. After they butchered the dead, the survivors wrapped and labeled the pieces so no one would have to eat their kin. Brenda would have made a joke. She would have said, *Donners, Donners everywhere, and not a bite to eat.* But the most amazing thing about the Donner Party and its sad story was the Gold Rush a year later. Not that they ate each other's flesh, not that they were forced to stop only 150 miles from safety on the other side of the Sierra, not that George Donner wanted to move his entire household at the venerable age of sixty-two, not that it took weeks, *weeks,* to gather a rescue party, not that the human heart is always wanting some strange novelty, not that most of the women survived, not that the Donners' wagon axle broke on Halloween, not that one of the children said to the rescue party, "Are you men from California or do you come from Heaven?" Not even that the winter of 1846 was the harshest in recorded history. But gold. Think of it. Gold right there where the snow coffins for half-eaten bodies melted and ran into Sutter's Creek.

* * *

The eastern rise of the Sierra Nevada out of Reno, Nevada, and into Truckee, California, is five times steeper than the western slope, and a driver feels it in the floorboards, in the gears, through the engine and out the steering column into the hands. The trembling of the vehicle's adjustments to altitude and to the drop in temperature became Mack Reinhart's trembling. He shook his way into the stillness of those stern granite faces and the higher peaks, still dusted with snow in the third week of August. It felt like falling into the open arms of California, the soft boughs of cedar, pine and fir held high to catch him. Mack Reinhart took in the scenery with great concentration—as if he were going to have to remember it in minute detail, draw it for someone, make a map. His skin was so pale that it glowed in the shadows of the truck bed and under the shadows of trees and high clouds. He was a ghost among the luggage, a mirage shimmering toward real water.

And so he drifted north of Lake Tahoe and over the first pass, down into Summit Valley, past Truckee and Donner Lake. He knew there was no stopping, not even for history, no tarrying in Soda Springs, or Cisco, or Emigrant Gap. He passed through Grass Valley and Gold Run, down, down, *hope the brakes don't give out* driving, to Citrus Valley, Orangevale, and finally the dust cloud of Sacramento. He thought if he looked in the rearview mirror, he'd see black smoke and char, the road he'd burned up getting that far, getting to his son, who had in the last few days taken shape before his very eyes, out of nothing, out of exhaustion. A son made of tiredness and road.

Down into California—and even on the valley floor, everybody and all their possessions seemed perched and ready to fall forward toward the ocean. He started leaning west at Truckee and didn't stop. He reached into the cooler, took out a beer, opened it, and drank half in one swallow.

"We made it," he said to no one. "We're here. I took care of business."

After that, he didn't move, didn't look away from the road running out behind him. Tears came into his eyes.

"You're welcome," he called out.

And still he dropped southwest from Sacramento to Vacaville, Fairfield, Vallejo, then wound along the East Bay, past towns named Rodeo and Hercules and Tara, along the water's edge, in sight of two bridges, the San Rafael, the Golden Gate far to the west, and aimed right for a third, the Bay Bridge. But at the last possible moment you could decide not to cross over, and you would be in Emeryville. And then he was there, at the address on the envelope he held in both hands, in a parking garage a quarter-mile from the Bay. Suddenly all he wanted to do was keep driving.

"It's your party now," he said and turned around, walked down to the marina where he could see the Bay Bridge and the foggy forms of tall buildings over in San Francisco. It was how silos had looked in the early morning in Kansas. Ominous, unwieldy in their towering over everything else. He'd never have thought Kansas and San Francisco would bear any resemblance to each other, but they did, and it felt like a lesson in humility.

If you lived in Emeryville, you'd learn to tell time by watching the Bay Bridge, charting the ebb and flow of fog in the guy wires, the crash of light on its spans, on cars crossing east to west on the upper level. The Bridge might turn out to be the only way you'd know if you'd slept, and for how long, because you'd stop keeping a clock in your bedroom. Maybe you'd come to believe that if you took your eyes off the Bridge, you'd die. Children learned something like that in Sunday school: if God stops thinking about any one of his creatures for even a fraction of a second, that creature, no matter where it was, what it was doing, would just disappear off the face of the earth.

He crossed through the parking lot and sat down on one of the wooden benches to wait, for what, he had no idea. Nearby, there was a man in a silver Honda, parked facing the Bay, eating his lunch, spooning soup out of a Styrofoam container, drinking from a split of red wine. When the man finished eating, he opened a newspaper, read for a while, then pulled the corners of the paper into his lap, reclined his car seat and fell asleep. Ten minutes later, two blonde women, both pregnant, walked quickly toward the car. "Dad," they called out, "Dad! Are you okay? Jesus, Dad. What are you doing out here? We've been calling all morning. We've been looking for you everywhere." He told them he drove to the marina for lunch every day. Parked under the same tree. It was the one place he thought he wouldn't be disturbed.

It was chilly by the water, so Mack Reinhart hiked back to the garage for a jacket and glanced up at Tommy's building. He couldn't imagine what was going to go on up there. Didn't want to. It was on the six o'clock news, splashed all over television, those tearful reunions. Miles and years erased with a couple swipes of a Kleenex. It made him sick. You weren't supposed to see two people that way. It was a rule, like being locked out of your parents' bedroom on Saturday mornings was a rule, the locked door a fact. Because you wouldn't understand what was going on in that room. Because you'd get it all wrong. Because you'd think those two people were killing each other.

There were shops along the marina boardwalk, food, clothes, boating supplies, a barbershop. For days, his hair had been blowing into his eyes when he needed to be able to look down the road and see what was coming.

"Layers?" the barber asked.

"Sure," he said. "Lots of them. As many as it takes."

I won't know what to tell him. I don't feel anything. Their rough stumble through all those years. The barber, the stylist, handed him a mirror so he could see the back, but he didn't look. He touched the spiky ends all over his head, and that was enough.

He went out and sat down again on a bench facing the Bay, then got up and moved out of the wind, under a tree, lay down with his face on the jacket, keeping the blue chop of water and the San Francisco skyline in one open eye. He fell deep asleep, the sleep of the just arrived. He dreamed the tall buildings of San Francisco were his suitcases, ranged beside the soft bed of Emeryville Marina park, and waiting to be opened.

II.

The trouble was, Tommy said, they would not have allowed him to teach their children. Every time he would say teach, they would hear touch. He hadn't wanted to run away from Santa Rosa, or anywhere else. He wanted to teach their children. Because he could. Because their children were just like him. He recognized something about them, some edginess. West of Santa Rosa, they had all seen the place that was the end of America, where all land falls away, where there was nothing but horizon, where a body had to stop moving, or else. They had seen it and were still seeing it, that end, their young eyes filling up with horizon and its peculiar geometry, the evening view: that last fraction of the sun's diameter as it slips out of sight. Tommy thought he could teach them better than he could children who grew up with nothing but open space, or height, or architecture or dawn, way over on the other side of the country. He believed that the part of a child that isn't bone or blood or tissue is geography.

So he kept to himself, kept quiet as long as he could. He understood it ran in the family. Quiet. Keeping to yourself.

And then the postcard from his father, absent from the beginning of Tommy's life, which said, I'm on my way. A funny phrase, leaving out the you, as in *to see you.* What if he's coming for the wrong reasons? Tommy couldn't help thinking. To win back my mother.

"But what are the right reasons?" his friends asked him.

All these years, silence, and now in under the wire. That first letter thirty years ago: he went to his desk and propped his flashlight so it shone onto the white stationery. *Dear Dad,* he wrote, *I'm writing to wish you a Merry Christmas and tell you that everything is o.k. with me and Mom. She told me you're an actor. Is there a movie I could see you in?* He didn't know what should come next. There was too much to tell in a single letter. He should have started years before. *You can send me a letter back if you want to,* he wrote, and signed it, *Love, Tommy.* He thought for a minute, and then added *Loftis.* He thought, this is like writing to the dead. This is like writing to the stars in the sky.

He had two distant cousins, more like old aunts, he called them that, "Aunt," one in Petaluma, one in Santa Rosa. They were twins, and even though they lived in towns fifty miles apart, they had a kind of accidental telepathy, an invisible wire running between them. They often dressed alike, without consulting, they might turn up at a party in identical black skirts and tiger-print blouses. You could trust them to have the same centerpiece on their dining room tables, send out the same Christmas cards. They never married. "We'd just outlive husbands," they said. "We'd be lonely for each other." One of the cousins, Caroline, told Tommy about his father. "He's an actor," she said. "A kind of a playboy. You might not like him." Later, she said to Tommy, about living in general, "The thing is, not to be ashamed." And the other cousin, Katherine, added, "or afraid." "The thing is, to be able to tell a good story after." "After what?" Tommy asked. "After anything," Caroline said.

And Tommy took that piece of advice with him, out into the world. He told it to his classes. He said if you could tell a good story, then all you had to worry about was whether anyone had told that story before. People would always try to tell you they had heard your story before, that it was an old, old story, and always you had to find a way to show them they had not heard it, and anyway, it was not an old story.

It was a serious matter, his Aunt Caroline said when he told her he loved men, and the thing was, she used that phrase again, she said it and smiled her most girlish smile, the thing is not to break any hearts. Or at least as few as possible. It was the Golden Rule, she said, it applied to everybody, no matter what, no matter who they loved.

Now half of his friends are dead. Half. Bodies no longer in this world. Tommy said that to himself for a while, "I can't believe he's no longer somewhere in this world." Then the words lost their meaning, turned to gibberish, the way words do when you say them over and over. The first few dead he kept on talking to, like a secret held close to the chest, he could feel them in the air. He decided what death must give you is an acute sense of humor. You could see all the comedy in the world, comedy as in chaos that gets set right. For the dead, the world was nothing but little comedies acting themselves out all over the planet. Which was why often the presence of the dead was so calming. They saw it happening where you couldn't, chaos turning to order, they saw its slow progress and they could wait.

Once in a hospital waiting room, he overheard a telephone conversation he was sure only the dead would find funny. An attendant was handling the phones, someone who would certainly be called an orderly, even though, Tommy thought, that's the last thing he is. The orderly answered a call and after a brief pause, said one word, a question, which was "Straight-jacket?" The orderly listened and then said, "For a play? You mean like on a stage?" He wasn't really stupid, Tommy knew, he was young and he wanted to do his job right. There was a longer pause, and Tommy could see the orderly's eyes fixed on the middle distance. He was thinking, and then he said, with the great dignity of the misinformed, "Well, no. I'm sorry. These are modern times and we don't use straightjackets anymore."

Max, the second man Tommy lived with, was German, used to speak it sometimes, prayed in the language of all those dark poets. *Bitte,* Tommy heard him say every night for almost six years, praying, on his knees beside the bed. *Bitte, bitte.* It made Tommy sad, though he knew Max was saying please, please, sad that he had to ask for anything at all. There was something, a kind of giving up, in the tone of his voice, asking please, the dark mass of his hair falling wetly over his eyes, dripping onto the shoulders of his light blue pajama top. He always took a shower right before going to bed, and so Tommy's last vision of him every day would be this one, as if he'd just walked in out of a rainstorm and fallen to his knees.

Tommy met Max at a party, high up at the Embarcadero. When they left, with several other people, they all walked north towards Fisherman's Wharf. Tommy walked next to Max and tried to look at him, but every time he'd glance over, he'd lose his footing a little and fall into him. Max's hair was the same blue-black of the night sky, and so when Tommy looked up at him along the darker stretches of street, it seemed Max's face was part of the heavens. Which it now was, he said, again.

They lived across the street from a Baptist church and on

Wednesday nights, they would sometimes turn out the lights and watch the Baptists come to testify, as they called it. Max and Tommy loved them, the Baptist families, followed the children through nearly six years of growing up, watched the women through pregnancies, watched the men through their mysterious lives of which there was so little outward show. They could not really explain their fascination to anyone. It had to do with faith, the assurance of things hoped for, the conviction of things not seen.

He started to bleed from his gums and his ears. In the morning there would be blood on the pillow. He said to Tommy, it was a German fairy tale, the one about tinkers, knife-sharpeners, pot-menders, that if they had to bleed, they could only do it at night. Why? Tommy asked and Max said, Would you let a bleeding man sharpen your knives? Tommy said absolutely, it was a sign of his talent. Max had to agree it was true. What's a tinker's damn, then? Tommy asked, and Max pointed to the pillowcase, said it was that blood on the sheets of a tinker's bed, the least bit, the beginning of the end.

The twins had been teachers all their lives, and Tommy knew it was from them that he got the idea. Caroline taught French, and Katherine taught science, using a textbook called *From Galileo to Cosmic Rays.* The French text was called *Parole et Pensée,* Speaking and Thinking. Caroline was what people called a francophile, she loved everything French. There was a mysterious Frenchman in the family, a soldier, no one would explain him or the force he still exerted over Caroline. It had to do with the war, with Normandy or Paris. It had to do with Chartres, bombed-out churches, with trying to find God inside a skeleton of broken glass. Whenever Tommy saw Frenchmen in the movies, they were drinking red wine from a dark bottle with no label. That was what French became for him, a dark bottle with no label. He learned the language by writing letters to Caroline, one or two a week, down to Petaluma. *Ça va? Je suis fatigué. Maman dit moi d'aller au lit. Merci pour votre lettre.*

And his grandfather, the one Tommy was named for, was a teacher, and so there came an invisible, inaudible command with the name Thomas. Tommy knew he was a good teacher, but it was always a struggle. How to let a child learn? He read John Dewey. He thought about truth. How could it change that way? Wasn't there anything that stayed true? Truth is relative to time and place and purpose of inquiry. Was it ever not true that he did not have a father?

Methode Champenoise. Tommy and Caroline liked to say that to each other and laugh, as if the phrase contained the essence of French, all its funny nasal pomposity. They drove—Caroline drove because Tommy had never learned how—up to Moet Chandon, in the Napa Valley, took the tour, and learned how the French monks first made champagne. There was a filmed reen-actment, and Tommy's father was the actor playing the monk. "There he is," Caroline said, and Tommy just stared, watched the film play through four times. They drank a glass of champagne, called brut, outside in the garden. Tommy said he just couldn't believe it: his father acting like a monk. They ate pâté. "How brutish of us," they said to each other, giggling, "to eat liver this way." They watched the live owl, the mascot, sleep on its perch.

"They're almost silent in flight," Caroline said. "They take over the nests of other birds, or else they live in burrows. When they call out at night, they say Quick, Quick, Quick.

"I'll tell you a story," she continued, "about your mother and an owl. You were just born, and your mother's mother had just died, both of those events within a year of each other. The only thing your mother wanted, the only person she would have anything to do with, was you. She didn't go to the funeral or listen to the reading of the will. She didn't want any of her mother's earthly possessions, not the house in Santa Rosa, not a single dish in that house. Not the collection of owls my sister and I split up, not a single one of those owls."

With their hard wisdom, Tommy thought, and their snapped-shut faces that say we knew all along, the day and the hour, we knew all along. Who on earth would want them?

"We tried everything to cheer her up: flowers, little gifts. What seemed to work was pastry, fancy French pastries, the kind with a thousand layers you can peel away. At least she ate them, or that's what we thought until we found six different kinds all together, palm leaves, napoleons, cream horns, bear claws, eclairs, profiteroles, pushed to the back of her refrigerator, so green they looked new, all curled into green fists, little green hearts come out of their bodies and sitting still behind the milk bottles.

"And then one Saturday in the very early morning, a live owl flew down the chimney. Your mother heard it and got out of bed. She saw it flap its wings twice and settle down on a curtain rod in the exact middle of the house. Stayed there all day, watching and listening. She called and I went over and spent the night. She didn't want to be alone with a spirit like that, she said. And I tell you, it was something, that owl. Pure white, incredibly long legs. We weren't scared exactly; in fact your mother was calmer than she'd been in months. She was relieved. When that owl settled in the house, something settled down inside her too. We didn't want to call the wild animal people right away, decided we'd do it Monday. I woke up Sunday night to hear your mother talking. She was saying, yes, we're doing fine. She was speaking to that owl. I'm getting along, she was saying, and the baby is growing right up. It was four o'clock in the morning. I was standing twelve feet away from your mother in that pitch black room. I heard her voice and I heard ice chattering in the glass she must have been holding. The sound was loud in the dark, and dry-sounding, hard like sticks knocking together."

Hard like the bones of the dead, too hard to break or crumble or disappear. Like Max's bones. Tommy thought he still bumped into them when he turned in his empty bed. He could still smell Max's body rotting, the overblown flower smell of it, when stems of flowers have been left too long, in water that has not been changed. It was in the mattress now, seeped through, inside the bedposts. How could you love a God who had made the world so porous? Of course there's no objective truth in such a world. Nothing stays where you put it.

He remembered everything Max said at the end, memorized it, carried the words around with him like they had form, substance, weight. He said he felt the words as if they were his own, the way people who live together for a long time come to look alike:

There's always some part of you that doesn't need anything and can't help a living soul.

How is it possible to want so many things and still want nothing?

At first I wanted to die every day. Lately, I only want to die now and then.

Imagine coming to a place where you could love anything you chose.

Fog, starlings, early sunlight, gold hills, stars like pinholes in black fabric.

I wanted a tattoo. All my life. But now, of course . . . You do it for me.

To reinforce trust in their real natures is the best you can do for people. The Zen Master said that. Or was it Everett Koop?

Dad, I'm involved in something I don't think you're going to understand.

Tommy's words.

His father was arrowing towards him across the United States of America. Quick. Quick. Quick. And then he was there. "And it makes me furious," Tommy said. "All that wasted time."

From his mother, Tommy said, he inherited precision and a light touch. He could ice a cake so it looked like it had come into the world that way. He could butterfly, stuff and tie a leg of lamb, bone fish so precisely they seemed de-evolved. Max said that, holding up a filleted salmon, he said, This was originally an invertebrate, right? His mother's precision made him good at magic tricks, sleight of hand. He still had an old copy of Harry Blackstone's *Secrets of Magic,* yellow and black with three collaged hands on the cover, making a coin disappear, and the claim, THE FAMOUS MAGICIAN REVEALS HIS MOST STARTLING ILLUSIONS AND SHOWS YOU HOW TO PERFORM THEM IN YOUR OWN HOME. "Right," Max said. "If you happen to have on hand a woman, a woman-sized box and a set of cavalry swords."

How are you at making things disappear, he asked Tommy.

A good magician never reveals his secrets.

I'm not asking you to reveal anything, Max said. Quite the opposite.

Magic is possible because people can see only one thing at a time. They see the effect and not the trick. The thing about making something disappear is that you always have to bring it back. Otherwise the audience gets uncomfortable. You do more tricks, elegant tricks, the French Drop, the Gypsy Switch, pull an ace of spades out of an orange. Still, the audience can't think of anything besides what's missing. They suspect you, first of being mean, then of being a fake, they decide you don't know how to bring it back, the thing that's disappeared. It makes them mad. Just now they were adoring you, thinking you could work miracles. They thought you had greater powers than they did. And suddenly they see you're just like them, you're not a diamond, you're a mirror, and they can't stand to look. They would kill you if they could.

Quick, quick, quick. Tommy could picture him, having seen him only once, as a monk. On the highway: hot, dusty, stops only for gas, for meals, for sleep. Go, he whispered to the air above him, go like hell. Fast as you can. He was seeing through his father's eyes the alarming sights of Kansas. Long views that run without finding the horizon. A lone tree, miles away to the north, starkly leafless in August. A white horse, white as his mother's owl. A round cloud, gray and knuckled like the fist of God. A hail of white, wet flies smearing the windshield for seven miles between Salina and Hays. How fast could an old man drive alone? Divide his mission by his age. A man's heart is traveling a million miles an hour in the direction of its resting place. There's a train going in the other direction. A riddle. A story problem. The thing is to turn it into a good story. He would have to take Highway 50, Tommy thought, which called itself The Loneliest Road in America. He would have to take it for quite a ways, across the wide and desolate middles of Utah and Nevada. That's what the map says: The Loneliest Road in America. Like it could be an attraction, and the tourists would come pouring in.

At first, but only for a minute, everyone wondered about trans-fusion, Tommy said. Why couldn't you just pump out all the old bad blood and pump in some new? Imagine the living body, bloodless and pure, lying alone on a cold table. In another country. Morphine could get you there too, but with morphine, as with disappearance, somebody always had to bring you back, looking just the same, without wounds. In the end, transfusion was just too miraculous for the modern world. No one believed in such marvels. Just like no one ever believed the owl story when he told it. What kind of owl was it? everyone wanted to know. Must have been a Snowy Owl if it was white. Sometimes they winter this far south. Quiet like snow. Or a Great Horned. Pale too. Did it have ears? It had long legs. That's all Caroline could remember. How could you forget a thing like that? people say. Tommy always told them, close your eyes. What color is my shirt? Most of the time, they couldn't tell him.

So it must have been a Burrowing Owl. Those long legs. Makes a strange mounded nest in the ground, like the Oven Bird. Sometimes a Burrowing Owl will take an Oven Bird's nest, before she's done with it. Then the Oven Bird will pace outside on her pink legs, saying Teach, Teach, Teach. But the Burrowing Owl will never learn.

In the movie at Domaine Chandon, Tommy's father, as the monk Dom Perignon, says, "Come brothers. I am drinking stars." Then he holds up his glass, and the liquid inside glitters and sparkles. But old Perignon can't see it because he is blind. The camera stares directly into Tommy's father's face, and a voice says, *He learned to have a countenance that was joyous but serious and modest. He was never to appear sad or frowning. Nor was he to speak too much, in too high a voice, or in between his teeth. He learned to enunciate when he spoke, and not to contradict or make impertinent questions or responses.*

He learned to keep to himself.

Part of the champagne-making process is called riddling, the vibrating and tilting of the bottles. Sediment slides down to the cork and is expelled during disgorging. Riddle, an enigmatic or dark saying. Riddle, to fill with holes. *I'm on my way.* Tommy's father, the great, blind monk Dom Perignon, wrote this riddle on a postcard.

Tommy loved the names of the bottles, the sizes: *split, tenth, standard magnum, jeroboam, rehoboam, methuselah, salmanazar, balthazar, nebuchadnezzar.* As if only the excesses of the oldest stories could hold champagne. And the seventeenth-century tools brought from France and kept safe in a glass case, picks, tongs, and sharp, dark probes, like ancient dentistry equipment. It was hard to see how pleasure could ever come out of such instruments.

"I miss my parents," Tommy said. "It comes over me sometimes. My parents collectively, too. My father. All these years, to have no attachments. When I watched other people bang up against each other. Little collisions, constantly. It seemed like it would hurt. But now. I don't know. It doesn't hurt."

Max watched him from the couch. He was afraid to go to him, didn't know if that's what he wanted.

"Let's do one on you," he said. He meant a tattoo. "Anything you want. Like one of mine. Or different."

"No," Tommy said.

"Why not?"

"I don't know. It's not for me. You couldn't wait to get yours, I know, but I never wanted one."

"You don't trust me."

"I do trust you."

But Tommy didn't. All that blood. That was the part that scared him. Other people's blood. You had to think about it. You had to be careful these days, when blood was poison. Even so, Tommy wanted to touch Max all the time, get some of him on his skin. There was this whole secret life he had on the road before he came to San Francisco, and Tommy wanted to get at it, steal it away. Max knew the world by traveling through it, and Tommy only knew what he imagined. What lay between their different kinds of knowing was Tommy's skin.

"You want me to have this bad past," Max said. "You're dying for me to be on the lam or something. Well, I'm not. I don't have a police record. I'm an open book. You can check. You need me to be a shady character, embezzler, dealer, even just a shoplifter. It's some weird romantic thing. And I think sometimes, Christ, if it would make him happy, I'll be anybody he wants."

And then he was dead. Tommy held Max in his own unmarked arms. Next to Max's, Tommy's body seemed too clean, too white. Untouched. In his grief, he thought, *Max, I'm so mad at you. Max, I don't want to be untouched for the rest of my life.*

"You think this looks primitive," the tattooist said, showing Tommy his tattooing equipment. "Well, get this. In Russian prisons, there are twenty-eight million tattooed inmates. It's like a second kind of punishment. Not like torture, but so that they wear their crime forever."

"How do you know?" Tommy said.

"I met a guy. He identified the bodies of criminals. They do it themselves, and maybe over seven or eight years. They use electric shavers that have been reconstructed to house needles and liquid dye, which is usually scorched rubber thinned with urine. Tattooing begins with the first crime and then multiplies as convictions increase. It says something about criminals. It isn't maybe so much an accident, you don't so much find yourself in the wrong place at the wrong time and make a mistake. It's as if being a criminal is a job, an occupation. A skill that gets honed. You always know the white collar criminals and the political prisoners because they have clean, marble-white skin. They're not as talented, or maybe not as driven, viscerally, not as obsessed. More intellectual."

He said that a professional criminal has an eight-pointed star across his chest. If this star is on his kneecap, he's an anarchist, he doesn't bend his knee to other powers. On a man's fingers, each tattoo stands for a conviction, a true sign language, making the fingers speak without even moving. A black-and-white diamond means a man pleaded not guilty and is bitter and dangerous. A domino with six dots signals a man who's broken and harmless. A murderer wears a skull with a knife or a lightning bolt through it. A drug addict will wear a needle, gin pouring out of a bottle, a beetle caught in a spider's web.

"How do you know all this?" Tommy kept asking him that.

"My friend. I told you. So what do you want?"

A skull, Tommy said, on the back of his neck, but the tattooist said, how about above your heart? How about somewhere where you can see it in the mirror without having to turn around, where you can see it, keep an eye on it, not where it's always about to sneak up on you, about to grab you from behind?

So he went to work. He wore sterile gloves, but still it was terrifying to watch. And then when the first cut was made, Tommy told him to stop. He said he'd changed his mind. He wanted an owl, could that be done? He'd just thought of it. An owl like the one his mother saw in her house, talked to in her kitchen, the mascot of *methode champenoise.* An owl to see in the dark.

Tommy watched, his chin fallen to his chest, stared at his own blood, beading up on his breast. It seemed to put him into a kind of trance, that blood. "I remember the oddest things," he said, "at the strangest times." His eyes closed, and the tattooist moved even closer to listen, moved into the web of Tommy's history. "The other day I remembered the 4-H Club pledge: 'I pledge my head to clear thinking, my heart to greater loyalty, my hands to larger service and my health to better living, for my club, my community, my country, and my world.' I remembered that it was hard to burn the palms they gave you on Palm Sunday, and it was sacrilegious to throw them away, so you spent a lot of time walking from room to room, holding on to them and thinking about what you were going to do. I remember my mother had a boyfriend in Santa Rosa who was a member of the Set Free Tribe, which was an organization of Christian motorcyclists, Bikers for Jesus, she called them, Hogs to Heaven. I remember when my mother was a commercial seamstress, I used to walk through department stores, looking for her identification number on the insides of clothes. I remembered having a dream, not too long ago, maybe last year, where I dreamed a whole poem, about three pages long, but when I woke up, all I could recall of it was the title, which was 'One Good Reason to Keep Women Around.'"

Tommy raised his voice just slightly to talk over the buzz of the needle.

"There you go," the tattooist said when he'd finished. "Now you're identifiable." He tore off a last piece of paper toweling and scotch-taped it over Tommy's tattoo. He peeled off the rubber gloves and threw them away. He said, "You're a brave guy. All that time and not a peep out of you. Not a single little sigh."

When he first taught in Santa Rosa, Tommy lived across the street from the high school in a house owned by a friend of his mother. One day that first fall, he looked up over his students' heads and across the street, and he realized he could see into his own room, see how the place looked when he wasn't there. How the metal on everything gleamed dully in the morning sun. How light gathered in the corner where he'd thrown a towel. He saw light shining on the edge of the chair he'd been sitting in two hours before, drinking coffee, reading the morning paper. It was like eaves-dropping. The room was ablaze with this awful blinding privacy, and he had to look away, it had so little to do with him.

And so he looked back to his students' heads bent over their work and suddenly he knew what they were thinking, the sentence practically hummed over their heads in clouds of comic book talk. He had just told them they would love the poems they were reading. And they were thinking, he says we love this, but we don't. His first term of teaching had been exhausting. It was all a test, in a season of tests, that's what fall was, the season of tests. Of memory: do you remember how to walk on wet leaves and then on ice without falling? Do you remember how to balance, throw your weight forward, how all walking on slick surfaces depends on not being in any one place for very long. And so he thought of his students as he had of his own room across the street: what would they come to look like in his absence? When he had finally stopped talking. When he had taught them everything he knew, and left the room. When his voice had died completely out of their ears.

Now, he had wondered about the sound of his father's voice, if parts of it could be heard in his own speech. He thought about sounds that stay with you, hang in the air. The sound of his mother and the twins singing harmony on "Silent Night," Caroline on the piano. The electrifyingly high note they hit on the word "peace." He wondered if his father could sing, if he would sing, crossing America, with the car radio turned up loud and the windows rolled down and the night air and sheer speed pulling his voice out of the window the way it does a girl's long hair, whipping it in the face of darkness, like a banner.

Tommy showed his classes how to translate a piece of *Beowulf* into modern English, making the hero appear from out of a forest of runes, like magic. He showed them how fragile this translation was, a work-in-progress. He thought of his father conjuring himself nearer and nearer with the help of a map and a car key. How fragile. And his voice, which was loud, Tommy felt sure. His father opened his mouth so it filled with highway dust. Then he spit it out and started over again. Taking it from the top. He was singing his heart out, singing into years of silence. He was appearing slowly.

Magic shows these days were all glitter and fog and blowing fans, lights so bright you could hardly see what was happening. David Copperfield, who made audience members disappear and never brought them back. He tried to distract you with nearly naked women, dancing suggestively—suddenly you were in Las Vegas. But you kept thinking about those people from the audience. Where were they? The lights were dazzling, there was a vague scent of gunpowder in the air. What happened to them? You were supposed to forget about it. And mostly you did. But in the oddest moments, there was that question. Were they really gone? Were they standing behind the curtain? Did they have to miss the rest of the show? Were they ever coming back?

III.

Mack Reinhart first saw his son standing outside on one of the second-floor balconies. They stared at each other, two men about the same height, both dressed in jeans and sweatshirts. Tommy's feet were bare, white against the cement. The resemblance was all in the way they held their jaws, their chins, their faces, raised a little, to say, *no, I would never do such a thing,* or to take a punch halfway, walk right into it. Tommy had a neat beard, but that didn't affect the cut of his chin, the angle.

Upstairs, the hallway was carpeted and dark, like the inside of a hotel, but the door to Tommy's apartment was open. Reflected

light from the sun low in the west and the last of the fog spilled
into the darkness, and he thought at the time it looked manufac-
tured, melodramatic—that one door open, the weakening light.
And then he was inside, he'd closed the door. He was shaking
Tommy Loftis's hand, it was thin, Tommy was thin all over.

And he got it right away, though once you know a thing, it's
hard to remember a time when you didn't know it, or at least have
some inkling. Tommy had sores on his face, not sores really, but
the same leechlike patches his father knew to be Kaposi's sarcoma.
They were scattered over his face like someone had thrown them
there, thrown some chemical on him out of an aspergil, what a
priest uses to broadcast holy water over the congregation. He felt
faint, Mack Reinhart did. He felt revolted, crowded by Tommy's
body: *Where did you come from?* he thought, *I was just now alone
in the world.*

"Are you hungry?" Tommy said, then turned away. "Are you
hungry? I stocked up." His voice was hoarse, rickety, ancient.

And he had stocked up, like the two of them made a whole
cocktail party: a table of food, a white tablecloth, bottles. Already,
Mack Reinhart was finishing a drink, fast, then he held out his
glass to ask for another, and Tommy made it for him. Tommy's
hands shook. He blushed when he spoke, and it made the sar-
comas darker, angrier. He seemed to know it was happening, and
he put his fingers to his face, took them away, studied them for
some sign. They didn't say much, please, thanks, this is good.
They looked out the window between sentences, and the view got
to be like a chattery person in the room with them. They enter-
tained it, listened to it saying nothing, got charmed by it, and
then it was too much for them, too bright, the setting sun
blinding.

"There's only so much you can take," Tommy said, and lowered the shade. He told his father the apartment belonged to his
friend Max, who had died a few months earlier and left it to him.

He said he'd only just moved in, he'd been living up in Santa Rosa, teaching high school, but he'd had to quit. He said he wasn't sure what he was going to be doing now that it was fall.

Every word he said in that old man's voice got swallowed up into his father's silence, the vacuum of it, the silence of his father trying to decide what to do, the absurd reasonableness of his silence, trying to figure out what he had done. Why had he come here? What were they going to do now? He knew Tommy was waiting for the answer.

"So what are we going to do?"

Rest. He wanted to check into a motel, but Tommy said he had a spare bedroom, and there was no sense in spending money for a nap. His father gave him a crazy look, the look of somebody trapped, but he followed Tommy down the hall. As they left the room, Tommy reached out, once, to touch his father on the shoulder, move him in the right direction. It was a gesture that looked, because of balance and physics and other kinds of laws, more like it would turn into a shove. Tommy saw it start to happen, and then couldn't watch. It was as if a big black bird flew right at his face. *Max,* he thought. It came into his head as a kind of plea. He stared at his father's back. *Max, I don't know this guy,* and then, *but if you were here, he wouldn't be.*

The next day, out on the Bay, there were sailboats, a crowd of them gliding and tacking, the wind and sun working on the surface of the water, like hundreds of silver fish were rising up to feed and then disappear.

"The famous San Francisco Bay," Mack said to his son. "I've never been out here before."

"It's really the mouth of a river," Tommy said, "the mouth of seven rivers. Sacramento, American, Wildcat, Alameda, Coyote, Rodeo and Pinole."

"Is that right? Seven?"

"Cross my heart. I have no idea. You must have been surprised."

"About the seven rivers?" And then he laughed. They both did. They whooped like kids, together, loud, like bad kids.

Then all Mack Reinhart wanted to do was talk, as they watched the Bay Bridge reveal itself wire by wire through the fog, like a huge, impossibly silent harp for the angels to strum. He told Tommy Loftis about his travel business, about the particular honey and salt accent of Atlanta matrons and their husbands, couples planning to visit western Europe, couples who spoke only English and were afraid of getting lost in the web of public transportation on a dark night in a foreign capital. So they came to him to book flights and then rent cars they'd never seen, in cities they'd never been to, cities whose names my father loved to say: Stuttgart, Lisbon, Oslo, Bellagio, Marseilles, Antwerp.

"You can picture it," he said, "a strange automobile with a glove box full of warnings in languages you wouldn't understand. Picture getting into such a car and driving away."

These couples always asked about the location of the steering wheel, left or right side, and the speed limit on the Autobahn. They had a certain look in their eyes, like they were sizing him up. A few people joked about his traveling to Stuttgart or Oslo as their chauffeur. He knew all the driving was at night, in the late summer, on steep mountain roads lit by full moonlight and bordered by olive groves, or some other bewildering fruit trees blasted nearly to pieces by the wind, leaves and petals looking like sparks on the ground. The passengers would have fallen silent hours before, drifting off in midsentence, their last words a kind of gibber and spit that might make one think they knew a little German or Norwegian after all.

And for a while before that, when Tommy was a baby, there was acting. Which he could remember almost nothing about.

What stayed in your memory was how it felt. The last part Mack Reinhart played was the son of a snake-handling minister—in the middle of the piece, he looked down and saw that the front of his shirt was streaked with blood. Coming on stage, he'd caught his hand on a nail or a stray wire and never felt a thing. The audience, who knew real blood when they saw it, was horrified, but as soon as he started talking, they felt they were meant to be caught up in precisely that way. He heard all this later, from the lighting technician. His first words, *My Daddy was gonna do this tonight, but the Lord froze his face, so he sent me,* brought on total silence. He was carrying a wooden crate that was supposed to be holding copperheads, and at the end of the monologue, he reached into it and said, *Maybe you can handle and maybe you can't, but there's one sure thing in this world . . . yer empty, yer gonna get bit.* He learned to say that last phrase like a grace note, looking up suddenly, and hard, straight into the faces he could see in the first row. But then one night, he lost his voice, and it never came back.

What stayed in your memory was how it felt. You wanted to be shattered by a performance, and you wanted your audience to be shattered, you wanted a houseful of people who couldn't move when the play was over. Who couldn't believe what they'd just seen. Who recognized themselves at last. The way to do that was to make it personal, make what you did seem so private that you would never dream of doing it in front of one single person, someone you'd known all your life, let alone a group of strangers. You wanted to make them feel like invaders when they watched you, make them almost want to look away in embarrassment, or get up and leave, be gone from that place.

Tommy said, I decided it is the nature of fathers to be gone. You think they're always at work, but really, they have retired in a way, from this world, but they lead a more difficult, shadowy life someplace else. They struggle against mysterious forces and overwhelming odds. He said, I have always thought of it this way:

fathers stand outside all day, working the world's implacable soil until their machinery goes to pieces, until their love for their children breaks down wheels and pulleys and chains, until blades and spokes and teeth lie in heaps all around them. Then they stand outside at night thinking, dreaming that the stars are the points and edges of their love-wrecked machines reflected upward. In the morning, fathers decide they're foolish, foolish men, and pray for wisdom they already have.

His father told him, in wild, lonely moments on the road, he thought about becoming a priest. Deep down, he knew he didn't have a vocation, but still his imagination chewed on the idea, and so he could picture himself holding the Host, the cup of wine, waiting for the elements to transform themselves. He wondered if you could feel transubstantiation, like being struck by lightning. It happened to hikers all the time in the Rockies, they came back with this distance on their faces, none of them could quite put it into words, except for one detail. They all talked about being thrown out of their fully laced boots, as if their feet had shrunk two or three sizes and slipped free. They told the story of walking back seven, maybe ten feet to their shoes, still laced tight, upright, one ahead of the other in the attitude of hiking forward, one slightly higher on the slope. Sometimes there'd be smoke rising out of them, two short puffs, ghostly. Incense burning inside the boots.

Or maybe it was more like light. He knew that light is nothing but a rapidly alternating electromagnetic field traveling through space in the form of waves, which he thought he could sometimes feel buzzing right by him. Especially in the evenings when the sky turned luminous, pink and then seemed to shatter. Pieces of sky got caught in the cogs and slowed down the speed of the world.

He tried to hear the still, small voice saying he had a vocation, telling him anything, but there was always silence on the line.

Beyond silence, like the world before there was sound in it. Something made him go outside to listen—what were mountains, after all, if not a place for God to exercise his voice, make it echo? But all he heard was wind, hush, whispering, and after a while he turned away disgusted. If he was ever going to hear anything, it had to be huge and loud, he would have to fall down in the face of it, be thrown out of his boots, his clothes, his skin, and after that, all human voices would sound weak, thin, pathetic. And he knew he didn't have the strength for that kind of longing, and afterward, that kind of loneliness.

What was his calling then? Not the Air Force, that was clear right away. He had the wrong kind of mind for it, a mind made up of hallways instead of rooms. One of the teachers at the Academy said that, a composition teacher: your mind is a huge room, which first you furnish, then you decorate. He was always going out the door of that room, walking off into a maze of corridors. Another teacher mentioned pharology, just in passing, in a long list of various -ologies. He wrote that down, looked it up, read up on lighthouses, signal lights. This led him to the Morse Code. You could get recordings of Morse Code, so that you could learn it in your spare time. Dot dash, he thought, translating someone's talk. Brenda Loftis said his eyes had that bottomless look, the same look as in the eyes of the man who had been blown out of his shoes by lightning. He had this idea of going back to the Midwest and becoming a contractor. He wanted to build houses with a lot of windows, even though he knew it wouldn't be very practical in a place like Chicago. This desire had to do with light, which was what he believed he would miss most when he left the edge of the Rocky Mountains, the way light at seven thousand feet came in from everywhere, zooming across the Great Plains of America and clattering down from Pike's Peak.

I always pictured you, Tommy said, as if I made you up myself, instead of the other way around. I could see you with my mother, and together you looked like mountains and coastline, the jagged and then meandering outlines of your bodies. Like a signature that changes, but is always recognizable. I used to see everywhere, your specific bodies, the flesh line of a leg, hers rounded and small, yours taut with just bones and muscle and tendon, all of it practically visible inside the skin. I saw your hands in the hands of strangers, hers which are large for such a small woman, and rippling with veins, strong from playing the piano and sewing. Yours which are delicate and pale. No rings, either of you. I saw her narrow waist, the slump of your shoulders. As if I made you up myself. No marks on your bodies, not even a freckle. Your faces are always in full sun. Upturned to catch the light, block it, and so your shadows fall straight behind you on the ground, like a woman's long hair, like a dark stain, blood maybe. Like blood, running behind you. From a wound no one can see but everyone can feel.

Tommy said, "You know, you don't have any accent."

"Because I've lived so many different places. Never for very long."

"I guess you're a good driver."

"It's true," his father said. "In all modesty. Fast and steady."

"There's two kinds of drivers in this world," Tommy said. "There's the ones who drive *away*, and the ones who drive *toward*."

His father said he knew what he meant.

"You'd rather travel with drivers away," Tommy said. "Safer. Not in such a rush. Once the offending object has cleared the rearview mirror. Off to something new. And you're an actor. Drivers away, all of them. *Look at me! Here I go!*"

"Which are you?" his father said. "Toward or away?"

"I never learned to drive."

"Never?"

"Never needed to. Now though. Well, I probably shouldn't anyway."

"You're pretty sick," his father said.

"Not as sick as I might be. But who knows?"

"Are you a Catholic?" There was a small crucifix hanging between the windows.

I go in sometimes and sit. Ask for forgiveness. A friend of mine lost his dog, a beautiful dog. Samoyed. So I stood out there on the balcony and said a prayer to Saint Anthony, offered him a generous donation if he'd find the dog. And man, it was deafening, the silence. Then I said, "I'll go back to church." And I did. It happened to be Mother's Day. Beautiful families all around me. Children selling corsages. All those mommies and daddies. I stuck it out. They found the dog on Monday.

When I was a little kid, I thought the priest was saying, This is my mommy. He was holding up the host. I couldn't get the words right. This is my mommy. And so I said Amen and stuck out my tongue.

And this is my daddy. Amen to that too. And I always thought the priest was saying, Body of light. Right before he put the host on your tongue. I couldn't get the words right.

It's easier to just keep saying Amen. Body of light. Blood of light. Untarnished in the veins. Amen.

"I was thinking about my mother," Tommy said the next morning. "I was wondering if you want to go see her."

"See her. Where is she?"

Tommy turned to see his father glancing over his own shoulder, ducking a little, as if he were making his body ready to take a blast to the back of the head.

"She's in Santa Rosa," Tommy said. "About an hour north. She'll be at a bicycle race tomorrow."

"Does she want to see me?" he said. He tapped his index finger on his chest, then he curled his hand and rapped on his breastbone, like his body was a room, and there was someone inside, a late sleeper. He looked away from his son, out at the Bay.

"Yes," Tommy said. "I think so."

He turned it over in his head, that one word, yes, and then her name. Tommy said his mother was doing well, that she'd been with a man named Hightower for going on ten years. He was the one racing a bicycle.

He wondered what his father was looking at, tried to see it reflected in the dark part of his eyes, his last view of Brenda Loftis, the back of her head receding into the already moving darkness of the train to California, her hair growing blacker in the doorway. She was going to Santa Rosa then, but first to San Francisco, where he was now standing, the very place, the edge of the continental United States. Maybe all along, *she* had been on his mind, a small part of his reason for making this trip. He was deciding yes, of course he would go to see Brenda Loftis in Santa Rosa. Tommy wondered if it was because he still loved her, or because by then he'd turned into sheer momentum, a body filled with moving.

And so Mack Reinhart was driving again, north this time, but not alone, along the edge of the Bay past Berkeley and the chugging, smoking industries of Richmond, crossing the San Rafael Bridge where for a second it looked like they would drive right through the gates of San Quentin. He could imagine those prisoners in the old days, craning their saved necks to see around the clenched fist of Tiburon, trying to get a look at their old friends in the exercise yard on Alcatraz. But they were free—Tommy said it as they passed, *makes you glad to be free*—and heading on to Novato and Petaluma, where they stopped to pick up Tommy's Aunt Caroline. She was a skinny seabird of a woman, a sandpiper, gray-blue hair, quick eyes that fixed their bright light on you, took in all your possibilities and all your failings at once. She rushed out on her little bird legs when they drove up and then fit herself neatly between Tommy and his father in the front seat of the truck.

"So," Caroline said when they were settled and aimed toward Santa Rosa, "Quite a reunion. You two. Look at you. You could be father and son." She laughed then, a giddy trill. "Oh my yes." Then she turned to Tommy. "What does your mother say?"

"Not much," Tommy told her. He and Caroline exchanged a look of deep alarm that made his father lift his foot off the gas pedal. They both felt the slowing down. Other vehicles passed, honking their horns.

"No, no," Caroline said. "It's all right. She's up to it. We'll see to that."

They came then into rolling hills and fields of grapevines, six weeks away from the harvest, the landscape punctuated by those golden hills, their dry grass a color that was startling. It was a particular, enticing shade you couldn't find any word for, not yellow, not brown, not even really gold, though that was the name the chambers of commerce seemed to have settled on, maybe because it came closest to getting at the feel of this landscape: rich, aloof, thousands of acres turning to something intoxicating, alchemical, a place on the near edge of ferment.

Tommy didn't know how they'd find his mother at the Sonoma County Airport, where the race started and finished, only that they would. Caroline believed so too, and she led them like a tour guide, saying we'll find her, we'll find her, over and over, like she was trying to comfort a child. Every woman—in the parking lot, clustered outside the airport terminal, at the finish line—became a distinct and gorgeous possibility. There was high color in Mack Reinhart's face, as if he were way above sea level again, back at seven thousand feet in Colorado Springs. Tommy and Caroline could see the rush, the hurry, imminence. He moved as if into heavy wind, leaning forward. He wanted to spot

Brenda Loftis before Tommy did and point her out—it was a kind of a race or a test. He believed surely he would know her right away, even after so many years.

Tommy said her hair was gray, then corrected himself: it was silver, but not white. Her skin was tan and leathery from gardening, from the dry climate. He said she was probably thinner than his father remembered, leaner. He'd seen it happen over the years, the consolidation of her flesh. Now she looked like a whippet, he said, and Mack Reinhart imagined a sweet-faced person, alert, like Caroline. His father stood still then, stared into the middle distance, and shook his head.

"You can't remember her face," Tommy said. "Maybe she can't remember yours either."

"Where else could she be?"

"Maybe she's out on the course with him," Tommy said. "A lot of people do that, cruise around until they find their person, then ride with them for a while."

They went back to the truck and drove out of the airport parking lot and east to Old Redwood Highway. The race course was a sixty-mile loop around the town of Healdsburg, and the bicyclists rode it twice. The riders were spread out, a race official told them—it would be hard to locate anyone in particular, maybe easier to find someone in a car following a bicyclist. The driver of the car would have to slow down, he said, and raised his voice slightly, and generally become a nuisance to everybody else. There were nice places to stop, though, he said. You crossed Franz Creek and Maacama Creek, and then the Russian River. And watch out, the official told us, for all the folks fishing—some kind of fishing rodeo going on today, out towards Geyserville. Bad planning, he said, shaking his head, two big events at once.

They stopped for a while at Maacama Creek. Tommy scanned the packs of bicyclists for Hightower, his father watched the fishermen from inside the truck, and Caroline watched him.

He might have remembered fishing with Brenda Loftis in the spring of 1956 in Piseco Lake, northwest of Saratoga Springs. He tightened his jaw and raised his chin like something was hurting him, a shooting pain through his chest. Then he closed his eyes. Maybe on Piseco Lake in 1956, Brenda Loftis was already more shadowy presence than flesh and blood woman. Already it was hard to get his arms around her. Even before Tommy was born, she became like the tension on a fishing line, or like the invisible wound where a line enters the water. He always fished with his head turned slightly to the side, as if he were listening for a sound, rather than waiting for the sensation of pull, listening for a break in the perfect pitch of his line. And then, without the least movement, there would be a fish—on the end of the line, in the air, in his hands. It seemed like magic. Fishing was a trick, it *was* magic.

All his memories must have suddenly seemed like a trick of light and water—even his memories of Brenda Loftis and their life together, their life with Tommy. He was having trouble drawing more than quick, shallow breaths—all those shadows swimming in the branches of his lungs, taking up space. Stand in a river like that and the veins would go watery, the arteries turn wet and dark. Fishermen wrote that all the time, though they never seemed to speak of it; they said you became part of the river you were in: its current, its unexpected, unholy atmosphere became the flesh on your bones, and you were flayed alive by water, your thighs turned to thin weeds, your feet hardened to stones. You were in another element, and it flowed over your body like mercury would. If you opened your mouth to ask for directions, to speak at all, you could get in trouble. You would swallow some mercury and you would die.

They stood in the shadow of those golden hills in Sonoma County, on that rocky shoulder of the road, for a long time, listening to Franz Creek and the Russian River in the distance, rising up out of their rocky beds and sounding at every turn like *wish, wish, wish.* He was tired of moving. He thought at the time the river's and his one wish for themselves was stillness. It seemed like the whole afternoon passed, while they stood in the exact moment of the season's passing, summer to fall, then the whole world changed its mind and moved back to summer. It had tired him out too, the hook of Tommy Loftis and his mother deep in his heart, so that even years later, it was still hanging there, fleshed over, something he couldn't live without, some tiny catch he'd feel with each breath he took, each mile he swam upstream. It was like a voice, a screech, a fingernail of cold metal.

And when Tommy said, there she is, he thought then maybe the hook might still be inside Brenda Loftis too, hook and eye now, holding them together, its lovely curve still sharp, sharp and surprising as the woman his father was waking up to see before him right then, right there, getting out of her car on Chalk Hill Road. She scanned the traffic in one quick movement and turned her head sharply, then glanced backward over her shoulder and saw Tommy, saw only Tommy. Brenda Loftis, almost forty years later. Tommy looked at his father and said, you'd know her any-where. And it was true: Mack Reinhart had been watching for her all these years, everywhere, remembering his last view of her, the back of her head, frozen still, her stillness, *she* was the river's wish for itself.

Tommy thought he could see all this in his father's face. He knew he could. It can be the most tender fiction of this life, to believe you know what someone else is thinking.

It was a scene that needed to be watched. It was so private. But still nothing prepared him for that moment—certainly nothing about acting did him any damn good, though it should have, watching those people make their way towards each other. It looked like trying to remember old lines, lines they learned years ago. You have to stand still until they come back to you, but you can't be preoccupied by the words, or you'll miss everything else. What stayed in your memory was how it felt, terror, mostly, or not knowing what would come next.

Brenda Loftis had Caroline's quickened, beady-eyed manner. She looked surprised and then glad, because at first she saw only Tommy and his aunt, her sister. She walked toward him with a peculiar gait of her own: her knees slightly bent and her arms out like she thought she was going to have to catch Tommy any minute, her whole center of gravity lowered and patient, like a woman carrying a child just before it's born. Then Tommy put his hand on his father's shoulder, and Brenda Loftis stopped in her tracks. She got a good look at Mack Reinhart and she turned her head and stared straight out over the golden hills of Sonoma County ahead, like she knew all she needed to from the move-ment of her son's arm up and away from his own body, the laying on of his hand. Then she dropped her own arms to her sides and moved backward a few steps, off the highway—she was smart enough to know that was the exact time and place a speeding vehicle would appear and knock her into the next world. She was a woman who did not want to die, had never, ever thought about dying in any determined fashion, not even when she stepped off a curb in Philadelphia, thirty-five years before.

Then Brenda Loftis started forward again, and took Tommy in her arms. She seemed to be only slightly shorter than he was, and when she held him, she turned her face to the right, away from his father. Then she was walking back to her own car, get-ting in it. Caroline leaned down and spoke into the window, and then Brenda Loftis drove away.

Men kept going by on bicycles, their bodies bent forward and tucked down against the wind the way they'd been trained not to create friction, drag. Bike shorts glittered on their legs, a hard muscular shining, their race numbers fluttered behind, like somebody calling after them, waving his one white arm, somebody who can never catch up. A pack of riders, ten or twelve, flashed by. It happened over and over again, at intervals of about a minute, so that the scene seemed to skip and falter, like it was recorded on film, but the film had grown old and was in danger of cracking and splitting. There was a strange counterpoint—Tommy and his father, both dressed in light blue and white, their hair two different shades of dark, and the bicyclists in bright colors, neon greens and pinks and violets, wearing mostly white helmets, and veering away at breakneck speeds, while the other two moved carefully, slowly closer, then apart.

"She didn't want to see you," Tommy said to his father. There was a rift in his voice, an odd satisfied relief.

"Well, Tommy Loftis," his aunt said his whole name as a reprimand, "why did you bring him here then?"

"She was furious," Tommy said quietly, more to himself than to anyone else. "I didn't think she'd do that. I didn't think she'd just go. What does she have to be furious about?"

And then he turned to his father. There was a drunken tilt to Tommy's face, as if he didn't know whether to laugh or cry. "Now you know what it feels like," Tommy said. "Now you know."

"Did you do that on purpose?" Mack Reinhart said.

"No. I didn't really know. I wanted to surprise her is all. I thought that would be the best way."

"Look at me," he said to Tommy. "Jesus. Just look. What the hell are we doing here? I don't even know you. I don't know who you are. You could be anybody."

"Except that I'm not," Tommy said. "And you do know it." He turned to Caroline. "You know it. She'll come around, don't you think? She will. She will."

They stood there by the side of the road. A huge shadow passed over, the shadow and belated roar of a plane making its final approach to the Sonoma County airport. Another wave of bicyclists blurred by, and then two women in a car, going the other direction. One of them called out a name, and a bicyclist waved, and she snapped his picture. They would be in it, those strangers in the background everybody asks about. *No, no,* she would have to say every time, *we don't know them.* Strangers in photographs were as troubling as absences. All those family pictures, in the mother's desk, in the father's closet, the missing member whose shadow fell across those who stood posing, boasting, *I am not the one missing.*

My father had a habit, all throughout my childhood, he would run out of the room just as the camera clicked shut like a door, like a tiny guillotine. He hated being photographed. Sometimes he was only half in the picture, chopped off, split down the middle.

How much you love something depends on its power to disappear.

IV.

Tommy remembered this: Max said there's a point that you get to on the morphine drip, when you know you should turn back the dosage, and you do. It's the point at which you feel like you're leaving your body behind, it isn't there to feel pain or be satisfied by pleasure. It's just gone. But you're not floating or flying or any of that. You're not paring away layers to become a soul. You still have a body, a shape—it's just empty. More like you're a spider or a butterfly or a piece of straw. Or fog. Something small but full of potential, a sentence fragment. Something *estranged,* that's the word for it. Something for someone to carry. Useful. Like a pocket dictionary, a phrase book. Fog. That's when you know to turn back the drip.

"Stay here," Tommy would say to his father. "Why don't you? Retire. Make a few phone calls. I've found that most things can be settled by making a few phone calls. Less than five usually. I mean *fewer* than five."

That was the answer to everything, it seemed like. Tommy imagined again how he would be struck by the blue of his father's eyes, the clearness of them, like all those Caribbean seas advertised in the dead of winter.

If you were willing to put your face underwater and open your eyes, you could see the whole lost world down there. You would get used to it, and you'd let yourself sink, see yourself sinking, feel your blood turned to skeins of stone and helping you down. You would come to believe that this was not a valley but a true *veil* of tears, the water opened for you, rent like the clothes of mourners, parted to reveal the body, pure, made perfect by sorrow, gleaming in sorrow's intractable light.

Tommy would ask his father to teach him to drive. He'll say he wants to take the test and get a license.

The next day, they would locate the nearest Department of Motor Vehicles office and get Tommy a learner's permit. He already had a copy of the state drivers' manual. Then they would cut loose in the mostly empty parking lot behind Tommy's apartment, screeching and lurching through the gears all afternoon until he was beginning to get the hang of it. They'd laugh so hard the tears would run down their faces. Tommy would be a natural so it wouldn't matter much if his father had a hard time explaining exactly what he was supposed to do when.

The driver's education manual explained that California has a transportation system second to none. Our mobility, it reads, so important to the California lifestyle, is dependent upon our ability to move.

During the driving test, only you and the examiner may be

in the vehicle. No animal may be in the vehicle. The examiner may ask you to simulate hill parking. You have to sign a document that says, "I agree to submit to a chemical test of my blood, breath or urine for the purpose of determining the alcohol or drug content of my blood."

Just because you make eye contact with a pedestrian doesn't mean the pedestrian sees you.

It is illegal to shoot firearms on a highway or at traffic signs.

There are certain people you should give a lot of room to. Here are some of them: People who may be confused. People who may be confused include: Tourists, often at complicated intersections. Drivers who slow down for what seems to be no apparent reason may be tourists.

Steer in the direction of the skid. Do not drive over paper bags, as they may contain glass objects, explosives, or an abandoned child.

There was a picture of every road sign you'd ever see, ever, in your entire driving life. You never knew there were so many of them: warning signs, regulatory signs, guide signs, right-of-way signs, speed limit signs, parking signs, hazardous materials signs, of which there are five. Tommy's favorite was any sign with a pedestrian in it. Pedestrians always appeared to be moving, he said, uphill, against an overwhelming invisible force. Instantly, you admired them. You would always stop for such people, maybe even invite them into your vehicle. You wanted to make contact with them, tell them someday it would all be easier.

You wanted to make contact.

They took a day trip out east to Donner State Park. It turned out that Tommy's father had always wanted to see the place too. East of Sacramento, the highway began to rise and turn, the air thinned out and cooled down. There was the sensation of climbing out of a dark hole into daylight, but you didn't feel any of the relief that should come with it. You felt as if you might fall. Or burn, which was far more alarming, surrounded by all that willing tinder. Tommy told his father it had been something, the Oakland Hills fire, the way the sky turned black, like doomsday. He thought about what he'd have to do to escape—he actually wondered if he and Max could swim the Bay. Up here though, if there was a fire, you'd have to turn and run downhill because you are mortal and wingless, downhill, through the low-slung heart of the fire, in order to get out of its way. Only the foolish or the monstrously brave would try going uphill, try to outrun the fire that way. What you should do if you become trapped, the Forest Service advised, was build an escape fire and then lie down in its ashes. The main fire would leap right over you, finding that where you lay, there was nothing left to burn.

At Donner Lake, there is a park and a campground, a memorial to the Donner Party and all pioneers, twenty-two feet tall, as high as the snow drifts were in the winter of 1846–47. Tommy's father stood beneath it for a long time, thoughtful and moved by its inscription: "Virile to risk and find: kindly withal and a ready help—facing the brunt of fate. Indomitable—unafraid" words that sounded as if they had been spoken by someone whose face was frozen almost beyond the point of coherent speech. Beyond the ranger station and museum, a trail winds through the woods and past a ten-foot-high slab of granite against which one of the Donner cabins stood. You can stop there and read all the ninety-odd names, almost equally divided between the survivors and the lost. Which is what Tommy and his father did. It was quiet, even though there were ten or fifteen other people standing with them. Maybe a couple whispered to each other or a child asked questions, but there was mostly that same chastened silence people feel in church. As if everyone is thinking, *This is sure hard to believe, but I'll try.*

The woods around the Murphy Cabin rock, though, split and crackled with noise, burst wide open with birdcall and small-animal scurrying. These woods were full of watching eyes, heads cocked to listen, stick-thin fingers parting the leaves. Full of children's low moans for food. Sometimes it was the wind, but sometimes Tommy was quite sure he heard the voice of Tamsen Donner, the hungry mother of us all. You could look across and see other campers or tourists on other parts of the trail, and for an instant, it was exactly who you expected to see, a Donner or a Breen or a Murphy, walking quietly, thinking about pie, maybe, or potato salad, thinking about God and Heaven and hunger, as if they were the real trinity.

They walked back to the visitors' center to see a filmstrip about the Donner Party. The theater was already packed and everyone in it seemed to be old. A man in hiking boots holding a clipboard addressed the group and explained that he was leading an elder hostel that had been studying the Donner Party for two weeks before making this trip. And they knew it all, far more than Tommy or his father did. When the likeness of Lanford Hastings, the maverick explorer who had led the Donners astray, flashed on the screen, they all hissed, as if it had been planned, but then they laughed at themselves, and Tommy and his father did too, and afterwards they spoke to Tommy, recognized his illness, and asked him how he was feeling. There was suddenly a roomful of grandparents, something neither of them had ever known. Tommy felt a strange falling away of time. If he had looked in a mirror, he would have been a child again, seven years old, gangly but robust. And his father, what would he be? Talking, rallying for a hike around the lake, and glad.

Tommy and his father drove over to Donner Lake, making half of the four-mile circuit, so that they could stop at the beach. The sky was the unnatural blue of travel brochures and promotional material, and the sun, which would have been unbearably hot, was diffused by a stiff breeze. They sat on the sand and watched the families unpacking lunches, untying sneakers, running after little ones. They hardly spoke, the conversation of awe. Tommy was reading *David Copperfield,* Max's favorite novel, which he hadn't had the heart for until now. He was twenty pages from the end, and his father waited, sunning himself, while Tommy finished.

"Well," he said, slamming the back cover shut, "gosh. All that."

"Can you see why it was his favorite?" his father said.

"No," Tommy said. "Yes. He wanted to understand the English. I mean the people, not the language. But no. It was something about names. I think he tried to tell me once. Doubting your own name."

They stood up then, walked to the car. It took a minute to get Tommy inside, situated, his legs stretched out at a comfortable angle. In that time, Tommy's father put *David Copperfield* on the roof of the car, and then got in and drove away. He was in a hurry, Tommy thought later. You get enough of the Donners and their unaccountable history—it comes over you suddenly, and you flee. He didn't miss the book until they got just west of Sacramento, and then Tommy let out a long wail, and his father really and truly thought he was dying, going to die, right there.

People were always doing that to themselves, losing their valuables because they couldn't keep still. There was no stopping it. You saw it happen, saw a book fall off the roof of a moving vehicle, as it backed out and turned around, and then you stood out in the middle of the road and flapped your arms, mouthed the words *come back, this is yours,* really enunciating. But the drivers of those cars would wave and smile, call out *same to you,* and fly right on by.

And isn't it funny, how there could be so much suffering in one place and then it could pass away without any sign. Just a rock, dust, the get-on-with-it of tall trees.

The radio said there'd been a new moon discovered around Neptune and the station was running a call-in contest to name it. Where has this moon been all along? the DJ asked. Why hasn't anybody been able to see it? There was a startled sound to his voice, like he had a personal stake in those questions, as if he'd sworn loudly and publicly, just the day before, that there were no new moons to be found anywhere in the universe. Static buzzed louder and louder. It closed in like a voice coming toward your face, then drawing away, toward and away, up over the hills and into the valleys. Sometimes only a single word came through, one word every eight or ten seconds, a frantic message. If you could only put it together, you might save someone's life.

The night before he took his driver's test, Tommy dreamed the police officer in charge would make him parallel park in San Francisco, on the steepest street in town, Telegraph, or that crazy twisted street near Coit Tower. But what happened was he took the officer to the post office to mail a birthday card to his brother in Idaho, and then to Burger King and back to the DMV. He said knowledge of drive-thru protocol was more useful these days than parallel parking. He asked if Tommy had a health problem that would make his driving unsafe. No, sir, Tommy said, not that would make my driving unsafe. Then he had his thumb printed and his photo taken. It was going to be a beautiful picture. You can tell that sometimes, right as the flash goes off.

They sat in the truck with a bottle of cheap champagne. Tommy took two or three little sips, but his father did most of the damage. All of a sudden, he said, he felt very tired. He leaned his head back and closed his eyes while Tommy drove them home. And it was then that his father taught Tommy the true language of driving, the vocabulary he really needed: fuzzy dice, switchback, mice building a nest in your muffler, gunrack, fender-bender, jackknife, bench seat, women climbing out of their jeans (What do I need to know that for? Tommy said. Respect, his father told him. It's tough to disrobe in a moving vehicle. It's hard work. Ask any woman), macadam, road flare, 6 percent grade, cop out of nowhere, open 24 hours, cash only, sunrise in the rearview, check your fluids, transmission, brake, chains required, soft shoulder, oleander, arrowweed, cottonwood, sage, roadhouse, sticky vinyl, cooler (both senses), remembering Esso, woman-faced cows crossing the road at night, no services, black-fingered genius mechanics, passing lane, spillway, cruise control on 65 and the air on max. Max. There forever, his name written right on the dashboard, glove box, wing window, the two substances that may legally fly out of a moving vehicle, which are clear water and feathers from live birds. And finally: when you wave good-bye to somebody, keep one hand clearly visible on the wheel.

In her retirement, Caroline was working as a volunteer in the county hospital. Neonatal. She said she wished she had a way to tell the babies not to struggle so hard, that what they learn at first they'll have to learn all over again anyway. She said she couldn't stand it sometimes, couldn't take her eyes off the babies, their tiny, perfect fingers, the soft fuzz on their faces, it broke her heart that they looked so beautiful under the garish hospital lights. They'll never be so sweet, she said, they'll never hold the attention of their parents so completely. Sometimes, a volunteer worked the nighttime shift with her, another woman in her sixties, whose job it was to hold the babies, the ones whose mothers wouldn't or couldn't. One night she told Caroline about a medieval potion called resurrectine, a dose of which would keep a corpse alive so it could repeat over and over the most important act of its life. The woman wondered whether she'd swallowed some by accident, absorbed it, if there were traces somewhere in her body. All those years holding her five children, changing their diapers, and here she was, doing it every night, making herself stay awake, repeating her most important act for the comfort of perfect strangers. She said there was something soothing about sleeping all day and holding newborns in her arms all night—it was like living off to the side of the world. With her own children, years ago, she would drive them until they fell asleep, drive out through Sebastopol to Bodega Bay and the state beach. Often it would be evening, then night, too dark to see the faces of her children in the backseat. But she could hear their breathing, hear it in and out, regular as the clench and splay of waves on the beach below, the breath of her sleeping babies seeming to balance her there on a bluff above the Pacific Ocean. Tenderly. Precariously. In the dark.

Picture the two of them out there as well, Mack Reinhart and Tommy Loftis, driving through the rest of their shared days along the edge of America, high above the Pacific Ocean. They would drive up and down the coast, from Half Moon Bay to Pacifica, along the Devil's Slide, admiring the way Mother Nature had ended the long California drought by soaking the highway, then gathering it down into her wet, curving arms and flinging it out to sea. They would laugh at the local merchants and the Sierra Club fighting over the road's carcass there—save the highway or save the hillside?— each one thinking it could stop time's various erosions that way. Tommy's father would find his whole true voice again, and he would say to Tommy, *Water, water everywhere, and not a drop to drink.* Every day, every single day they took their drive, he would say it, and about the eleven millionth time, Tommy would sigh and roll his eyes to Heaven, but he would never get tired of hearing his father rail against the pointless abundances of this life.

In the end, this dream:

They would ride in Mack Reinhart's truck one day out to Pleasanton to see an internist who would write Tommy a prescription for Seconal and then a second prescription, and then another. In case it got too hard at the end. They drove north past El Cerrito, through Richmond, over the San Rafael Bridge and down to Sausalito to meet Tommy's mother for lunch, but when they got there, the hostess told them a woman named Brenda Loftis had just called the restaurant and said she couldn't make it. They each had one margarita, blended, extra salt. They talked about a trip eastward so that they would be blinded in the morning instead of at the end of the day, blinded and their mouths burned by too soon sips of fast food coffee. They would make a song out of it: *Coffee is hot everywhere, and still we just don't think.* Or they would go south. When they merged left onto Interstate 80, a quarter-mile from Tommy's apartment, they first headed west, crossed the Bay Bridge and sailed down Van Ness Avenue as it became Highway 101. They thought they might try Los Angeles, Mack Reinhart might find work there, even though they knew the town eats actors alive, sucks the lifeblood right out of them.

"But you've had your life blood sucked out by the best," they said to each other. And so they went, in their shiny truck, in the night. South of Palo Alto, they took back roads, the ones that show up as tiny gray veins on a map: Middlefield Road and a long, straight run called North-South Road, then Camino Cielo down to Gibraltar Road. East of Santa Barbara, they stopped and got out and gazed south, to L.A.

"All those starlets," Mack Reinhart said, shaking his head, "and nobody knows who they are."

So they didn't stop anywhere near Hollywood, not right then. They kept going, down to Mexico, Tijuana, Baja, almost all the way to Cabo. They do a lot of driving after sunset, even though it doesn't ever seem much cooler then. They talk about sending a postcard up to Caroline, to Brenda, but they haven't yet. Most nights, as soon as it gets dark and the roads get empty, they open the windows and drive like that, through wind and strange little points of moisture that must be what's left of everybody's prayers for rain.

ACKNOWLEDGMENTS

I am deeply grateful for the guidance and insight of my editor, Kathryn Lang, and the careful and attentive copy editing of Freddie Jane Goff and Paul Spragens.

My thanks also to Kathy Fagan and Michelle Herman for believing in my work from the beginning, to Phil and Franny Levine, to my writing colleagues at Fresno State and the State Center Community College District and their spouses, to my family, to Cassie and Monica.

Daniel V. Stanford

LIZA WIELAND was born in Chicago in 1960 and grew up in Atlanta, Georgia, the setting for her award-winning first novel, *The Names of the Lost*, published by SMU Press in 1992. Her first story collection, *Discovering America*, was published in 1994 by Random House. She teaches Creative Writing and American Literature at California State University, Fresno.